D0901791

THE RIO AFFAIR

MICAH BARNETT

 GenreWerks

Cover art by: James A. Ross

PART ONE
THE GRINGO

CHAPTER
ONE

THE SMELL IS what woke her. It was a sweet, acidic smell so thick and rich that it made her gag. She'd smelled it before, but where? Then she remembered. It was at the *sítio* or country house that her father had rented during summer break. It was the smell of the neighbor's pig being butchered. Next came the sound. A dull, squishy thunk. Over and over. This too brought her back to the country house and the farm worker's machete sinking into the pig's flesh.

She checked the clock. Three in the morning. She'd only been asleep for a couple of hours. She'd tried to go to bed sooner but the Brazilian ritual of leaving a party, even in your own house, can last forever. Everyone needs a hug. Everyone needs a kiss on the cheek.

"Mais um beijo!"

Her mother would also insist on a photo with each guest. Secretly hoping that her beautiful daughter would appear in their posts.

Her father of course avoided the camera. He *never* appeared in pictures. He would laugh and claim that he was part Navajo Indian and that the camera would steal his soul. He didn't look like an Indian. At least not like any of the photos she'd seen of them. He was a gringo. An old White man. Seventy one years old. Tonight was his birthday. When people first saw him with her beautiful dark skinned mother they always assumed money was in play. But the assumption was dismissed as soon as they heard him speak.

His voice is what she loved most about her dad. A booming, laughter tinged voice that, combined with his thick gringo accent, made everyone love him. Men and women. He was an American. Originally. This much she knew. However the story of his life and how he'd ended up in Brazil changed every time he told it. Some day she promised herself to go to America and find out the truth. One thing she did know about him is that he was a force. He wrapped her and her mother within this power. They belonged to him and as such were protected from any danger or uncertainty the world could offer. And for this they adored him.

He never seemed to work but he always had money. They moved often but always to beautiful homes. Always hidden behind high walls and security fences. Growing up in Rio de Janeiro she was taught from a young age to be aware of danger. Everyone was at some time touched by the crime and violence of the city. A car jacking. A mugging. One time she'd been held up on the street by a dozen gun toting boys with no shoes. She immediately handed over her purse and they went on their way, cackling in delight at having pulled one over on the rich girl. She'd shook with rage for two days. But her Father's calm assurances made her feel right again. He called it a street tax. In one of his few serious moments he told her, "There are only two guarantees in life: death and taxes. And if you're forced to choose between the two, always choose the tax. Whatever it costs."

They'd moved to a new house a week after the purse incident.

Everyone in Rio had a story like this and most of them were true. She and her friends joked that people from Rio, the *Cariocas,* had real life spidey senses.

Right now those spidey senses threatened to burst through her eardrums.

"Mamãe?" she called out for her Mom.

Her thin, brown feet padded silent on the polished floor. Her pink toenails almost glowed in the dark. The modern house had tall ceilings and cement floors to keep it cool. But tonight there was a deeper chill in the air. Like in a hospital. Or an asylum. The metronome "thunk" suddenly stopped.

"Pai?"

At fifteen years old the shape of the woman she would become was apparent. In her panties and thin sleep shirt embarrassingly so. She crossed her arms across her breasts and held herself tight. Standing in the dark and calling for her parents, she was still very much a child.

"Pai? É você, Pai?" Dad? Is that you?

A point blank flashlight blinded her.

"Pai?!"

A canvas bag dropped over her head. A sickening void opened in her soul as she realized that even if she were to survive the ordeal to come -- she would never see her parents again.

CHAPTER
TWO

"LOOK at the camera and state your name."

"Miles Ronan."

"What is the purpose of your visit? Business or pleasure?"

Such a simple question. So why did it feel like I'd skipped straight to the cavity search? I had given the Customs Agent my blue passport. I should have used the red government one. Then there would have been no questions. No need to put a name to whatever the hell it was I was doing here. I tend to get lost in my own thoughts. At least that's what both of my ex-wives will tell you. And the 12 hour flight from D.C. had left me even more spaced out than usual. As an FBI Agent in a foreign country I had no special powers. But at least if I declared myself with my official passport I wouldn't be accused of running an illegal op; and just maybe the U.S. government would be kind enough to bail me out of trouble. But this wasn't an official mission. Besides, I had a flight home tomorrow morning. How much trouble could I cause?

"What is the purpose of your visit, sir?" the Customs

Agent asked again. This time with an edge as he sat up and took notice of me.

"It's a personal visit," I replied. "My dad died. I'm here to identify the body."

———

The defining moment when visiting a foreign city is always that first step out of an airport. Rio de Janeiro was hot and humid. But not an intense heat. A slow, go at your own pace heat. The Taxi drivers didn't rush at me with life and death stakes. Rather, they leaned on the side of their cars and wagged a questioning index finger. As if my business wasn't worth a full handed wave.

The driver didn't try to test his English on me. Which was a relief. I liked to let a new city wash over me in silence. I've been to a half dozen countries through my work as an FBI Hostage Negotiator, but never to Brazil. The opportunity had arose of course, Brazil being one of the kidnap capitals of the world, but I'd always found a way to turn down the assignment. Considering my history, the Bureau never complained.

At first Rio was a disappointment. But like a good story-teller the city made you earn its riches. The first gauntlet, the smell. It smacked me in the face upon leaving the airport as we drove past miles of slums, *favelas*, that spread out from the freeway like a crumbling human ant colony. The concrete houses were in a constant state of construction, rising up and sideways and on top of each other with tangles of pirated electrical wire that seemed to hold them all together. Clearly there was no plumbing system as the stench of feces was thick enough to cut. And the bay of water along the freeway was coated with a black, tar-like substance. I tried to imagine what the area looked like before... when weary ship-bound explorers arrived to an oasis of fruit and fish and open armed natives... but I couldn't. Thankfully the pay off was worth holding my breath for a few minutes. We zoomed through a moss lined tunnel and emerged into a fairy tale.

Turquoise waves crashed on white sand beaches. The winding beach path hummed with tanned bodies as they reveled in their daily exercise. Rising from the beach was a forest of stylish 60's era high rise apartments interspersed with the occasional vine covered stone mansion dating back to the Portuguese. But the most striking element were the granite mountains that loomed over it all. Like living, breathing stone sentinels that regulated the throbbing pulse of the city below. Even their names were magical. *Páo de Açúcar. Corcovado. Pedra da Gávea.*

After only a few minutes it was easy to forget that the outside world existed. Suddenly, thirty years later; I understood how my father was able to disappear and never look back.

CHAPTER
THREE

THERE WERE TWO BODIES. A male and a female. The man was caucasian. Francesco Silva. Seventy one years old. The female was of mixed race. Aparecida Silva. A swirl of African and European ancestry. She was forty seven years old. Both victims had suffered multiple deep lacerations. Several bones were broken and nearly every organ punctured. The coroner had made a heroic effort to stitch their faces back together.

Despite the damage the man was clearly my father. Thirty years had softened the features and he'd lost most of his hair; but it was still the face of my childhood. There was also the matter of the ears. He'd been a wrestler growing up and both ears were lumpy with cauliflower ear. Just like mine. Curiously he hadn't bothered with plastic surgery. He even maintained an identifying scar above his left eye, the result of a head butt from one of our living room wrestling matches. He'd always been proud of that scar. "Look what my boy did! Eight years old and knocked my ass out!"

"I'm sorry about the smell. But our refrigeration is limited."

The Coroner spoke passable English. This was a city of

eight million with morgue space in the single digits. It had been only three days and the bodies had already gone sour. He was a sympathetic man but wanted to move things along. The bodies needed to be in the ground.

"Yes. That's him," I replied. "But his name isn't Francesco Silva. It's Frank Ronan."

The Coroner noted the name change. "I did a complete set of photos. They'll be with the Detective if you need them." He zipped the body bags and as an afterthought added, "I'm sorry for your loss."

"I lost him a long time ago," I replied, more to myself than to him.

"Do you plan on burying him here in Rio? I can give you the name of a funeral service," he said and moved to dig through his cluttered desk.

A funeral was the last thing I wanted to deal with. The last thing he deserved.

"How much just to burn 'em?"

"Cremation? I can refer you in that direction too," he said.

I pulled out my wallet. I hadn't bothered to change any money. I wasn't sticking around. I handed him all my cash, four hundred dollars if he was lucky. "Can you take care of it for me?" I said.

He let the outstretched money hover in the air. "He was your father, right?"

He didn't approve. But I didn't care. I had to get out of there. I couldn't breathe. I set the cash on the body bag. "Do what you want with him. Throw him in the dumpster out back. I really don't give a shit," I said and turned to leave.

As I reached the door he called out, "At least there's still hope for the girl."

I stopped. My fingers fell away from the doorknob.

"What girl?"

He stood up and took the cash. Four hundred dollars was enough for him to dispose of a body; but not enough to spare my conscience.

"Their daughter," he said. "I guess that would make her your sister. They think she got away."

CHAPTER
FOUR

"I CAN'T BELIEVE IT, Frank fuckin' Ronan. Right here under our nose the whole time." David Barry was the Deputy Consul to the U.S. Consulate in Brazil. His reaction to my father was typical. Starstruck. "What did he make it to, the top five?"

He was referring to the FBI's Most Wanted List.

"Last time I checked he'd fallen out of the top ten," I said.

"Still, Frank Ronan. The man's a legend. The Rio Police are calling it a robbery gone wrong. But it had to be cartel, right?"

I'd buried this crap so deep. But it kept bubbling up. "Does it matter?" I said.

"I'm sorry," he blushed. "You're right. Your Dad just died... completely inappropriate."

We were eating a late lunch on the patio of *"Bar Lagoa"* a century old German sausage and beer joint with career waiters in white jackets and black ties. The restaurant sat on the shore of a small lake or technically lagoon if you counted a narrow drainage ditch running to the nearby ocean. From the patio, across the water, I looked up at the towering Corcovado Mountain with its iconic statue, Christ The Redeemer. From down here the statue appeared to be an inch tall. But of course in reality I was the bug, the statue was the giant.

My father's crimes had hung over me for most of my life. It was a simple story, really. He'd been working the drug beat for LAPD when he and his partner stumbled on a storage unit filled with cash. A pallet stacked with plastic wrapped hundreds. Afterward, the DEA estimated the haul to be upward of $50 million. You see these types of scenes in the movies and wonder, what would you do? Would you take a little for yourself? Just a little? Well, Detective Frank Ronan at 40 years of age with an ex-wife and a kid to support and a city pension to look forward to -- he took it all for himself. Over the course of 24 hours he and his partner removed the entire cache and stored it in the hull of a sailboat down in Long Beach.

His partner was the stupid one. He bought himself a Corvette. A week later he was dead in a Sunset Strip hotel with his pants at his ankles and his throat slit in a big red smile. The police fingered Dad as the killer. But I never saw it. He may have been greedy but he wasn't a killer. At least not that type of killer. Besides, that wouldn't explain what happened next.

It's not an accident that I ended up on the FBI's hostage rescue team. After the money was taken a strange van began to appear outside our house. They snatched me the day after Dad's partner was found. I was twelve years old and in the seventh grade. It was a Monday. The sky was a bright blue, the kind of blue that appears in L.A. in the movies and in real life about ten days a year. I was held in a trailer with boarded up windows parked in the high desert. The kidnappers wore masks, carried guns and spoke Spanish. After twenty days they stopped coming to bring me food. It took another day for me to gather the courage to test the door. It was unlocked. I walked a mile to the freeway where a car stopped and drove me to the Barstow police station.

It was during these twenty days that my dad, the hero I'd been counting on to save me, had disappeared. Him and the sailboat and the $50 million in cash - had vanished into thin air.

Later, with years of experience in my pocket, I came to the conclusion that Dad's disappearance had actually saved my life. He was their goal. Him and their $50 million. But you can't very well negotiate a ransom with thin air. So when all they got was radio silence they were left with a choice: kill me or let me go. Kill a cop's kid, even a dirty cop, and LAPD would've torn the city apart. Letting me go was the logical choice. A corporate write down. When I'm feeling generous I tell myself that this was Dad's plan all along.

"Did you know he was in Brazil?" Barry asked.

"I assumed. They found his boat up north in Bahia. There's no extradition, so the Feds never looked too hard. The cartel probably looked in the early days; but about a year after it went down they ended up killing each other. After that there was no one left who cared enough to get their hands dirty."

The Deputy Consul chewed on this as he moved the sliced sausage and onions around on his steel plate. I knew what was coming next. Barry was in his late fifties and had ogled every woman who walked by our table. He wasn't a bad guy. Just obvious. He would make a horrible card player. Which is why he'd probably survived so long as a diplomat. Everyone liked a loser.

"What do you think happened to the money?"

There it was. The fifty million dollar question. I took a

drink from my beer. It was ice cold and light as air. A perfect contrast to the humid heat. I made a note to never underestimate these Brazilians. When it counted they knew what they were doing.

"Don't you think the important question is what happened to his daughter?" I said.

"Oh, absolutely. I... I assumed she was with family," he stammered, but then smoothly switched to diplomat mode, "If you want to make contact I can get the ball rolling. Of course we'd have to engage with Rio Police. Social Services. Human trafficking isn't just a conspiracy theory down here. They get sensitive about things pertaining to children. By the way, did you come in on your government passport?"

If I had been traveling under my government passport Barry would have the power to dictate my next move. This must be the reason that he'd invited me to lunch.

"No, tourist. Why? Looking to get rid of me?"

"Of course not," he said with a forced grin. "That's perfect. I was going to say, take a few days. Enjoy Rio. I'll get you a list of sites..." he trailed off.

"I'm sensing a 'but'."

"I know you know this, I just need to say it officially. The FBI is forbidden from conducting investigations in Brazilian territory. So, if you're thinking about digging into your father's death -- please don't. Let the locals handle it. And I'll do my best to keep you apprised. There. I said it."

"Don't worry," I assured him. "Revenge is the furthest thing from my mind. Whatever happened to my dad was a long time coming."

"Good. And his daughter? Did you want to try and make contact?"

I'd been avoiding the question since I left the morgue. Should I let her keep her own memories of her dad? Or track her down and tell her the truth? I took the easy way out. "I doubt she knows I exist. Probably better it stays that way," I said, ashamed as soon as I said it.

"Agreed. Definitely for the best," Barry replied. He took a congratulatory drink from his beer. He had an agenda. What I couldn't tell was whether he simply wanted to save himself from a mountain of paperwork - or was it something deeper. He grinned at me and waved for the waiter to bring another round. The smug bastard. He was going to make me go there...

"When will I have the police file?" I asked.

One lesson I've learned through my work is that hostage negotiations are basically a life and death version of our every day interactions. By asking Barry to answer *when*, and not *if* -- he'd accept that I *will* see the file and that the real question was a matter of timing.

"Oh Man, that could take a while. I've dealt with the Rio Police a bit, and they don't take kindly to strangers. Or *nonprofit* police work, if you get my drift. How about this, I promise I'll forward it to you in D.C. as soon as I have it?"

Someone, somewhere didn't want me digging into this case. And they'd sent this cheap suit to send me packing. Why had I agreed to meet him for lunch? I should have just turned around and got on the next plane home. I looked out over the Lagoa. Like at the beach ten blocks away, locals in their colorful exercise gear and toned, tanned bodies jogged and biked and walked along the path that encircled the water. I was struck with the surreal feeling of being trapped inside of a giant mechanical watch. Constantly moving without going anywhere.

"You know, I have some days coming," I said. "I think I'll stick around. Wait and see that report before I leave."

CHAPTER
FIVE

"YOU FUCKING FAGGOT." The cop was in plain clothes. Tank top and jeans with a badge hung on a gold chain around his neck. He jammed his gun into the small of my back and ordered me to walk across the street and down to the beach across from my hotel. The area was crowded with locals and tourists who all stopped to stare. None of them, especially the locals, dared to intervene. He had a tattoo on his upper right arm of the BOPE coat of arms, a skull with a knife impaled through the top and two revolvers criss-crossed pirate style along the bottom.

The letters B O P E stood for *Batalhão de Operações Policias Especiais*, the special forces of the Rio police force. Royce Mirza was their poster child. Thirty four years old. Six foot tall. Muscled. Buzz cut. Gnarled ears. And that drunken sense of immortality unique to people who faced death on a daily basis. The BOPE were the front line in the city's never ending drug wars. They're the ones who went up into the favelas in full body armor and attempted to enforce some semblance of order. They were considered heroes by the silent majority, justified in their use of force. But at the same time labeled violent, lawless and unaccountable by a vocal minority. The truth probably laid somewhere in the middle.

I met Royce five years ago when he came to Virginia to take part in an FBI training. We'd bonded over a shared love of grappling and entered into a debate over which was better in a street fight: wrestling or jiu jitsu. Round one went down on the mats of the FBI training center. I hadn't wrestled in years but I'd once been good enough that it paid my way through college. The fact that I held my own against his jiu jitsu black belt for five minutes before tapping to a rear naked choke won me his undying respect. It also marked my own personal journey into a martial art that I equated to human chess. Or as my Professor liked to call it: yoga for bad asses. Round two of our rivalry would go down right now on the beach of Rio.

"Dude, I told you, you can't call people 'faggot.' In English it's really fucking offensive."

"Shut up, faggot."

He was incorrigible. He also seemed to have no sense of irony as the two of us stripped our shirts off and latched onto each other half naked in the sand. The match ended the same as the first time around. Although I did threaten a couple of legit submissions which earned me a post fight nod as we sat on the sand catching our breath.

"You've been practicing."

I grinned, "Purple belt."

"Yeah? I was gonna say blue," he said, referring to the rank below purple.

"Screw you. I almost had you."

"In your dreams." But he knew I was right and offered up the slightest of nods.

"How's the family?" I asked.

"Good. My baby just turned seven."

"Already testing for her black belt?"

"No, Man. Ballet."

"Are you kidding me?"

"I know. I know. It hurts. She took one jiu jitsu class and walked out halfway through. 'Too sweaty' she said. What about you? Still living all alone in that depressing apartment?"

"It's not depressing anymore. I bought a plant."

"We need to get you a Brazilian woman. Someone to take care of you."

"I like my plant."

"You can't fuck your plant."

"Maybe you never had the right plant?" I grinned.

"Maybe. What do you call those plants in the desert. With the spikes?"

"A cactus?"

"Yeah, I think a cactus wasn't such a good choice."

"Dude, you can't start with a cactus. Cactus are strictly for professionals."

"Now you tell me!"

It felt good to laugh. It had been a while. The humor dissipated as fast as it had arrived and we sat in silence watching the sun drop over the ocean.

"Hey, I'm sorry about your dad."

"Thanks, Brother."

My fellow FBI Agents had always kept me at arms length. I rarely worked with a partner and never stayed at one post for long. It's not that they didn't trust me, it was a sense that I was contaminated. The Brazilians who I met during training were different. They knew about my father. Hell, everyone knew. The story preceded me. "Hey, that's Miles Ronan, you know that FBI Agent whose dad is on the FBI Most Wanted List?" But the Brazilian visitors seemed to consider it a badge of honor. And the fact that Dad was likely hiding out down in Brazil; well, in their book that made me an honorary Brazilian.

"Want to go see his house?" Royce asked.

No. I want to run away -- that's what I wanted to say. But I didn't.

"Yeah. I'd like that," I replied.

We waited a few more minutes until the sun finally set and then jumped in the ocean to clean off the sweat and sand. Afterward we dressed and he drove us along a narrow highway cut into a cliff above the ocean to an area called "*Barra da Tijuca.*" A thin spit of land bordered by the turquoise of the Atlantic on one side and a dark murky channel on the other. The area was booming with new construction. High rise after high rise. Because of security concerns these high rises were the preferred form of living; however there were also a few gated housing developments that the Brazilians called, condominiums.

The security for my father's condominium was impressive. The walls were fifteen feet tall and lined with razor wire. The entrance was secured with a gate and manned by a security team who sat behind bullet proof glass. Cameras covered the common areas. In order to pass through the gates Royce, even with his BOPE credentials, had to wait as they confirmed his identity. It seemed impossible that a potential killer could have gained access undetected.

The house was sleek steel and polished concrete. This was architecture not housing. Which made the condition of the interior all the more jarring. The walls had holes. The furniture was ripped apart. Even some of the floor had been smashed open. Royce explained that it wasn't like this when the bodies were discovered. The house had been pristine. Spooky clean. As if the killer had been a ghost. The front door had been locked. The alarm had been set. The only disturbance had been in the master bedroom where the murder took place. The damage we were looking at was the result of the Rio Police searching for Dad's money.

"Did they find anything?" I asked. I wasn't angry. I was curious.

"*Nada.*" Nothing. He replied. "But I hear it was a feeding frenzy. Now they're embarrassed. They want this to go away."

The master bedroom had also been torn apart but it was still possible to picture the murder scene. The cement floor and bed frame were stained with blood. The walls and ceiling had long, straight lines of blood splatter. The splatter would have come from the swinging of the machete down onto the bed. Based on the nexus there was only one person doing the killing.

"The bodies? How were they positioned?"

"They were on the bed. Your Dad was killed first. Then your Mom. Or, sorry, his wife."

"But he didn't stop there," I pointed out. "That would've taken one or two blows. At the morgue I counted at least a dozen hits on each body."

I stood beside the bed. There were no footprints within the blood. The killer must have worn fabric booties over his shoes. Which meant the killings were premeditated. I re-enacted a chop with an imaginary machete. "See how the splatter lines are straight. Almost like they're painted on. Methodical. There's no sense of panic. The killer has done this before. He's at least killed before."

Royce stood back. Respectful. This wasn't his world. His best work was done at the end of a gun. "Why all the trouble?" he asked. "Why not just shoot them?"

"He's sending a message."

"Message to who?"

"That's the question." Another thought occurred, "Or, he's fucking insane."

The daughter's bedroom had also been ransacked for treasure. Her name was written on the wall in colorful block letters: L E T I C I A. I was drawn to a shelf of framed photos in which she posed with her Mom. Posed with her friends. Dad appeared in none of them. Which made sense. But at the same time was a little surprising as this was a happy and loved girl. He must have given some kind of an explanation for avoiding family photos. Did the girl know about his past? Doubtful. She looked too carefree. Gotta give him credit. Dad did it right this time around.

I picked up what looked like the most recent photo and slipped it out of the plastic frame. The girl was doing a tourist-y "Christ" pose while standing at the base of the Christ The Redeemer statue. Smiling. So happy. Despite her coffee complexion I could see Dad's nose and freckles.

"She has your eyes," Royce noted.

He was right. They were a piercing blue that reminded me of every school photo I'd ever taken. Before she could suck me into a black hole of nostalgia I folded the photo and put it away in my pocket.

"What are they saying about her?" I asked.

"They think she woke up, found the bodies and then got scared and ran away. That's their explanation for the locks and alarm being set. Her Mom's family is from Bahia. They think she went to stay with them."

"They think? They didn't follow up?" That sounded sloppy even for the Rio Police.

"It's Bahia. If she wants to disappear up there, they'll never find her."

I hoped that was the case. That she was safe. With family that cared about her. Not locked in a windowless room waiting for a hero who no longer existed - who had never existed - to come and rescue her.

As we left I walked slow along the hallway from her

bedroom and looked for signs of a struggle. I didn't find blood but there was a stain on the cement floor just before the master bedroom. I bent down on my hands and knees. Some kind of liquid had spilled. I spit on the floor and rubbed my finger in the spit. I kneeled low and inhaled. I was hit with the faint but unmistakable scent of... "Urine."

A bowling ball of fear landed in my gut. I looked up at Royce.

"They took her."

CHAPTER
SIX

THE MAN HAD BEEN awake since five in the morning. This was his regular routine and he did not require an alarm. His body was his art and he devoted the first two hours of every day to its perfection. He was thirty seven years old, six feet three inches tall and possessed 7% body fat. A number he measured every day. His routine began with a three mile run on the beach. Actually a sprint. He didn't believe in doing things half way. He then performed an hour of weight training via functional pattern exercises. Many in the family were stuck in the old ways. They had isolated themselves and had inevitably begun to stagnate, not only physically but ideologically. Meanwhile he insisted on exploring the latest innovations. Functional patterns was one example. The method eschewed the static, repetitive movements of traditional weight lifting. Instead the weights were moved in swinging or pushing and pulling movements that simulated real life actions. The results were undeniable. He'd never felt so powerful. So explosive.

He finished the routine with twenty minutes of deep breathing while sitting on the floor of the steam sauna. Then, with his pores open, he injected his "vitamins." The original cocktail had been designed by a longevity doctor in Miami. But he'd tweaked the formula himself as new technologies came to his attention. The main components were micro-doses of various growth hormones and a designer steroid called ostarine which increased muscle density without adding weight or size.

After his shower he finished by standing naked in front of his floor to ceiling mirror. He was a physical specimen. Each muscle lean and clearly defined. His skin was clear with a light tan, inevitable in this tropical climate. He had very thin body hair as a result of regular waxing. He detested tattoos. His sandy blond hair had begun to thin but he'd quickly halted the process. He now had a full head of hair which he slicked back with a slight part. His face was handsome. His nose straight. His eyes blue. His cheekbones high. He was perfect. The pinnacle of four generations of selective breeding. The *Ubermensch*.

His penis, not overly large, was substantial and more importantly in perfect proportion to his body. Uncircumcised of course. This final part of the ritual was the most important. With his hands to his sides he stood completely still and stared at himself until he became fully erect. He could feel the rush of blood flowing to his groin. He imagined the semen being generated. Oh how he wanted to bring himself to release!

But his control was exquisite. It was not yet time. The process was exact and could not be rushed. She would be ready for him soon.

Very soon.

CHAPTER
SEVEN

THE MANILLA ENVELOPE was left under my hotel room door early in the morning. The yellow stick-it note read: *"Miles, It was wonderful to meet you. Have a great flight home! All The Best, David Barry."* The envelope contained a photo-copied summary of the police file on my dad's murder. Someone in the Consul's office had even been kind enough to translate it into English. Although the summary was flimsy, three pages long, I doubted that the Rio Police were holding back information. Based on what I'd seen this *was* their entire case.

Unfortunately for Deputy Consul Barry, by the time I'd woken up my flight had already left.

After leaving the scene last night Royce was called out on patrol so I returned to my room where I ate a $50 room service hamburger, drank half a beer and passed out. Looking back I realized it had been twenty four hours since I'd last slept. I was now re-charged but still moving slow. The initial rush of a new country had dissipated and the jet lag was working its way through my system.

Despite the hardening realization that Dad's daughter had been kidnapped -- my first order of business was to change hotels. My current room offered a stunning view up and down Ipanema beach, but at four hundred dollars a night my finances would be depleted within a week. I moved five blocks off the beach to a grungy hotel one step above a hostel. The view was a brick wall and the sheets would never be changed but it came with air conditioning. And at fifty bucks a night it meant I could see this through. At least until I ran out of vacation days.

My next step was to call my boss back at FBI headquarters in Virginia. Special Agent In Charge Peter Wills was a year younger than me but light years ahead when it came to playing the game. A big Black man with a shaved head and the bark of a football coach. He'd been an All-Ivy linebacker and was now married with, at last count, four kids. All boys. When he laid down the law his people jumped. It was early in our relationship when he realized I wasn't like the other agents. We were in Oklahoma meth country. I'd been trying to talk down a tweaker with a gun to his girlfriend's head when the local Agent In Charge gave up and called in the door kickers. Wills ordered me to pull back but instead I took off my vest and stripped naked and walked into the trailer. The Tweaker was so shocked that he set the girl free and we proceeded to spend the next hour chatting about how the NSA had hard wired the ant colony beneath his house in order to tap into his brain waves. There's a powerful intimacy that comes from talking to someone when you're naked. Hell, by the time we had him in cuffs I was almost convinced of his theory.

Wills suspended me for two weeks. But when he learned that I'd used the time for a long delayed surf trip to Ensenada he flipped out again and cut my suspension in half. To his credit Wills soon realized that for me the work was more important than the career. Ever since, he's tried to adjust his managerial style accordingly. Right now I could hear him gauging just the right ratio of carrot to stick.

"The Deputy Consul called," said Wills. "The guy just about crawled through the phone and up my ass. Says you've been interfering with a local case. Says he warned you to stay clear and then you turned around and broke into the murder scene. C'mon, man. Rio Police want you out. And I don't blame them."

"It's complicated, Sir. There's a missing girl. And they don't seem to have her on the radar."

"Yeah. I read the file. You think she's really your sister?"

"Half sister. And yeah. She looks like me. I have vacation coming."

"Sixty fucking days worth. I checked. You haven't taken a day in three years. But the way it works is you need your vacation approved through your supervisor." He let the threat hang for a moment. "I'm granting you five days. Get this out of your system, and then get your butt back to D.C. There's plenty of people for you to rescue here at home."

"Thank you, Sir."

"Just remember, you're in the wilderness on this. You get yourself pinched for interfering with a police investigation -- ain't no one riding to the rescue."

"Understood, Sir. And Sir..."

"What?"

"If she's my sister - that means she's an American."

I knew that the implication would be clear. About two years ago Wills had invited me to his house for a BBQ with his family. It was an attempt to re-set our relationship after the tweaker incident. Four beers in he told me how his father and a group of Vietnam Vets had recently traveled back to Vietnam to collect the remains of an old buddy. The conversation moved on to the state of the American identity. Once upon a time it actually meant something to be an

American traveling abroad. There was a sense that our country had your back. You felt safe venturing out into the world. Because once upon a time - there were consequences for waking the dragon.

Wills was silent. For a moment I thought I'd lost the connection. Then with three words he sent us both over a cliff from which we'd never return.

"When you find them... *make them pay.*"

I returned to *Bar Lagoa* for a late lunch of rice, black beans and *bife milanesa*, or breaded filet mignon. The waiter was happy to let me linger and for the next two hours I ate, drank shot glass sized cups of dark coffee and absorbed the case file.

The murder scene was like a magician's puzzle box. As I'd seen last night the outer walls of the housing complex would've been impossible to breach. The house itself was locked and had its own independent alarm which had been set from the inside. Per the report, the house had hosted a small birthday party for my dad earlier in the evening. There were five guests. Each guest was logged in at the front gate upon arrival and each guest was shown on video leaving by 1:00 A.M.

The first sign of trouble had been when the family's maid arrived at 9:00 the next morning to find the doors locked and no response from within. At that point the condominium security was called to break through a window and the dead bodies were discovered in the master bedroom. Other than the dead bodies there was no sign of struggle or forced entry. The Rio Police, based on a hunch that the daughter's body was hidden within the house, then proceeded to dismantle the interior. This last part was a stretch. But I had to admit it was a good cover story for what must have been a mad scramble to find Dad's missing millions.

The Rio Police had interviewed each of the guests at the party. They were all respectable types. A lawyer. A doctor. A college professor. An executive. And a housewife. It was confirmed that all five had gone directly home after the party. None of them seemed to be aware that their friend, Francesco Silva, was actually an American fugitive named Frank Ronan.

The missing daughter, Leticia Silva, aged fifteen, was now believed to have escaped the house in the early morning hours. It's assumed that she's the one who locked the doors and re-set the alarm. However the report was unclear on how she could have escaped the condominium grounds without being seen on camera. There was also no indication that she was taken by duress as there had been no calls for ransom. Her school mates had been interviewed and none of them had heard from her. It's believed that she fled Rio via an unregistered gypsy bus to stay with her mother's relatives in the northern coastal state of *Bahia*.

The important questions, the questions that would solve this case, weren't addressed in the report. How had Dad survived so long without being identified? Thirty years is a long time on the run. Why would someone want him dead now? Was it new enemies or old? Was it a rage killing or a message killing? What *had* happened to his money? My dad had become a stranger to me. I needed to speak with his friends.

"You is Miles Ronan?" The Waiter appeared at my side.

"Yes. That's me…"

"*Policia,*" he said and pointed to the entrance where two Rio Police Officers stood waiting.

The Officers had even less English than the Waiter. But it

was clear that I was to go with them. For a second I was tempted to make a run for it. I wouldn't have made it to the end of the block. Screw it. Let's see what they had in store. I slipped the Waiter R$100 and asked him to hold the manila envelope with the case file and my notes. I promised I'd be right back. Wishful thinking. I got into the rear of the tiny squad car and scrunched between two officers each one holding an assault rifle which poked out the top of their windows. Two other officers sat in the front. A driver and a man whose name patch I recognized from the case file. Detective *Roberto Amalero,* the lead detective on my father's murder. Unlike the other officers' threadbare uniforms Detective Amalero's shirt was crisp and pressed.

"Hey, Detective. Can you tell me what's going on?" I asked, cheery and as innocent sounding as possible.

He slowly turned and gave me a silent look which bore into my soul while at the same time failing to acknowledge that I even existed. The kind of look that they seem to teach in every cop shop in the world. He then faced forward, smacked the dash and barked at the driver, "*Vamos!*"

CHAPTER
EIGHT

THE BOY WAS THRILLED to be home. Two weeks traveling in Argentina with his bickering parents had been torture. To make it worse they'd enforced a no video game rule for the entire trip! The front gate guards at the condominium knew them well and waved them through. The car pulled in front of their house and as his parents dealt with the driver and the luggage the boy darted ahead. He knew the security code by heart.

Once inside he paused. The place felt different. But then he remembered that the vacation had been scheduled around a construction. His mother was always coming up with remodeling ideas. The workers had finished but there were some supplies and tarps left behind. The boy's reunion with his game console was suddenly forgotten. There, poking out from beneath a painter's tarp was the coolest thing he'd ever seen. A sword! It was a small sword. He'd seen farm workers use them. They had a name... machete? This one didn't seem to be a farmworker's tool. It was soo sharp.

But the real reason that he knew it was a sword... is that it was coated in blood.

CHAPTER
NINE

MARIÉ ALVES and her mother sat in front of the tiny kitchen TV waiting for the weather report to end. The weather was her mother's favorite part of the morning news so Marié felt a jolt of pride as the segment wrapped and her mother sighed, "*Finalmente.*"

Next up was Marié's segment. Her very first on-camera spot. The report was a stand-up outside the entrance of the "Golden Gate" condominium where a brutal double murder had taken place five days earlier. Marié's intent had been to use the high profile case to shine a light on the corruption that made Brazil a haven for fugitives like this dead American. But the piece had been trimmed, more like butchered, down to under a minute and it focused entirely on the salacious elements. "Machete!" "Fugitive!" "$50 Million!"

"*Filho de puta!*" She shouted at the TV as it cut to commercial. "They didn't even mention the missing girl!" Her producer had promised that depending on the response they might throw her a follow up spot. She would have to insist on final cut. "*Desculpa, Mai,*" she apologized to her mother who was startled by her outburst. "That wasn't the whole piece. Not even half. But, what did you think?"

Her mother's eyes filled with tears. She was so proud of her daughter that she didn't know what to say. Instead she grabbed hold of Marié's hand and squeezed, "You were beautiful. And you spoke so well."

"*Obrigada, Mai,*" Marié thanked her mom and now she too was starting to tear up. It had been a long journey. She'd started her career as a child actor and had become ingrained in the country's psyche at age seventeen when she co-starred in a popular tele-novela. The nightly *novelas* were viewed by up to 70% of the country. This intimacy of appearing in their homes six nights a week caused the Brazilians to become possessive of the actors. As if they were a part of their family. Feeding off this obsession was a rabid tabloid industry that documented every step of their off screen lives. Marié had not been prepared for the intensity of the fame. After the novela ended she stopped acting and enrolled in the *Universidade do Rio* where she studied journalism. She would report the news. Not be the news.

At twenty nine she was still recognized on the streets and called by the name of her teenage character, but the intensity had faded. People were now interested in her more because of her ex-husband, Gabriel Borracha, another actor currently starring as the villain of the country's top novela. The marriage had lasted a year and he'd cheated on her three times that she was able to confirm. She weathered the tabloid storm with a grace that endeared her to millions of Brazilian women. It was this hard earned persona: serious and trustworthy, that Marié intended to bring to her journalism. Which is why her producer's hatchet job was so frustrating. But she wouldn't cause a scene. She'd do like she always did. Put her head down and work harder. And in the end she would prevail.

At the *Jornal do Mundo* studios Marié was given a round of applause by her co-workers. She was touched, and a little embarrassed. Her producer offered a half hearted apology for the edit. He explained that the orders came from the top.

"You should've told me," she scolded.

He shrugged in reply. He had a career to think of. She was the flavor of the day. It was a good lesson. From now on she trusted no one.

She had asked them to post her e-mail at the end of the story in order to solicit tips from the public. She opened her computer to find over 500 e-mails. The report had only aired an hour ago! But as she scrolled through the e-mails her excitement faded. There wasn't a legitimate tip in the bunch. Marriage proposals. Critiques of her clothes. Comments about her ass. Fans urging her to go back to acting. There were even naked pictures. Both men and women.

She prepared a mass delete when one e-mail jumped out. It was the only one written in English. But before she could open the file her producer rushed over to her desk. He'd just got off the phone with a contact at the police station. "They have a suspect! BOPE's on the way to pick him up right now!" he said.

She jumped into action. They'd need a camera man. She could do her own make-up on the move. A driver...

"I'll drive," the producer offered with a grin. "But only if I'm forgiven."

"This better be real. Otherwise you're back on my list," she said and gave him a quick hug and kiss on the cheek.

"Oh, it's real. Let's just hope they don't kill him before we get our money shot."

CHAPTER
TEN

ROCINHA. When we arrived at the base of the city's largest favela the BOPE team was already geared up and waiting. The favela, home to over 200,000 souls crammed into less than one square mile, covered the side of the mountain like a drunken quilt. The concrete houses were two, three or four stories high and painted in a dozen different colors. It made me dizzy. Like trying to watch an I-Max movie from the front row.

I wasn't under arrest. But I still had no idea what was happening. The officers let me out of the car and Detective Amalero motioned with a finger, "Come."

The BOPE team was a dozen strong. They stood at military attention as Capitão Royce Mirza walked the line inspecting their weapons and gear. They were dressed in their iconic black combat fatigues with skull insignia on the shoulder. They each had a bullet proof vest and ankle high leather boots. Their backpacks were filled with ammo cartridges. Their belts held a holstered 9mm. Strapped over their shoulder and cradled in front like a baby was their primary weapon, the semi-automatic AK-47. On their head they wore soft black berets pushed to the side. On lesser men the berets would look costume party silly; but they somehow perfectly fit the team's espirit de corps. I made a note to ask Royce if he could get me one. But not now. Now Royce was all business. He introduced me to the team as a special guest observer from the FBI who'd come to study urban guerrilla tactics. The men visibly swelled. They were proud of their work. Royce then handed me a bullet proof vest and pulled me aside with Detective Amalero for a quick briefing.

The target was a construction worker named Jose Galvão. He'd been sleeping and working inside the house next door to my dad's place. The neighbor family had been on vacation but when they returned they'd found a machete and a pair of girl's underwear hidden amidst the construction supplies. It's believed that he snuck over the adjoining wall, committed the murders and then abducted the girl. It turns out Galvão had a history of rape. He'd been locked up two years earlier when the teenage daughter of a neighbor became pregnant. But after she miscarried, the girl's family refused to let her testify and the sick bastard was released.

"Have you had contact? Does he have her now?" I asked.

"We don't know. We flew a drone over his house and confirmed that someone's there... but that's all we have."

I took in the BOPE team's firepower. It felt obscene in contrast with the locals casually walking past in shorts and flip flops. Kids. Women. Elderly. All going about their daily routine. Royce guessed what I was thinking.

"Galvão's protected. His cousin is head of the drug gang that runs the community. That's why no one's pressed charges in the past. We won't take him without a fight."

"And they already know we're coming," I noted as I looked up at the wall of houses. Thousands of them. Each one dotted with black voids in place of windows, like a beast with a million eyes. "Royce, if she's not there we need him alive."

"We'll do our best," he said. He then turned to his men and barked, "*Batalhão!*"

The men snapped to attention, "*Sim, Capitão!*"

"*Quem somos?!*" Royce called out. Who are we?

"*Somos as caveiras!*" Their refrain echoed off the buildings. We are the skulls.

"*Então, vamos,*" Royce said. He pulled off his beret, placed it in his pocket and headed up on foot into the favela. In unison the men fell in behind.

Pop-pop. It sounded more like popcorn than gunfire. And like waiting for the last stubborn kernels in the pan the sound would come in unexpected intervals. Pop. Pop-pop-pop. Pop-pop. Pop. The BOPE team moved in single file military precision and cleared each corner before proceeding. Jose Galvão's house was only a half mile hike up the mountain but it took us 40 minutes in the hot, muggy afternoon sun. I was soaked in sweat by the time we arrived. The resistance had been minor. Shots were fired from far off and none of them came close to hitting. Either they didn't care too much about protecting a child rapist -- or they were luring us into a trap.

"Take this," Royce said and handed me his 9mm side arm. "And stay put."

His men needed even less instruction as they moved into position. They could do this in their sleep. Four of them entered from above, climbing down from the neighboring rooftop. The rest of them entered from the front door. I could hear them scream instructions in Portuguese as they moved through the house. But there were no gunshots. Thank god. Suddenly...

"'Ta *correndo!*" *Em baixo! Em baixo*! He's running! Below! Below! The man on the roof pointed to a figure darting down a narrow corridor two houses over. "*Vai! Vai!*" Go. Go.

The team took off in pursuit. Their careful formation dissolved into a full on sprint down and through and over the houses and rooftops.

There was no way I'd be able to keep up so I moved into the house tucking the 9mm into the back of my pants. Detective Amalero was already inside questioning an elderly woman. She was rocking and crying.

"She know nothing," Amalero said and threw up his hands. He stepped back and lit a smoke. In his first show of solidarity he offered one to me. I declined. He shrugged and went outside to check his walkie for news of the pursuit. As the old woman quietly sobbed I studied the house. It consisted of two rooms. The living area doubled as a kitchen and a bedroom for the old woman. The other room was a bedroom with a bathroom attached. Men's clothes were washed and folded on a shelf. This must have been Jose Galvão's room. I flipped over the mattress. Beneath it was a shoe box. Inside the faded cardboard was a collection of girls' panties. They were all used. Some with urine stains. Others with blood stains.

My heart raced as I was flooded with anger. I marched into the living room and dumped the panties on the Old Woman's lap. She knew what her grandson was doing. She had to. The house was too small for secrets. "Where is she?! Where's the girl?!" I struggled to recall some rudimentary Portuguese, "*Onde esta a menina*?!" I took a bloody pair and jammed it in her face. "You know! You know! Tell me!!" She fell to the floor crying. I didn't care. I pulled the gun and jammed it into her face, "Where?! *Onde*?!"

Terrified she glanced toward the kitchen. It was a microsecond. But it was enough. I whirled as a burly mass flew from a gap in the wall and slammed into me.

Jose Galvão's body was soft but his hands were strong. The hands of a construction worker. I landed hard on my back and he clenched those stone hands around my neck. I couldn't yell for help. I couldn't breathe. He was heavy. At least 240 lbs. He wore only a pair of shorts and sweat from the roll of fat beneath his chest dripped into my eyes. His breath was a rancid mix of fear and day old alcohol. I felt myself losing consciousness. This was the test. The first time I would be able to use jiu jitsu in a real world situation. And if it didn't work I was going to die before I could hold it over Royce. Think, damnit! Calm your mind. I got control of my breathing and then I moved my legs up around his waist and shifted my hips to the side and with the last of my strength I swept him over and suddenly I was on top. Startled, he let go of my neck and tried to crawl free. But he wasn't going anywhere.

"Where is she?!" I screamed. He spit at me. I snapped and punched him in the face. Over and over. "What did you do to her?!"

Detective Amalero burst in and saved me from doing any serious damage. He pushed me off and flipped Galvão onto his stomach where he secured his hands behind his back with plastic zip ties.

"*Bom, Gringo. Bom,*" Amalero said. He gave me an approving nod as I crawled to my feet gasping for breath. Then he and two returning BOPE dragged both Galvão and his grandmother out into the narrow roadway.

Shaking with adrenaline I proceeded to tear the house apart. Every drawer. Every box. I ripped open the cushions and mattress. I dumped out the small refrigerator. But there was nothing. Other than the box of cotton trophies that I'd already found, there was no sign of the girl.

My dad's daughter.

Leticia.

My sister.

CHAPTER
ELEVEN

SHE HAD no idea how much time had passed. The masked Man allowed her out of the box for only a few minutes at a time and the small, silent room had no windows. Had it been days? Weeks? In the beginning she'd thrown herself at him in a rage, desperate to escape. But he was too strong. And oddly, kind. He never struck back. When she'd finally collapse with exhaustion he'd hold her in his lap and feed her and then bandage the sores on her fingers and knees. The skin was shredded and her fingernails were torn off. She knew that she wouldn't be able to scrape free of the steel box but the panic drove her to try. Every time. And each time he would gently clean and bandage the wounds.

"Guten Abend, gute Nacht, mit Rosen bedacht,"

He spoke only German to her. She understood nothing except that this lullaby was the sign that her time out of the box was coming to an end.

"Por favor! Não!" she begged and clung to his neck. She promised to do anything he asked but when the song came to its gentle end he firmly pushed her down into the box.

"NOOOO!"

The lid closed. Locked. And as she had done every time before she burst into a panic induced frenzy as she clawed at the lid.

CHAPTER
TWELVE

MIDNIGHT. Five days. Five days since my father's murder and my sister's disappearance. I paced outside of the Rio Police station where Detective Amalero and his team were interrogating Jose Galvão. They had obtained a confession within the first three hours, but Leticia's whereabouts were proving elusive. I had a sinking feeling.

"Excuse me? Hello?" the reporter called out. She had been waiting at the station when we arrived with the prisoner. Initially there had been a mob of news teams but they all left after the first hour. Even her own camera man had left. As she approached I realized that I recognized her. I'd seen her segment on the murders while scrolling local news. She'd offered a tip line and I'd sent her a Hail Mary e-mail asking if she'd be willing to share information. That had been just this morning. A lifetime ago.

"I heard you speak English before, with the police," she said. Her own English had an accent but like most of the upper middle class in Brazil she was essentially fluent. "You're the American's son, right?" she asked. She read from notes on her phone, "Miles Ronan?" She pronounced Miles, "Me lees."

"Miles," I corrected her.

"I'm sorry. Miles. Miles," she repeated, committing my name to memory. I got the sense that she didn't make mistakes twice. She offered her hand. Professional and confident. "I'm Marié Alves. You sent me an e-mail." She pronounced Marié like the French, "Ma-hee." She looked younger than she probably was. She wore a button down blouse and slacks. Her hair was pulled back. But from up close no amount of down dressing could hide the soft, natural beauty in her face. And when she smiled she was almost too pretty for the grungy, real world surroundings. The effect was that of an actor playing the role of a "serious" journalist. But one thing I've learned in years of sorting through lies is that looks were deceiving. Action counts.

"Have you heard anything? Have they found the girl?" she asked. She seemed sincere. Not just fishing for a story.

"Not yet," I replied.

"Do you think they have the right guy?" she followed up immediately.

The question hit like a sucker punch. It was at that moment that I realized the answer was no. That Jose Galvão, while undeserving of sympathy, had been set up. The murder and abduction had been too clean. Too perfect. If committed by one person it would've required a high degree of mental focus and physical skill. If committed by a team, they would've been experienced military professionals. Galvão was none of these things. He was clumsy. He was uneducated. He was impulsive. Yes, he would confess to the crimes but there was a reason that he could produce nothing on Leticia. He had nothing. The suddenness of the realization left me vulnerable for a second.

"You don't think he did it, do you?" Marié pounced. Damnit. I was groggy. And she was too cute to be this

sharp. *Did they get the right guy? You don't think he did it?*
She'd trapped me between a negative and a positive. It
forced me to provide more than a yes or no answer.

"I'm hopeful."

"Hopeful for what?"

"Deixa ele! Sai," Royce walked out from the police
station and waved Marié off. She stepped back but refused
to be intimidated.

"Capitão, Mr. Ronan here thinks that you have the
wrong suspect. Do you have a comment?" she spoke in
English for my benefit.

Royce looked at me, "What the fuck, dude?"

I rolled my eyes. "I didn't say that. She's playing you."

Royce whirled on Marié, finger in her face, *"Fica longe.
Fica longe mesmo. Jornalista cachorro."* Get away you journalist dog. Marié flashed fear. Her college journalism class
hadn't prepared her for the fact that not everyone was
impressed with her intrepid reporter routine.

"Royce. She's just doing her job," I said. I pulled him
away and as we headed off to his car I looked over my
shoulder. Marié had already recovered. We locked eyes for
a second and I realized that she and I might be the only
people in this entire country who wanted to uncover the
truth.

"He'll be dead by morning," Royce said as he turned the
meat over the flame. I agreed in silence. Royce lived in a
two bedroom apartment on the tenth floor of a fifteen story
building. The apartment had a small balcony about four
feet wide on which we stood and drank beers as he grilled
strips of meat on the charcoal grill set into the brick wall.
He'd built it himself and it was his pride and joy.

Day or night, Rio was a city of views. Below us the city lights spread down and up and around the dark shadows cast by her stone monoliths. In one direction the lights ran to the ocean. In the other direction, high above, the Christo stood with arms spread. A glowing beacon. Visible from any place in the city. As each piece of meat was deemed ready Royce sliced it into sashimi thin strips and we ate it right there with our bare hands. The day's adrenaline had finally begun to fade. I looked at my watch, 2:00 A.M. Royce's wife and daughter where asleep. They were used to his nocturnal behavior. And with the air conditioner humming in their rooms we could speak freely.

"Amalero wants the case closed. Which means they need to make sure Galvão doesn't change his story," Royce said.

"He didn't do it. You know that," I said.

"No, my friend. He did it. Even if he didn't do it."

Royce looked out over the balcony. It bothered him I could tell, this fluid sense of justice. But it was ingrained in the city's DNA. And his own. It was such a beautiful city, hardly worth razing to the ground just to satisfy a random gringo's desire for revenge.

"What about Leticia?" I asked. I turned down another round of meat. I'd lost my appetite.

"We're on day six, Brother," he replied. "We tried our best."

He was right. The Rio Police and even BOPE were under-staffed and under-funded and that was before corruption siphoned off much of their budget. Besides, six days in a disappearance like this, without a single shred of evidence… almost never had a happy ending.

"I have a present for you," he said, pulling me back from the abyss.

He reached into his pocket and handed me a Brazilian

passport. I opened the book and stared. It was my dad's photo. It must've been taken within the last five years. He was smiling. It was a real smile. A life is good smile. Even his eyes were happy. It was the face of my childhood. But that was all that I recognized. The rest of the page described a complete stranger. This person was named *Francesco Silva*. He had been born three years earlier than my father in *Salvador Bahia, Brazil*.

"I took it from the evidence box. They don't need it anymore. I figured you might want a picture of him."

"Thank you," I said. It was nice to have an image of my dad. The picture proved that he had been a flesh and blood person and not some mythical character.

But more importantly, it provided me with my first real clue.

CHAPTER
THIRTEEN

THE TAIL WORKED as a three man team rotating every other block. I spotted them as I stepped out of my hotel. They must have followed me home the night before. By the time I'd arrived at *Bar Lagoa* to pick up my envelope with the case file I'd identified all three of them and their car, a beat up Fiat with the windows tinted pitch black. They were cops. I recognized one as Detective Amalero's man. They were keeping tabs on me, making sure that I'd given up the case and reverted to tourist mode. I at least looked the part. Shorts, tennis shoes. T-shirt. Dodgers cap.

I slipped into a corner bike shop. They mostly rented clunkers by the day but what drew my attention was a wall of skateboards in the back. I grew up on a skateboard in L.A.. The last time I rode was five years ago when I went back home for Mom's funeral. I'd found an old board while cleaning out her garage. I was lucky to escape that outing with a half dozen stitches. Now at 42 years old it was probably even more foolish.

I exited the store with the new board and with a quick salute to my tail, the chase was on. Within a block I'd regained my teenage form and they had no chance. The streets of Ipanema were narrow affairs lined with five to six story apartment buildings and canopied with the waxy, green leaves of century old Eucalyptus trees. Parked cars and trucks jammed into every open space and the traffic moved at a crawl. I pumped like mad and zipped down the wrong way of a one way street, neatly swerving out of the path of on-coming cars. After three blocks of kamikaze maneuvers I'd lost them. Sweating and breathing hard I eventually popped out of the shadowy maze onto the squint bright, wide open avenue that ran along the beach. The crowds of people gave me plenty of cover as I slowed my roll and slipped into the jet stream of locals flowing along the smooth, well maintained beach path.

Ipanema Beach was a white sand treasure shaped like a three mile long smile. The northern tip of that smile, known as *Arporador,* was dominated by a low granite hill that provided a stunning view back over the swooping beach. At the end of the day the rocks would be covered with blissed out beach goers politely jostling to view the sunset, like fans at a Grateful Dead show. But now, in the middle of the day, it was ruled by skinny local kids diving off the rocks and fishermen dangling homemade poles.

"A skateboarding FBI Agent. That has to be a first."

Marié Alves was "incognito" in brightly colored jogging gear. Spandex short. Sports bra. A floppy baseball cap pulled low. She was sweating and slightly out of breath but in better shape than any journalist I'd ever met. Which meant that every male set of eyes within 30 yards had been clocking her since she arrived. Luckily the rocks kept us hidden from the main beach path.

"I didn't know I still had it in me. Feels good," I grinned, still buzzed from the ride. "Here," I handed her the envelope with the case file summary. "You can hold onto it. But we need to come to terms."

She eagerly flipped through the papers. "Did you hear about the suspect? Jose Galvão?"

"Yeah," I replied. "He hung himself in his cell." Deputy Consul Barry had texted me the news first thing in the morning.

"Have you ever seen a jail cell in Rio?" she asked as she sealed the envelope and gave me her full attention.

"No. But at the rate I'm going I might get my chance."

"It's the size of your hotel bathroom. With at least ten prisoners per cell. It's not a place where a person can just hang themselves."

"Don't worry. I didn't think it was a voluntary suicide."

"Just so we're on the same book."

I smiled and gently corrected her, "The same page. Just so we're on the same page."

"You know what I mean," she said. Despite her confidence she was a little shy about her English. "But thank you. I did a foreign exchange in Seattle when I was in high school. All of your sayings, I still get them confused."

"Are you familiar with the concept of off the record?" I asked. We needed to set the ground rules if this relationship were to be of any use.

"Yes. Of course. I won't use your name if that's what you want."

"That is what I want. I also want you to promise not to run *anything* until we find Leticia Silva."

This condition didn't go over as well but I pressed on, "Thanks to Jose Galvão's confession whoever's holding her just might assume that the police have given up. This means they just might relax their guard. And just might keep her alive long enough for us to find her."

She understood the logic. I could also tell that she wanted to make a difference. If she was interested in fame there were plenty of other avenues for a girl as attractive as Marié Alves.

"Understood. But when it's over I run with everything. That means your story and your dad's story." The counter-offer. She'd been used enough in her short life. No more.

I didn't like the idea of becoming famous. Famous FBI Agents were either fired or promoted. Either way my life would be turned upside down. But fuck it. My career wasn't going anywhere anyway. Plus, I didn't have time to waste and I needed a guide. Someone who knew this world. Who spoke the language. And by offering her the story that would launch her career; it meant that I just might be able to trust her.

"Deal," I said and offered my hand. She juggled the case file envelope and hurried to shake. Her hand was smooth and soft but her grip was strong. She ended the contact on a brisk formal note before I could get any ideas. She then burst into an infectious grin, "Awesome!" I got the sense I was her first secret source. Her first undercover investigation. "Where do we start?" she asked.

"With Francesco Silva." I showed her my dad's Brazilian passport. "This is a real passport. It's not a forgery. That means he was able to open bank accounts. Purchase property. Sign contracts. How does a fugitive American named Frank Ronan become a real, living, breathing Brazilian named Francesco Silva?"

"For the right price anything is possible in Brazil," she replied.

"But who did he pay off? Who was helping him? Based on the degree of difficulty of the murder - let's assume they didn't choose my dad by random. They killed him for a reason."

"Which means that they must have known who he really was," she replied.

"The police report lists five people that attended his birthday party the night he died. We start with them."

CHAPTER
FOURTEEN

DETECTIVE ROBERTO AMALERO was 34 years old and had been with the Rio Police since he'd finished the two years of military service required of all 18 year old Brazilian males. He'd risen to the rank of Lieutenant Detective faster than anyone in recent memory. The reason for his success was equal parts competence and political awareness. Since coming onto the force he'd made it a point to find out what his superiors wanted - and then got it done.

His latest coup was winning the confidence of Bruno Pesado, the populist Mayor of Rio who was in the final year of his second term. Pesado, affectionately known as *Gordinho*, or little fat man, was tall and thin with huge hands and a shaved head. His nickname came from a play off his last name *Pesado* which meant heavy. Now at 55 years old he was at a crossroads. Move on to politics on the national stage? Or retire? Eight years as Mayor of one of the most corrupt cities in Brazil meant that he had a nice little nest egg; however dirty money was expensive. It cost half a million a year for his lawyers to keep the various Federal investigations at bay. It was money well spent. The last five Rio de Janeiro mayors had ended up in prison following their terms. He had no intention of joining the club.

"Amalero! Stop lurking, Man! Come," Pesado waved for Amalero to join him at his regular table in the back of iconic *Confeiteria Colombo*. Amalero had been patiently waiting in the wings as Pesado held court for a group of reporters and fawning city deputies. The restaurant, located in the Centro district of the city, was a replica of a Parisian confeiteria with a décor heavy on mirrored walls and brass railings. The glass bakery counter was legendary. On Sundays the line snaked around the block as people came for post mass cake and coffee. Pesado had made it his daily lunch spot because he liked to get his picture taken in a place that held happy memories for voters.

"But first, a picture with the hero of the day," he bellowed as he stood and put an arm around Amalero's shoulder. Pesado's social media assistant snapped photos for the day's feed. "Perfect. Now everyone beat it," he ordered. He waited until the black suited Security detail cleared a perimeter around his table.

"Good work, Detective. I'm told our suspect has confessed. Resolution is good. Anything I should know about the interrogation?"

"Like we thought, Jose Galvão had been sleeping in the neighbor's house the night of the murders. He said he heard the girl scream. Just once. And then it was silent. Said he looked out the window and thinks he saw the killer leave."

"Just one man? Not a team?"

"One man. A white man dressed all in black. He was carrying the girl."

"So he didn't leave with the money?"

"Just the girl," Amalero replied. "He must've come back to frame Galvão on a different day."

"Interesting," Pesado replied. "What about the gringo, this FBI Agent? I hear he knows what he's doing."

"We're on him," Amalero assured. There was no need to explain that his men had lost track of Agent Ronan this morning. "If he finds anything we'll be the first to know."

Pesado motioned for Amalero to lean close. "If he finds anything, he ends up like his dad. The same goes for the daughter. No loose ends. Understood?"

Amalero nodded, "*Claro.*" Of course.

"*Excelente,*" he said and patted Amalero on the arm. "I talked to your Captain. You're on this full time now. Dive into the mud. Get dirty. But find the money. I assure you it's much better to retire in dollars than reals."

As soon as Amalero left, the Mayor welcomed his next guest. His good friend and tennis partner, Deputy Consul David Barry. As he sat down Barry slid a piece of paper across the table.

"What's this?" Pesado asked.

"A receipt."

Pesado took a minute to read. "For a travel visa?"

"Frank Ronan's daughter went to Disney World on a school trip two years ago," Barry explained. "The visa fee was paid via a credit card linked to an anonymous LLC. Tell your men to get smarter. Frank Ronan didn't bury his money in a damn hole in the ground."

"It's in a bank," realized Pesado.

"Do you know how much $50 million dollars would be worth after 30 years of compounding interest?"

"How much?"

"A lot."

The mayor leaned back to consider the possibilities.

When Barry first came to him with his wild story of a gringo's hidden treasure they were smoking cigars after an afternoon of tennis and private massages. All of it on the Mayor's tab. Barry wasn't the type to pick up the check. The information had felt like a favor. An attempt at paying him back for countless requests that the mayor had granted. But now that the treasure had crystalized from fantasy into reality, the Deputy Consul's tone had changed. Did he really think that Pesado was working for him?

"How long have you had this receipt?" asked Pesado.

"How long have I had the receipt? What do you mean?"

"A day? Hours? Weeks? It's a simple question."

"I don't know. I have a million things come across my desk. Yesterday, maybe..."

"I have this feeling that there are things that you're not telling me. I don't know why. Maybe it's your tone. But when people lie to me it makes me angry. I don't want to be angry at you, my friend. And you definitely don't want me to be angry at you," warned Pesado.

"Of course not," Barry stammered. "I swear, I'm not hiding anything." Despite Barry's many flaws, and he was aware of them all, one thing that he prided himself on was an ability to read a room. "My bad," he backtracked. "You're right. I'm just a passenger on this train. You know how to handle your men. I'm just excited is all. This could turn out to be big. Much bigger than I thought."

Pesado poured himself a fresh cup of coffee from a small silver pot on the table and took his time as he spooned in a mound of sugar. He liked Barry. He was a good gringo. One that knew his place. "I can see you having a very nice life here, Mr. Barry. With friends like me Rio de Janeiro can be a paradise on Earth."

"I'm ready, my friend. Oh, am I ready," Barry grinned.

"But with an enemy like me -- it can feel like you've

been dropped into the pits of hell. I suggest you stop smiling so much. And recognize that I've been playing this game my whole life while you've just laced up your first pair of shoes."

Barry wiped the smile off his face with his hand and pretended to place it back in his pocket. Pesado considered reaching across the table and slapping the man. But instead he humored him with a laugh. He raised his coffee cup. "To compounding interest."

"To compounding interest," Barry replied, raising his own glass.

Pesado took a sip and then leaned in close, grasping Barry's hand as if they were sealing a blood bond. "We are both smart men. Sometimes too many smart men in one room is dangerous. So we must work together if this is going to play out. We must be able to trust each other. Do you understand?"

"Totally. One hundred percent. Anything you need. Anything. Just let me know," Barry assured him.

"Good. I may hold the keys to hell; but our mutual friend -- he's the devil."

CHAPTER
FIFTEEN

FOLLOW THE MONEY. It's not just a cliché. It's standard operating procedure at the Bureau. As Marié drove us across the city I kept returning to this phrase. In my experience the motives for murder are limited. Money was almost always the winner. Revenge or rage second. Bat shit crazy came in third. Based on the gruesome crime scene all three were in play. Revenge and bat shit crazy tended toward the bloodier side. But there's a reason the wealthy of Brazil walked behind security details and drove bullet proof cars and lived in gated condominiums. Everywhere I looked the inequality was in your face. The poverty was real. The wealth extreme. And if you had it - you could assume that someone else was gonna want it.

Our first visit was with Dr. Fatima Santiago. A dermatologist who catered to Rio's movie and TV industry. My new partner was already proving her worth as it took her just one call to get us a same day appointment. After the obligatory cheek kisses we sat down in the stylish office for our consultation. The doctor had been friends with my dad's wife, Aparecida. They'd bonded over a love of botox and the fact that their daughters were in school together.

"My daughter has been crying non-stop since it happened," Dr. Santiago said. "She and Leticia weren't close but they were friends. I think it's the shock more than anything, the fact that this could happen to someone you know. And then the news today that this... this, what was he? A handyman? How he confessed to killing all of them. I guess we'd been holding out hope that Leticia got away."

Marié leaned in and said, "We think there's still hope."

"Oh? Really?" Dr. Santiago said. I could see her mood lift. "If there's anything I can do," she offered. "Please. I want to help."

"What did you know about Francesco Silva?" I asked.

"Not much. Just what Aparecida told me. That he was a retired investor. You know like stocks and things. I only met him a couple of times. But of course, now it turns out he was..." She looked to Marié for confirmation, "It's true what they say? That he was a criminal? A fugitive?"

"It looks like it," Marié replied. "Did Aparecida know the truth about her husband?"

"I really don't know. But if she did, she was good at keeping a secret."

"How was their relationship?" I asked, "He was a lot older. Was there anyone else in her life?"

The doctor shook her head, "Oh no. Never. Aparecida looked glamorous but deep down she was a simple person. Loyal. She adored Francesco. He'd pulled her out of a fishing village in Bahia and gave her everything. And if you ever met Francesco, he was how you say, virile. He had this power that drew people. No. Even if he had a dozen lovers Aparecida still wouldn't have looked at another man."

And just like that, the mythical character returned.

"What can you tell us about their daughter?" Marie asked.

"Leticia? I think she was happy. I mean, she had everything. I spoil my daughter but they really spoiled Leticia. And it didn't seem to change her. From what I could see she was still super nice to everyone she met."

"Any boyfriends? Anyone that might be trying to manipulate her?" I asked.

"I don't know. I can ask my daughter. But I can't see her being involved in anything dangerous. She really seemed to be sheltered. Too much if you ask me. I mean these kids need to be exposed to the world. They can't be treated like a fairy tale princess forever. I told that to Aparecida once. She didn't want to hear it. It felt like she and Francesco were determined to extend Leticia's childhood as long as they could."

"Why, do you think?" I asked.

The doctor looked around her office. The walls and shelves were devoted to brochures about anti-aging laser peels and rejuvenating botox treatments. "Immortality," she shrugged. "As long as your baby is still living at home, you don't have to grow old."

Our consultation ended soon after, as the doctor had patients waiting. As we left she insisted on a selfie with Marié and promised to forward her photos from the night of Dad's birthday. The visit had revealed no real clues but it had provided the first real truth about my father. That he hadn't changed. Up until the end he'd been trying to play god.

"He always picked up the check and never made you feel lesser for it." Gabriel Martins was a professor of South American literature at the Rio extension of the *Universidade do São Paulo*, the country's elite university. "I would call him a classic renaissance seeker. Always asking questions.

Always picking people's brains. Every time we'd go out it would be with a whole new group of people. I'd watch as he sucked up their knowledge and then once they were empty, I'd never see them again. I felt lucky to be invited so many times. I think he liked to visit with me because of my English -- I lived in America for a decade while I taught at Princeton. Don't get me wrong, his Portuguese was quite good but in English, he was able to relax."

"Did he tell you about his life in the U.S.?" I asked.

"He mentioned that he'd been a police officer. He had a lot of stories from those days. But, did I know he was a fugitive? No. I never pried to be honest. Don't kick a free lunch in the mouth is what I say. But I did sense that he'd left family behind. You're his son, I assume? You have his eyes. You, Francesco and your sister. All the same eyes. Shiny. Piercing. Like very observant sparklers." He was proud of his literary flourish. Then embarrassed. "Forgive me, like all literature professors I'm really just an aspiring writer at heart."

The professor's office was small but tidy. Certificates and diplomas were prominently displayed. He was a man who was proud of his opinions, but had few people to give them to.

"What is your take, Professor?" I asked. "What do you think happened?"

"What do I think? Oh my. Well, if I were to put on my Sherlock Holmes hat… It had to be someone that he knew. Right? That would be the only way to enter the house. You know who I would look at is his lawyer. He would know where the bodies are buried, so to speak. I met him for the first time at the birthday gathering. A real stand-offish fellow. At one point the two of them snuck away for a private conversation. When they returned Francesco was different. Subdued."

"Any idea what they were talking about?"

"Honestly, I drank a lot that night. I *will* miss Francesco's wine cellar. I just know it was some time before he reverted to his jovial self."

"How did the lawyer react? Did he seem upset as well?" I was trying to determine who had delivered the bad news. My dad or the lawyer.

"Now that I think about it he did seem a little more upset than Francesco. I think he left the party soon after."

The lawyer's name was Paulo Heinrik. He was an exclusive criminal and immigration lawyer with an office in downtown Rio. His secretary politely took a message but made no promises that he would call back.

The final guests from Dad's birthday party were Daniel and Tanya Gonsalves. We arrived at the restaurant to find them already waiting at the table. Introductions were followed by elaborate hugs and double cheek kisses and by the time we sat the entire restaurant had been made aware that a minor celebrity was in their midst.

"I can't believe I'm having dinner with Serafina," Tanya gushed. "Please. I have to have a selfie. Is that OK?"

"Of course," Marié said. She leaned in and allowed Tanya to take a grinning photo of the two of them.

"Aparecida would be dying. She loved *Guerra das Gêmeas*," Tanya said, wiping her eyes which had begun to water as she recalled her recently dead friend.

Marié clocked my confusion and explained, "Serafina is the name of a character I played in a TV show."

"Serafina *and* Katarina," Tanya said. "They were twins. *Guerra das Gêmeas*. War of the twins," she translated for me. "It was one of the most popular novelas ever."

"Wow. You really are famous," I teased Marié.

"That was a long time ago," she insisted.

"So, let me guess, one twin was evil and one twin was good?"

"Yes!" Tanya squealed and then jumped in to relay the plot, "And they were separated at birth and never knew that each other existed."

"Until they both fell in love with the same man?" I offered.

"Exactly!" she chirped. "He was the son of this super rich businessman and the bad twin, Katarina, was trying to steal his money while the good twin really loved him. But it turned out that the bad twin was being used by her adopted father in order to get revenge on the businessman. So in the end, the bad twin ends up sacrificing herself in order to save her sister... Serafina."

"Who I assume goes on to marry the son of the super rich businessman and lives happily ever after?"

Katarina clapped her hands in mock applause.

"I love it. Can't wait to see it," I teased.

"Too bad it's in Portuguese," said Marié.

"Damn. Can I get a selfie at least?" I asked.

"Don't even think about it," she warned.

Daniel and Tanya loved the banter. They also loved being the restaurant's center of attention. This fleeting connection to Marié and the scandal of the week was as close to celebrity as they would ever get and they'd eagerly cleared their schedule for us. Daniel was a vice president with a Brazilian soft drink company. He was in his 40's and well traveled. Tanya was a housewife who prided herself on keeping up with the latest movies and tele-novelas. Both of them were upper class born and raised and were proud to show off their just passable English. And while neither seemed torn up over the brutal murders of their recent hosts; neither of them seemed capable of murder.

According to Tanya they'd met Francesco Silva and his stunning wife Aparecida at an art exhibit a little over a year ago. "They invited us to a dinner party right after. I think Francesco wanted to use Daniel for business. But me and Aparecida, we really hit it off."

After a long but enjoyable meal the dishes were cleared and the coffee and check were delivered. Daniel insisted on paying. I let him. The place looked expensive. Besides, the couple had begun to share urgent glances. He wanted something from me. Paying for dinner made him feel more comfortable to ask. I drank my coffee in silence, allowing the tension to build. Finally Daniel couldn't take it any longer.

"I would like to talk serious with you because your dad... No easy way to say this... your dad owes me money." Daniel had been speaking in English most of the night but now he was nervous and stumbling over words so he turned to Marié and spilled the rest of the story in Portuguese.

It turned out that Daniel had invited my dad to invest in a start-up idea. A website that bought and sold crypto currencies in Brazil. The two of them had created an LLC with the help of Dad's lawyer and Daniel had gone ahead and sunk his life savings into the website construction. Dad's investment was to be R$500,000 which would be used to buy the first offering of Bitcoin. Unfortunately he was murdered before the wire transfer was complete. Now Daniel needed to get a hold of Paulo Heinrik in order to approve the transfer. But Heinrik had stopped returning his calls.

"Por favor, can you make Heinrik send the money. He is your Dad's lawyer. Your dad is dead. That means he has to do what you say," Daniel begged.

"I'm not sure it works that way," I apologized.

"Please, can you at least talk to him? Tell him to call me?" he pleaded.

"My friend, Paulo Heinrik isn't returning my calls either. It might help if I had some kind of leverage. Is there anything you can tell me... something about him or his relationship with my dad?"

Daniel considered. As he wrestled with himself I studied the man. He was a trim, healthy type with a deep tan. One of those locals that I'd seen taking their daily exercise out on the beach. His Rolex was real. His wife's phone was the latest model. She was better looking than him and despite being a successful executive he seemed to look to her for his social cues. And now she was giving him a wide eyed nudge. He took a deep breath of courage and spoke in Portuguese for Marié to translate. When he was finished Marié held back a smile and told me, "He thinks that Heinrik is gay. He says he saw him at the beach in Leblon walking with a much younger man who was in really good shape."

"Gay?" I tried not to laugh. "I don't know if that counts as leverage these days."

Daniel expanded on his theory, "No. No. He saw me. I was playing volleyball. This was just two days ago. After the murders. And when he saw me the two of them took off in different directions. He didn't want me to see them together. He's hiding something. I know it."

"Maybe he just didn't want to pay you your money?" I suggested.

Marié stepped in, "Maybe this friend of his might be able to provide some clues? Can you describe him?"

"Tall. White -- but not a gringo. He looked like he was from the South. His hair was short, close to blonde. He was in very good shape. Like a model."

As Daniel and Tanya tried to impress Marié with insights I let their Portuguese flow past and slipped into my own thoughts. It had been a long day. But productive. Paulo Heinrik was the key. But the key to what? $R500,000 was not worth killing someone over. Not when they're potentially worth tens of millions. And who was this mystery friend? An accomplice? Physically it sounded like he could have pulled off the murders and kidnapping. There was also the question of why Dad would want to invest in Daniel's crypto scheme? Was Heinrik trying to talk him out of it? Did he see Daniel as a money pit? The questions had begun to pile up. Which was a good sign. At least they would keep me busy.

It was after midnight when we left the restaurant and there was still a crowd waiting to sit down for dinner. As Marié drove me back to my hotel we both fell silent. Outside the car window the daytime flow of bikers and joggers had been replaced by restaurant goers and nightclubbers. The thick heat of the day had begun to cool and the energy of the city had shifted into a new gear. Faster. Edgier. The traffic had thinned but continued to unfold like a complex multi-player video game. When the day started I'd clenched the door handle so tight I was afraid it would break off. But now I'd come to respect Marié's driving. She drove like she thought. Always looking for an opening. She paused at a light and snuck a glance. I didn't look away.

"How old were you when your dad left?" she asked.

"Twelve."

"Did you hear from him much?"

"Never."

"Never? Not even on your birthday? Not even a call? Or a card? Or like a mystery present with no name?"

"Nothing. He just disappeared."

She had to digest the idea of a parent disappearing into thin air. "I'm so sorry. My dad died of cancer when I was twenty. It was hard. It's still hard, when I think of him... But I always had him with me right up until the end. I can't imagine if he'd just disappeared."

"It was a long time ago. I hardly remember to be honest."

"Or maybe you blocked it out?"

"Remind me, are you a therapist or a journalist?"

She laughed. It was infectious. Like a pop song. "My college professor made us all take therapy. He said that if you do your job right an interview should be like a therapy session."

"Except that a journalist turns around and blabs your secrets to the world."

"It's not a perfect system," she shrugged. And then added, "Does the FBI teach you to ask easy questions?"

I smiled, "Only when the other side is holding a gun."

"Funny. My professor also said that the best way to get an honest response is give a little bit of yourself."

"Sounds fair. You go first," I said with no intention of holding up my end of the deal.

She considered how much to give as she gunned the car through a busy left turn and swerved around a loitering taxi before neatly sliding the car into the lone parking spot in front of my hotel. She then looked me in the eye with a disarming confidence.

"I'm twenty nine years old. I'm divorced. I live with my mother who I adore and will never abandon. And I hate that I'm famous for being in a soap opera when I was seventeen."

It was my turn. I cringed. This shouldn't be so hard. Normal people share their deepest secrets all the time. "OK. Let's see… I'm forty two. Divorced twice. I live alone in a one bedroom rental with no furniture to speak of," I offered. And then quickly added, "It's not as sad as it sounds. I get to travel a lot."

She took in my pitiful existence and then pointed out, "That means Leticia is the only family you have."

"It looks that way," I admitted.

Then, as if on cue, her phone pinged. She checked the screen. "It's the party photos from Dr. Santiago." She did a quick scroll and something jumped out at her. "I think you're going to want to see these."

CHAPTER
SIXTEEN

"HEY. HEY. WAKE UP," Marié said as she gave me a nudge. She then walked to the window and pulled open the blinds revealing the bright mid morning sun and my stunning view of a brick wall. I groaned. Everything hurt. My penance for taking up skateboarding again in my forties. It didn't help that I'd given the bed to Marié and had fallen asleep in a hotel room chair.

Last night we'd gone through Dr. Santiago's photo roll. My dad had clearly become an expert at avoiding the camera. Out of twenty photos he appeared in only one, and it was of the back of his head. The rest of the photos captured a small but happy gathering similar to what the others had described. Leticia appeared in several of the shots. She seemed to be a mature and friendly girl. Comfortable in social settings. The life of the party. Like our father. Even though we'd never met I felt like we were becoming friends.

The most interesting photo of the bunch was a group shot at the end of the party. In the background was the figure of a man. The figure could be seen through the sliding glass door as he stood in the back yard. Like the boogie man in a horror movie. He was tall. A white man. Dressed in dark pants and shirt. Although we couldn't make out the face, based on photos from earlier in the party he looked to be a similar body type to Dad's lawyer, Paulo Heinrik. However the time stamp on the photo read 1:00 AM. Two hours *after* Heinrik had left the party.

"I called Heinrik's office again. No answer," Marié said.

"Don't tell me the Marié Alves magic has run dry."

"The one time I want it to work. Go figure," she grinned.

I walked over to the small table where our growing pile of evidence was gathered. I had drawn up a time line of the night of the murders. According to the police report Heinrik was the first to leave the party. His car was seen on security video driving out the front gate at 11:30 pm and there was no sign of him or his car returning to the condominium.

"Speaking of magic… I would really like to know how this guy appeared in my Dad's backyard an hour and a half after he left the building?"

"He seems to be full of tricks," Marié said.

We were finishing each other's thoughts now. It felt good.

"I sent the photo to a tech here in the FBI lab. He should be able to pull up a face. But you'll have to wait your turn. This is a personal favor, not an official case so the tech needs to do the work on his own time."

"Thanks, Boss," I replied. "Anything on this Paulo Henrik?" As we spoke I tried to gauge Agent Wills' mood on the other end of the call. I needed to know how long I could rely on him. For now I sensed no reluctance. But for a career agent with a family to support there would eventually be a line he wouldn't cross.

"There are no flags in our database. He's never even been to the U.S. Which is unusual for a rich Brazilian. So I threw the name to a guy on the South American desk and he found some interesting family history..." Wills paused, as if someone had entered the room. "I can't get into it now. I'll forward you the summary."

"Thanks again. I owe you a souvenir. Maybe one of these speedo looking swimsuits the guys wear down here."

"Sounds good. I'll use it at our next pool party. The kids haven't been embarrassed of their dad in a while. I'm an extra-large by the way."

"The horror. The horror," I replied.

Wills rewarded me with a laugh. But then grew quiet. The *Apocalypse Now* reference was a little too close for comfort.

"Keep your head on a swivel, Agent Ronan. I'll be in touch." And the call went dead.

I set my phone down and looked across the bustling open air plaza and up toward a glass and concrete high rise office building. Paulo Heinrik's office was on the tenth floor. With Marié's help I had made an appointment with a dentist on the seventh floor. She'd told them I was a tourist friend with a dental emergency and I'd be paying in dollars. Amazingly a spot had suddenly opened on their schedule. I still had a few minutes before I was expected.

Enough time to read through the FBI summary that had just landed in my e-mail box.

CHAPTER
SEVENTEEN

DETECTIVE AMALERO HAD TAKEN over surveillance of the FBI agent. He had been on his tail since he and the journalist had left the hotel at midmorning. It was now noon and they'd made a winding circle through the beach area and downtown and then over the massive suspension bridge spanning the bay to the subdued neighborhood of *Niteroi*. They had made no efforts to disguise their route and Amalero finally realized that he'd been duped. He threw a flasher on his roof and waved the car to the side of the road. As he expected, Marié was driving but the passenger seat was empty. Agent Ronan had jumped out at some point during the drive.

"Detective! So good to see you!" cried Marié as she propped her cellphone in the passenger seat to record their encounter.

"*Filho de puta,*" muttered Amalero.

"I've been wanting to ask you so many questions!" she continued. "Like, how is it that Jose Galvão was able to hang himself in a cell with dozens of witnesses? Did you and your men force his confession? Or how about, why have you stopped searching for Leticia Silva? I would also *love* to know how a fugitive like Frank Ronan was able to live unmolested right under your nose for all these years? Are the Rio Police selling protection to international fugitives?"

Amalero stared at her with dead eyes. He had to remind himself that she was just a kid. All this idealism. She was so shiny and new that she almost glowed. He blamed the movies. In the real world journalists weren't heroes. They were parasites.

"Your mother was worried when you didn't come home last night," he said.

"Excuse me?"

It made him feel warm inside to watch her condescending smirk disappear. She wouldn't be the first reporter he'd broken. She was just the next. "Don't worry, I sat with her. I let her know you that you were working on a very important story."

"You were at my apartment? Inside? She let you inside?"

"Of course. I'm a police officer. I'm here to protect. And there had been a threat."

"I can take care of myself. I don't need any protection from you."

"I'm sorry. I was unclear. The threat wasn't against you," he waited a moment so that he had her full attention. "It was against your mother."

Marié froze.

A decade ago Detective Amalero, and almost every man in Brazil, had dreamed of taking the teenage Marié Alves' virginity. Today that dream would come true. He leaned into the car window and whispered in her ear, "Now turn off the camera so that we can have a real conversation."

CHAPTER
EIGHTEEN

I SHOWED my I.D. to the lobby security and they called up to the dentist's office to confirm my appointment. I then passed through a metal detector to get to a wall of elevators. The level of security felt cartoonish for a mid-level office building. But in Rio safety sells.

I rode in the phone booth sized box up to the tenth floor. I figured that I had about fifteen minutes before the busy dentist office realized that their gringo patient had gotten lost. Plenty of time. The tenth floor was quiet. I walked down the row of offices until I came to a thick wooden door. The polished gold plaque read, *P. Heinrik. Avogado.* The door was locked. They would have to buzz me in from the inside. I glanced up at the camera above the door. I didn't have time to wait for someone to exit... I'd have to take my chances on human curiosity. And perhaps some distraction. I dialed the office on my phone. Then as soon as I heard it ring I pushed the buzzer and looked down at the floor. Inside I could hear the Secretary, "*Halo? Escritorio de Senhor Heinrik?*" I put her on hold and called the office on a second line as I pushed the buzzer again and again. "*Halo?*

Halo?" Finally the Secretary gave up and the door clicked open.

The office was modest. A cramped waiting area with a reception desk for the Secretary and another door leading to Heinrik's private office. The Secretary was a middle aged woman who seemed to be good at her job. She immediately recognized that I shouldn't be there. That in fact I was the gringo that she'd been warned about. I aimed a finger at her and commanded, *"Senta!"* Sit! She obeyed - but at the same time her hand moved beneath the desk to push a silent alarm. It didn't matter. By the time security arrived I'd have what I came for. I made a bee-line for Heinrik's office. The door was closed. I ran at full speed and kicked. The door jam cracked open. I kicked again. Again! The door fell inward and I was inside.

Paulo Heinrik at 60 years old was a formidable presence. He was strong and tall with a relatively full head of brown and grey checked hair. His tailored suit was impeccable. His white shirt contrasted with his rich tan. He was tall. Imposing. I wasn't going to physically intimidate him. But the shock of me busting through the door was sure to light up his adrenal gland flushing his brain with endorphins. For the next three seconds it would be impossible for him to do any of the mental calculations necessary to deceive.

"What happened to Leticia Silva?! Where is she?!" I shouted.

It took him exactly four seconds to formulate his response, "I… I don't know."

During these four seconds Heinrik's eyes subconsciously glanced up and to the left multiple times as the left side of his brain attempted to kick start its rationalizing functions. If he were able to give a truthful answer it would have blurted out immediately, as a defense mechanism. I'd got what I came for. He was lying. He either knew where she was or knew what had happened to her. Both were chilling prospects in light of the short bio that I had just read.

"Agent Ronan. Won't you have a seat," he said, motioning to the chair across from his desk. Heinrik had regained his composure. He'd now tell me nothing that he didn't want me to know. "I was just about to return your call. Your father was not only a client, but a friend of mine. I'm deeply sorry for your loss."

"The loss was more yours than mine. I didn't know the guy," I replied. I glanced toward the open door and the frantic Secretary who had gone into the hall to await the Security Guards. I had maybe two minutes. Not enough time to be subtle. "I know you killed him. Or had a part in it. The way I see it you helped create his new identity and helped stash his money. Probably through a series of shell companies. And after he died you planned to end up with control of the accounts. But he started to burn through the money. Fancy houses. Stupid investments. So you killed him."

I could hear the elevator ding.

I continued, "I'll make you a deal. Keep the fucking money. I don't want it. Keep the money. But give me my sister. And you'll never see me again."

"There is no money, Agent Ronan," Heinrik said. He was an excellent liar. His marble blue eyes bore into me. "I assume you were told that your father and I argued the night of his murder. This is true. Francesco, excuse me, I knew him as Francesco, had spent or lost almost all of his money. I begged him to downsize his life or he and his family would be out in the street. But he'd convinced himself that this clown Daniel Gonsalves would save him. I argued otherwise."

Two Security Guards ran into the office. Heinrik held up a hand to stop them. He wanted to finish, "Your father's murder - his family's murder, was tragic. But it had nothing to do with money. It had nothing to do with me. It was, for lack of better words, an act of god."

"Since when do Nazis believe in god?" I replied.

He sneered and flicked his hand for the Security Guards to take me away. A gesture that seemed ingrained in his DNA.

———

Agent Wills' brief had been gathered by Israeli intelligence. It turned out that Heinrik's Brazilian roots were established in the late 1940s when his grandfather, Gustof Heinrik, fled Europe after the fall of Berlin and came to Brazil to join an enclave of fellow Germans in the Southern state of Santa Catarina where the cool, mountain climate reminded them of home. They would go on to build a self contained community that, from clothes to food to housing, resembled an idyllic village in the German Alps. Albeit one with a dark secret. During the war Gustof had overseen many of Hitler's human experiments. It's believed that he brought hundreds of research files from Germany and that he was using this hidden community in Brazil to plant the seeds for a new movement.

Lucky for the world, Mossad Nazi hunters eventually caught up with Gustof. He was assassinated in the summer of 1965 while dining in a restaurant in São Paulo. The file contained actual photographs of the body. One shot in the forehead. Two shots in the heart. All of them point blank. The killer had looked him in the eyes as he died.

The Mossad has since kept track of the Santa Catarina village which is why they were aware of Gustof's grandson,

Paulo Heinrik, who operated a secretive law practice out of Rio de Janeiro. Paulo rarely tried a case in court. It seems that his entire practice revolved around obtaining Brazilian citizenship for foreign nationals. Or in other words, creating new identities for fugitives. A skill that his family perfected three generations ago.

Just as interesting as the Heinrik family history was the name cc'd at the top of Wills' e-mail: *Jaime Gold*. The same name as the Mossad agent responsible for locating Gustof Heinrik in 1965. Wills was sending me a message: Gold was still alive and I needed to reach out to him.

But that would have to wait. Right now two enthusiastic security guards were grinding my face into the sidewalk as they waited for the Rio Police to come pick me up.

CHAPTER
NINETEEN

ROYCE ARRIVED JUST IN TIME. Exactly twenty seconds earlier I'd watched Heinrik's Mercedes pull out of the building's underground parking. The windows were tinted pitch black but I recognized the car from the security footage from Dad's party. Royce badged the security guards who immediately let me go. He told them to get lost and then he turned on me, "I get about five hours sleep every two days and you just wasted two of them."

"I'm going to owe you even bigger. I need to borrow your car. Like right now," I held out my hands for his keys.

"You got somewhere to go? Get in. I'll drive."

"Sorry, Brother. I can't tell you why but I need your car. I need it right now. You have a wife and kids. Go home and give them a hug and I'll call you when I'm done."

As Royce struggled with this epic decision I watched the Mercedes turn the corner at the end of the block. I was going to lose him.

"Name your price. Travel visa for the family to go to DisneyWorld? I can put a word in with the Deputy Consul. He loves me. On your salary no way you meet the income threshold; and I'll bet you every kid in your daughter's class has already gone. Here's your chance, man. Dad of the year."

"You're such an asshole." Royce reluctantly held out the keys. "Don't fucking scratch it."

I snatched the keys and ran. "I'll call you tonight. Get some sleep. You're going to need it!" Hopefully the promise of future action would sooth his ego.

Royce's car was a fifteen year old VW Golf. The car was well maintained and had serious zip and sliced through the crowded, narrow streets. It took less than five minutes to catch up with the bulky Mercedes. I followed from a distance using the shifting Rio traffic as cover and thirty minutes later we arrived in the exclusive neighborhood of *São Conrado,* a pocket of beach front luxury high-rises nestled at the base of a looming wall of jungle. The Mercedes pulled into the basement garage of one of the buildings and disappeared. I parked along the beach to assess my next move. The apartment building had even more security than the downtown office. It would take an assault team to breach the entrance. Which also meant that it would have been difficult to sneak in a kidnapped teenage girl. No, if Heinrik was holding her, she wasn't here.

"Follow the money…" I reminded myself.

My phone rang. It was Marié. She explained that she'd led the police on a wild chase but they must've eventually caught on and gave up. It was a long story full of unnecessary detail. Either she was still wound up by the adventure; or she was hiding something. She wanted to come meet me but I told her no. I had another job for her.

"Heinrik's involved," I said. "Leticia's not here but

wherever she's at I'll bet he owns the property. Is there a way to find property records linked to Paulo Heinrik?"

"I can check with the city," I could hear her brain spinning, "I have an architect friend. He'd know how to begin."

"The properties won't be under his name," I warned her. "They'll be under LLCs or shell companies. Start with whatever entity owns his office and his apartment here in *São Conrado*." I then had another thought. "You should also check the house where my dad was living. I'll bet Heinrik was the landlord."

"Got it. What about you?" she asked.

"I'm not moving until he does. If Leticia's still alive that means she's been held captive for seven days. Mentally she'll have gone numb, but her body will be stressed. Her health will start to collapse. It's actually a good thing. It means her kidnappers will need to devote more attention to her. They'll need to feed her. Bath her. He won't be able to go much longer without paying a visit to the site."

"O.K. I'll get on the property records. Hey…"

"Yeah?"

"Be careful," she said and then quickly hung up.

"You too," I replied to the dead line.

I looked out over the beach. Young kids from the nearby favela were surfing on busted surfboards held together with duct tape. I found myself out there with them. Mind surfing. Slipping back to the summer before Dad disappeared. He and Mom had been divorced as long as I could remember but he'd always been around. I was about ten when he taught me to surf. I could barely swim. Dog paddle at the YMCA was as far as my lessons ever went. But he dragged me out past the breakers in Venice by forcing me to hold on to his ankle leash. The waves were probably shoulder high. Nothing serious. But I was terrified. He wouldn't let me get out until I'd caught a wave. We sat out there bobbing on our boards for two hours. Me: crying and shivering. Him: waiting for me to get over my fears. The lifeguard at one point grew concerned and waved at us to come in. Dad told him to mind his own fucking business. The lifeguard, all of 20 years old, wasn't going to mess with him. I eventually caught my first wave that day. One of many that summer. I wondered if he'd kept surfing here in Brazil. If he taught Leticia to surf. I wondered if she was the type of girl who sat on the beach; or had Dad drug her out past the breakers and taught her to face down that snarling wall of water and do whatever the hell it took to survive.

An e-mail appeared on my phone. It was from Jaime Gold. It read: "*We need to talk.*" And provided a local phone number. He was in Rio. The guy must be over 80. What was a former Mossad Nazi hunter in his 80's still doing in Rio?

Suddenly a beautiful, peaky left rolled all the way to the beach and spit the laughing surfers out in the white water. It was the middle of the day. Shouldn't they be in school? Naw, their fairy tale world imposed no rules -- and for them, nothing existed on the other side of the city's jungle clad ring of stone sentinels. I was starting to appreciate the feeling.

I wanted to talk to Jaime Gold; but it would have to wait. Heinrik's Mercedes had just pulled out of the garage. And this time it was moving fast.

CHAPTER
TWENTY

SHE WAS CRADLED against her mother's soft yet strong body. Her mother's voice, like warm honey, sang in her ear. It was a song from *Bahia*. One of her favorites. It told the story of the daughter of a fisherman who waited at the shore for her father to come home each evening. And how when he came home he'd gather up all of her troubles from the day and wrap them into his net. He would then cast the net far, far into the ocean where the troubles wriggled free and turned into glittery fish jumping and skipping across the waves.

She floated on her back. The shore was long gone and she rolled with the waves deep in the ocean. The night sky was star-less. Pitch black. The silence at first had been terrifying but now if she tried really hard she could hear the lapping of the water. She could even hear the fish swimming alongside her. Keeping her company.

Friends had told her what men wanted. Her friend Gabriella Santiago had even gone all the way with one. Gabriella said that it didn't really feel good but that it had made the boy so happy that he wouldn't stop calling her.

She was determined to make the Masked Man happy.

Maybe he's shy. This is why he wears the mask. Why he locks her away. She didn't care what he looked like because she'd seen his soul. He was the one who came to fish her out of the deep dark sea. The only one who cared about her.

Footsteps. Faint at first and now right above her. He was here!

She shivered. Then a jolt of panic. What if he didn't open the box?! No. He always opened the box. Today she would make him so happy. She would do everything he asked. Last time she'd scratched him. Or was that the time before? She'd learned her lesson. She was a good girl now. She was his... She worshipped him. And if only she could show him how much... She was sure that he wouldn't put her back in the box.

CHAPTER
TWENTY-ONE

I'D BEEN FOLLOWING for almost two hours when the Mercedes slowed and turned off the main highway onto a small dirt road. We'd left Rio and driven up into a large tropical mountain range beyond the suburbs of the city. Without the cover of highway traffic I had to slow and allow the Mercedes to pull far ahead. It was now late afternoon and the sun was behind us, which hopefully created enough of a glare that Heinrik wouldn't see me in his mirror.

The narrow dirt road was lined with jungle and wound like a broken corkscrew up into the mountains. Every hundred yards or so a side road would appear and slice down to a residence. These were weekend country houses or *sitios* where Rio's elite would come to escape the heat. The air up here was crisp and wet and rich with oxygen. A world where the crackle of fireplaces replaced the drone of air conditioners. The properties were large, often with manicured grounds and pools. Many of them doubled as small hobby farms. They were all isolated and private and indistinguishable from the main road.

Eventually Heinrik's Mercedes pulled into one of the

gated driveways. I continued past for half a kilometer and stashed Royce's car along the road. It was still light out but the sun dropped fast in the jungle. I needed to hike down through the brush and case out the property. It would be hopeless to try and find the farm in the dark. I scoured Royce's car in hopes of finding a stash gun. I hated the idea of moving in without a weapon. The only thing I could find was a tire iron. It would have to do.

The rainforest was wet and choked with sharp needled underbrush. The tire iron came in handy as a make-shift machete but I was scratched and soaked by the time I arrived at the tree-lined edge of the property. It was a complex of three modest houses. All of them faux alpine design. A barn and corral were set to the rear of the property but they were empty. The place was poorly maintained. A small collection of fruit trees wound between the buildings. The fruit lay rotting on the ground. An algae tinted swimming pool sat half empty. Directly in front of me was a field with rusted goal posts and knee high grass that once served as a soccer pitch.

There were two cars parked at the main house. Heinrik's black Mercedes sat next to a black Porsche Cayenne SUV with black out windows. The shutters were closed on all three houses making it impossible to detect any movement inside. But I could feel them. They were here. Heinrik and his friend… and Leticia. I needed to get closer but in the daylight it would be impossible to approach undetected. I settled in to wait.

The night arrived like a bomb. One moment it was light. The next all was dark. With the cover of darkness came an unexpected bonus, the forest erupted with the electric buzz of insects. It was deafening. A wall of sound to muffle my approach.

My first objective was to clear the smaller buildings. The barn was empty. It hadn't been used in years. The two guest houses were both locked and the lights were turned off. I listened at the window and they seemed empty.

A glow emanated from the shutters of the main house. He was inside. *They* were inside. I moved around the house to a rear door. It was cracked open. Were they waiting for me? I could hear a TV. I slipped through the door and moved through the kitchen shadows to the arched entrance of a cozy living room. Heinrik was sitting on the couch watching TV. I stepped behind and pulled the tire iron tight around his neck.

"Who else is here?" I whispered in his ear.

But he didn't reply. His head lolled to the side. My hands came away wet. A bib of red rested on his chest. Someone had slit his throat.

A door slammed shut behind me.

I whirled. The house was small enough that I could see it was empty. Whoever had killed Heinrik was outside. Waiting to pounce as soon as I stepped out the door. I used the crowbar to smash the lamp in the living room. Then I went into the dark kitchen and scoured the drawers. I found a nice sized butcher knife. It was sharp. Whoever lived here knew how to care for their blades.

I clenched the knife and waited beside the kitchen door. I tried to listen for movement but all I could hear was my heart pounding in my chest. I closed my eyes and took deep breaths to get my panic under control.

"Do you speak English?" I called out. I've talked down hundreds of criminals. This first exchange was crucial. If I could just get them to reply it meant that they were open to negotiation, whether they knew it or not. A simple response, even just one word, meant that there was something that they wanted. My job was then to find out what it was and give it to them.

Tonight there was no reply.

"Hello?! My name is Miles! Do you speak English? Can we talk?"

Silence.

The fear that I'd tamped down began to well up again. I realized that he already had what he wanted. Plan B: threaten his treasure.

"Leticia! Can you hear me?! Hang on! I'm coming for you!"

A door slammed closed in the distance. He was on the move. I sprinted out of the main house and across the open yard to the first guest house. And then I froze.

There she was.

Standing outside the open door of the guest house was a teenage girl in her underwear with a black leather mask tied over her head. The eye holes and mouth were zipped shut. She stumbled as she tried to walk. Her legs were weak as if she hadn't used them in a while. She was thin. Her ribs jutted out.

"Oh god…" I dropped the knife and ran to catch her before she fell and hit her head.

"*Agora!*" A man's voice shouted from behind.

As I turned toward the voice the girl blindly swung her arm at me and I saw the glint of a blade as it cut into my shoulder. I grunted in pain but she was too weak to do much damage. I moved to grab the small knife out of her hand but before I could secure her; the man's voice shouted again, "*Corre!*" Run. And she took off into the field. Blind. Barefoot. Stumbling.

"Stop! Leticia!" I moved to give chase but my legs gave out. A sharp pain radiated from my lower back. I'd been punched from behind. It had been a perfect, almost surgical strike to the kidney which temporarily shut down my nervous system. A powerful looking blond Man in a skin tight black shirt stood over me with my tire iron. He was so fast. He'd come out of nowhere.

I looked up toward Leticia. She'd run out of strength and stood still, wobbling and then sitting down in the dewy night grass. I struggled to pull myself to my feet. "Leticia, run! Go! Get out of here!"

Thud. The man hit me across the back with the tire iron. I collapsed in pain.

"Please. Let her go..." I gasped. When all else fails, beg.

He raised the tire iron to strike again. Instinct took over and I dove at his legs, trying to bring him down and secure some kind of advantage. But his legs were like steel poles rooted into the earth. He reach down and shoved my face in the wet grass. I clawed at his arm but his strength was freakish.

I felt the prick of a needle in my neck. Instantly my body relaxed. No more pain. No more strength. I tried to talk but nothing came out. It was as if a dark cloak had rose up behind me and settled over my head. Shutting me off from the world. Morphine? Heroin? Some kind of opioid. I went limp as the Man grabbed me by the collar and dragged me across the ground.

Inside the guest house, in the middle of the floor, was a steel door. The Man lifted the door to reveal a coffin sized box.

"No... NO!" I screamed. But no words came out.

He dropped my limp body into the box and as he closed the door he cracked the slightest of smiles and replied, "Yes."

CHAPTER
TWENTY-TWO

THE PROCESS HAD BEEN RUSHED. But the Man was confident. He'd followed the steps that had been laid out in the journals. Of course the inferior breeds were more suited to the process. And the younger the better. His subject had responded beautifully. The American had reminded him that he would need to give her a new name. This had been the next step. The one that his father had ruined with his fretting.

Greta. Back home in the family village in Santa Catarina he'd once been in love with a girl named Greta. He'd sat next to her at school. He'd tried to talk to her a few times and she'd even smiled, encouraging his attempts. But he always struggled to say the right thing. Instead he decided to give her a gift. He'd overheard her say that she was allergic to cats. So he killed one. Wrapped it in a box. And gave it to her. It was his way of letting her know that he'd do anything for her. The girl had screamed and threw it back in his face. Stupid bitch. From that point things had changed. Even his parents began to look at him differently. But he would show them. He would show them all. He was chosen. Not them.

The powerful Porsche pulled out from the dirt road onto the highway. The German engineering flowed from the cement to the tires and up through the steering wheel into his hands. He'd never felt more alive. He glanced to the backseat where the girl in the mask lay wrapped in a blanket. Sleeping. Happy to be with her master.

Yes, Greta was a fine name.

CHAPTER
TWENTY-THREE

SHE MOVED HER HANDS. Slowly. Slowly. Until they came to the clasp at the back of her neck. She loosened the belt. A centimeter at most. It was enough to peer down and out through the bottom of the mask. She breathed deeply.

"No," she said to herself. "My name is Leticia."

CHAPTER
TWENTY-FOUR

"MILES, I think I found something. Call me when you get this."

"Dude. Where's my fucking car?! Seriously."

"Hello, Agent Ronan? This is Jaime Gold. Please call me as soon as possible. There are things you should know about Paulo Heinrik before you attempt an approach."

"Miles. This is Wills. The photo enhancement came through. Sending it to you now."

"Hello, Miles? This is David Barry. With the consulate. Uh, just checking in. I hope you're enjoying your vacation."

———

Marié threw herself into the property record search. It was a welcome distraction. Her encounter with Detective Amalero had left her shaken. Not only because of the threat against her mother; but the fact that she had given in so easily. Her career as a journalist had been inspired by a desire to expose corruption. Brazil's systemic graft was a disease that impoverished millions. It was a cancer on the soul of her beautiful people. The siphoning of public money. The perversion of the rule of law. Even worse, the acceptance of this corruption. "Oh, it's just a little off the top." "Stop complaining, that's just the way it is." She wasn't so deluded to think that she alone would save the country. But maybe she could start a movement, a wave of outrage... and the courage to say, *basta*! Enough!

Then, her very first chance to stand up to the monster and she withered without a fight. Argh! It made her so angry! She'd promised Amalero to keep him informed of their investigation. But now, from the safety of her own company, her courage returned. She'd play along she rationalized, but just until she was able to find out Amalero's game. What did he want? Who was he working for? Once she had this leverage her mother would be safe. Her integrity would be safe.

Where the hell was Miles? Her wrist was sore from checking her phone. Why hadn't he called her? It was 9:00 in the morning. She'd been sitting in her car outside his hotel for the past hour. According to the hotel clerk he hadn't come back last night. Where the hell was he? Rio was a city of temptations, had he met a girl? It wouldn't have been hard. He was handsome. And an American. But more than that he had a charm. Swagger combined with sensitivity and also a little bit broken on the inside. A deadly combination. No, if he'd been the type of guy who trolled the night for girls he would've tried something with her, right? They'd technically spent the night together. She'd assumed that he would've tried to kiss her. She wouldn't have let him. But it would've been nice if he'd tried. He even insisted on sleeping in that ridiculous chair. Maybe next time she'd --

A bang on the car window jerked her back to the real world.

It was Royce Mirza.

"*Merda*," she cursed. Just what she needed, another cop come to make demands.

"Open," he said pointing to the passenger side door.

"Get lost!"

"Open!" He banged again. Harder. He wasn't going away.

She gathered herself. This time she wouldn't be caught off guard. She set her phone mic to record and dropped it in her purse.

"Where's your boyfriend?" he asked as he slid into the passenger seat.

"He's not my boyfriend. I thought he was yours."

"I'm not in the mood for funny. He borrowed my car yesterday and never came back. Something happened." He noticed her notebook on the dashboard. Before she could object he grabbed it and flipped through the hand written notes.

"That's mine." She tried to yank it out of his hand. He held it a second before letting go.

"Those are addresses. For what? What are you two working on?"

"I don't have to talk to you," she pointed out. "Get out of my car."

He rolled his eyes, "Listen. I don't give a shit about you. But it looks like our gringo friend has got himself lost. He can't speak Portuguese. Probably doesn't have much money. We're the only ones who like him. And he's poking his nose around some dangerous people. How about we call a truce?"

"You're the one who started it. *Jornalista cachorro?* Remember?" she pointed out.

"Me? O Mundo's been running bullshit stories about BOPE killing innocent people for years."

"Bullshit? Hey, I've seen the photos. You guys have turned the favelas into your own private shooting gallery."

"They're fucking drug dealers. Why don't you walk your fancy ass up there and see what really happens? You want a crusade? That's your fucking crusade. Clean those cockroaches out and everything changes in this town."

"Why don't you show me? Take me with you on a raid."

He considered her for the first time, "You're serious?"

"One hundred percent."

"Any time," he challenged.

She held out her hand to seal the deal. He rolled his eyes at her serious little gesture but shook anyway. Now that they had their truce she flipped open her notebook to a page of handwritten addresses.

"These are all properties owned or associated with Frank Ronan's lawyer, Paulo Heinrik."

"So?"

"We think he's involved in the murder. And if he is, then he's likely using one of his properties to hold Miles' sister."

"Which one was Miles going to look at?"

"I don't know. I haven't given him the list yet."

Royce ran his finger down the list of four properties. He recognized one, "This is the office where I saw him yesterday."

"There's also a *São Conrado* apartment which is his primary residence. And two houses in the Golden Gates Condominium complex. All of them technically owned by a holding company, *Catarina Imoveis* LLC."

"Two houses at Golden Gates? You got to be kidding me."

She was glad to see that he was smarter than he looked. "One of the houses is where Frank Ronan and Aparecida Silva where killed."

"What about the other one?" he asked.

"I don't know."

But she did know. They both knew. The second house is how the killer was able to get into Frank Ronan's house without passing through the front gate. It's also where they could have held Leticia Silva after taking her captive.

The front gate security remembered Royce and waved them into the condominium. Heinrik's second house was located at the far end of the complex. It was locked. Royce smashed a window and they climbed inside. The furniture and decorations were generic. Rental property decor. It was big. Five bedrooms. But only one bedroom had been used recently. The occupant had left behind some clothes. Men's clothes. High end. There was no sign of a struggle or of a hostage. The garage was empty but it had been recently used. Royce kneeled down and studied the tire tread on the glossy cement floor. It was a wide tire. An expensive one. Probably a SUV. There was also a trail of mud leading to the drain. The vehicle had been driven off road.

Royce returned to the living room. "There's mud in the garage. He probably held her here for a few days and then moved her, somewhere out of the city."

"Check this out." Marié was looking at an impression-istic painting of some jagged mountains. It was the type of rushed, generic art that you find at a street fair.

"Do you recognize these mountains?" she asked.

He shrugged, "You said that he was from Santa Cata-rina. They have mountains there."

"No. This is from here in Rio. It's *Teresopolis*."

CHAPTER
TWENTY-FIVE

THE FIRST TWO hours were easy. Thanks to the drugs. The next hour was pure horror. The Man had left my phone in my pocket and I'd made the mistake of turning it on. There was of course no signal but the light allowed me to see the extent of my coffin. The steel walls of the box were so tight I couldn't turn or even lift my knees. The panic hit like a boulder falling from the sky. I tried to scream. Nothing came out. I was sure that I was having a heart attack. I turned off the phone and didn't touch it again.

I soon learned that if I kept my eyes closed I could calm myself enough to control my thoughts. Royce's car was sitting off the side of the road. Someone would find it. They would contact the local police. The local police would then contact Royce. I worked through the various scenarios in my mind. They each ended with me being found. They were coming. They wouldn't find the car until morning. It may then take a full day for them to find the *sítio*. I just had to survive until then.

I thought of Leticia. She'd been in this box. I could smell her. But she didn't have the luxury of an impending rescue.

She'd been in here for six days. Six days and six nights with no hope of rescue. An eternity. Enough to do real harm.

"Leticia. Leticia. Leticia..."

My mantra. I had to survive; for her.

I learned later that it was five in the afternoon when they finally entered the guest house and heard my muffled screams. It took another 20 minutes for them to find a drill and drill open the lock. Royce was there. Marié was there. The local police were there. The bloody gash on my arm was infected. I screamed when they lifted me. The box had been filthy with urine and feces and vomit. I shook from dehydration. They put me in the back of a car. Marié sat with me. Holding me. We drove so fast. Then a hospital. An I.V. was inserted. And with one push of a syringe the dark cloak returned, wrapping me in its embrace. This time I welcomed its arrival.

CHAPTER
TWENTY-SIX

AFTER AN EIGHT HOUR NAP, a massive dose of antibiotics and twenty stitches I felt much better. But now I had another kind of head-ache.

"Look at it from their perspective," said Deputy Consul Barry. He stood across the hospital room and looked out the window at the jagged Teresopolis mountain peaks reaching like fingers into the sky. "We'd do the same thing if one of them came to the U.S. and interfered in an active murder investigation."

"The key word being active," I snapped. "They gave up! They beat a confession out of some throw-away loser and tied it all up in a bow."

Barry was here because the Rio Police had ordered me out of the country. I was to be escorted directly from the hospital to the airport. They were even nice enough to bring my suitcase from the hotel.

"Agreed. But now, thanks to you, they're going to take a second look. Consider it a win. But the fact is you have no jurisdiction here. It is *illegal* for an FBI Agent to conduct an investigation on Brazilian soil. Illegal as in against the law. You're lucky that you're not already under arrest."

"Bullshit," I snapped. "They're going to sweep this right under the rug again. She's an American. We have a responsibility here!"

"Oh my god. Are you serious? She's not American. Her father--"

"Was an American."

"Not according to his passport. Her birth certificate says her father is a Brazilian named Francesco Silva. The amount of red tape you'd have to go through to get that changed..." Barry threw up his hands. "Peter, can you talk sense into him. This will look a lot better if they don't have to drag our boy onto the plane in cuffs." Barry was talking to my boss who was listening in via speaker phone.

"Sorry David, he's your problem. As far as my office is concerned he's officially on vacation," Wills replied. Bless his heart. "By the way, Miles. Did you ever connect with Jaime Gold?"

"Not yet. We exchanged e-mails."

"Ah... well, maybe you'll get a chance before you leave." Wills hadn't thrown this tangent out at random. It was a message.

"No! No chance, guys. Agent Ronan is not visiting anyone. He may have more days of vacation but they're not happening here in Brazil."

"Gentlemen, I'm a busy man. You two work it out," said Wills. "Miles, I'm glad to hear you're still alive. I'll see you back at work next week." With that he hung up and I was left alone with my new frenemy, career boot licker, David Barry. We stared each other down from across the hospital bed. Barry was a pleaser. He wanted to please his boss. He wanted to please the Rio Police. And in a way I think he wanted to please me. It was something I could use.

"Why is it do you think?" I asked.

"Why is what?"

"Why *am* I still alive?" I didn't think he'd have any insights but it was a sincere question. One that had been haunting me since I'd woken up inside the box. "Because it doesn't make sense. He killed my dad and his wife. He killed Paulo Heinrik. But he left me alive. Me and my sister. Why? There has to be a reason, right?"

"Who knows what goes through the mind of a person like that," Barry considered. I could tell he was happy to be asked his opinion. "I think the important take-away is that your sister is still alive. And the local police know that she's still alive. That's good news. That's a win."

"You're right, Man. I'm sorry for earlier. This whole thing has me going crazy. First everything with my dad, and then learning that I have a sister... A win is a win. Even if it's a partial win." I jangled my wrist which was hand-cuffed to the side of the bed. "You don't really think this is necessary do you?"

Barry sighed, "Of course not. Let me see what I can do." He left the room to talk to the Police Officer waiting at the end of the hall.

I knew that if I let them put me on that plane Leticia would never be found. She'd be swallowed whole. I surprised myself with how easy I'd come to the decision. Up until now I'd been operating in a grey area. But now I was about to defy a direct order not only from the Brazilian authorities but from the U.S. Consulate. There was no way to do this half way. And there would be no turning back. The moment I stepped off this ledge I would no longer be an FBI Agent. My passport would no longer protect me. I would become a fugitive.

"Here we go," Barry sang out as he returned with a key to the cuffs. He pulled the key back just as he was about to open the lock. "You promise to behave?"

"Cross my heart," I grinned.

Barry cracked himself up. "I'm just kidding."

He opened the cuffs and I was finally able to get out of the bed. I was wobbly at first but quickly recovered. The hospital had brought me back to life. My small carry-on suitcase was on a nearby chair. I changed out of the hospital gown into street clothes as Barry went over my travel itinerary.

"The flight is this afternoon. Which gives us just enough time to grab something to eat before we head down the mountain. The seat assignment isn't the best, but once we're at the airport I'll see about an upgrade. You'll have to make a connection in Miami but--"

His last words cut off as I stepped behind him and wrapped my arm around his neck in a rear naked choke. He was softer than I'd expected and barely struggled. Within seconds he collapsed as his carotid artery pinched shut and blood stopped flowing to his brain. I set him down on the floor and handcuffed his wrist to the bed.

As I walked down the hall toward the Police Officer standing sentry at the elevator I could hear Barry come awake and cry for help. I waved at the Officer to come quick. He ran past me to the room and I stepped into the stairwell and sprinted down the stairs.

The hospital lobby was crowded with patients. They filled the plastic waiting chairs and some waited on gurneys lined against the wall. The overworked staff had no interest in a healthy looking body. I tucked my head and moved toward the door when Marié appeared at my side like an exhausted guardian angel.

"There are two police officers outside. They just got the call that you're coming down."

I froze.

"C'mon. This way." She turned and led me back into the

hospital. We worked our way through the winding guts of the service area and emerged onto a loading bay.

"Thank you," I said. "For everything. I'll be in touch as soon as I can. I haven't forgot that I owe you a story."

"Don't even think about leaving me behind. I go with you or I pull this alarm." Her hand went up to a fire alarm on the wall. "Your choice."

"If you come with me that makes you an accomplice. That does nobody any good. I promise, as soon as I find her you'll be the first to know."

"You owe me a story. That means you belong to me," she said. Then without taking her eyes from mine she pulled the hospital's fire alarm sending a wailing clang through the entire building. And there was nothing left for me to do but follow as she walked out the service bay and down to the main road where we hailed a taxi.

We were four blocks away before the ringing in our ears had faded and the taxi driver, a small, elderly man with sharp eyes and tanned, wire strong hands that gently gripped the wheel, looked back at me in the mirror and asked in perfect English, "So how are you liking Brazil, Agent Ronan?"

CHAPTER
TWENTY-SEVEN

WHEN JAIME GOLD was recruited into the Mossad's Nazi hunting unit he was only twenty years old. He'd drawn their attention because of his proclivity for languages. At the time he spoke four. Hebrew. Arabic. German. English. A lifetime later he'd added a few more. Spanish. French. And of course Portuguese.

"It's like the Mafia. They never let you out," he said referring to the Israeli Intelligence Service. "But I wouldn't have it any other way. If I retired I'd be dead. My wife would kill me." He cracked up at his own little joke. His wife, a petite and nimble, light skinned Brazilian in her late sixties, brought out a fresh platter of fried fish. "Isn't that right, babe?" he said as he smacked her behind.

"*Para,*" she warned and promptly returned the smack to the back of his head. "*Não fique palhaço velho.*" Don't be an old clown. She then turned her attention to me and Marié, "*Desculpa, Queridos.*" She stepped close and without warning pulled down the skin beneath my eye so that she could study the white flesh beneath. She didn't like what she saw. "*Ta muito branco.*" She turned to Marié and instructed her to make sure that I ate everything on my plate. And then whirled and returned to the kitchen.

Jaime translated, "She thinks you lack protein. Eat up or we'll never hear the end of it. She's crazy, but she knows what she's talking about."

I didn't need to be threatened. The fish was delicious. The breading reminded me of the tempura at a Michelin starred sushi joint. So thin that it was almost translucent and once my teeth broke through the crisp outer layer the tilapia juices exploded in my mouth. I was content to do nothing but eat and pick bones out of my teeth as Jaime regaled us with tales of the Mossad in the 1960's and 70's.

Jaime Gold lived outside of a fishing village perched on a spit of land jutting into the Atlantic. The modest houses were two or three bedroom brick abodes all of them painted an identical bright white with matching red shingle roofs. It reminded me of a medieval Spanish village. The kind where old women passed the day sweeping the street in front of their homes. Jaime explained that the white paint could be seen far out to sea and the fishermen used it to keep track of their bearings. The town also had a colorful history as a pirate cove and in more recent years as an unloading base for drug dealers. "I like to think of it as a boring town with just enough excitement to keep one from getting bored," Jaime said as we took a post dinner walk along the beach. He held Marié's hand, claiming with a wink that he didn't trust his footing in the dark. She was charmed. I was just a little jealous. The night stars were brilliant. The ocean waves dampened any outside sound making it safe to speak freely.

"Thanks for your help, but I need to get back to Rio. If there's any way we could find a car," I asked.

"You've really stomped on the ant hill, my boy. Best to keep you out of the city for now. Besides, the prodigal son won't be going back to Rio just yet."

The prodigal son. Wills had forwarded the enhanced photo from the night of the murder to both me and Jaime. I recognized the man in the backyard of my dad's house as the same man who had drugged me and stuffed me in a steel box. Jaime recognized him as Paulo Heinrik's son, Gregor Heinrik.

Jaime's cover was as a semi-retired foreign businessman looking for investments. But his official brief with Israeli Intelligence was to track the small pockets of Nazi culture that continued to linger throughout South America. The days of straight up assassination were over as all of the original Nazi fugitives had died of various causes; almost never natural. But their legacy remained and it was Jaime's job to make sure that no sparks flared out of control.

"And how do you do that?" Marié asked. "I mean if you no longer kill them... do you report them to the police? Expose them to the media?"

"I see what you are doing," Gold laughed and waved a warning finger at me, "Watch out for this one, my friend. Always looking for a scoop."

"No fair changing the subject. You didn't answer the question," Marié pressed with a smile.

"I'm a businessman now, my dear. If I see a fire that needs to be put out - I do it as a businessman. Let's leave it at that shall we," he said and gave her a firm pat on the hand.

"What can you tell us about this Gregor Heinrik?" I asked.

"Yes. This is the important question," he said ready to

steer the topic away from himself. "The boy came onto our radar when he was a teenager; around the time the family sent him to a Swiss mental hospital. We believe to receive shock therapy treatment. We're not sure what brought the treatment on, but he was there for about a year. When he returned to Brazil he went on to have an unremarkable academic life resulting in a law degree from a mediocre university. After graduating he remained unremarkable and seemed to be on track to take over his father's practice."

"Do you think he'll make a run to Santa Catarina?" asked Marié.

"Possible. His extended family is like royalty there. They'd protect him," Gold said. "But the way to catch a rat is not to chase - it's to trap. For this, you must know what he wants... you must have bait."

"Paulo Heinrik told me that my dad was out of money. Which would have made him a liability... maybe he sent Gregor to get rid of him?" I said, thinking out loud. "But then rather than kill Leticia, maybe he kept her for himself... but why? As a toy?"

"Paulo was a parasite. Not a vampire. His business was not to suck his clients dry and throw them away. His business was to keep them solvent - extremely solvent - so that he could feed off them for the rest of their lives. A client of your father's magnitude would not have been allowed to go broke."

"But if there is still money to be made, then why kill him?" Marié asked.

"You're right. Leticia would be leverage - and what good is leverage over a dead man?" Another scenario suddenly occurred to me. "What about the argument at the party? Maybe Dad was trying to cut Heinrik off?"

"Based on the fact that Paulo Heinrik is now dead, I

think we can assume Junior is driving this crazy train," Jaime said.

Nothing was making sense. A memory of the man's wild eyes suddenly flashed at me in the dark. Maybe it really was just the work of a madman.

Jaime stopped walking and looked out over the moonlit ocean. Empty fishing boats dotted the water. Anchored for the night.

"I've hunted these monsters for my entire life," Jaime said. There was a contained rage to his words. For the first time I could see the cold blooded assassin behind the grandfatherly veneer. "Their sickness, it is a burden. But I carry this burden because with it comes blessing. The release that comes from ridding them from the world -- it is an almost holy feeling."

I realized that he knew more than he let on. "You know what he's doing, don't you?" I said. "If you're waiting for us to work through the easy scenarios so that we're prepared for the hard truth. Trust me, I can handle it." I glanced at Marié. She'd come this far, she wasn't going to run away now. "We can handle it. And we really don't have time for guessing games."

"Very well," he sighed. He looked out over the dark ocean as he spoke, "It is a process which the Nazis referred to as *das zombergun*. A silly name. Always with the silly names to make the horrific seem cartoonish. Loosely translated it means *zombification*. It is a brainwashing protocol created within the camps. What they learned is that if the psyche is broken down, brutally and completely... and then rebuilt in a methodical manner, then it's possible to shift the brain's neurological make-up in a way that mimics hypnosis."

"He's hypnotizing her?" Marié asked, almost hopeful. Hypnotizing didn't sound so horrific.

"No, my dear. He's torturing her."

Marié took hold of my hand.

"Another way to think of it is as a non-surgical lobotomy. A real world example would be... you are familiar with Charles Manson?"

Being a child of L.A. just the name sent a chill up my spine.

"Then you may know that Charles Manson was an aficionado of Mein Kampf. We believe that he had used a version of *das zombergun* on his followers - who were under his control when they committed the murders which made him famous."

"So he wants to control her?" I had to push down a rising tide of rage. "For what? Sex? A killing spree?"

"For this he could have grabbed any girl off the street," points out Marié.

Jaime nodded in agreement, "Don't be fooled by the madness of his methods. There's a reason she was chosen. I would guess it's the same reason that *you're* still alive, Agent Ronan. I don't know what that reason is. But there's something that makes the two of you unique."

"The only thing that we have in common is our dad."

"Then that is where you start. That is where you will find your bait."

PART TWO
THE PIRATE LIFE FOR ME

CHAPTER
TWENTY-EIGHT

THE SAILBOAT at night on the ocean was a place of sounds. Rigging clinked. Sails flapped. Water sloshed. Floorboards creaked. It had been a month at sea now and he was intimate with every one of those sounds. So much so that they had become like silence. Any alteration in their rhythms was a klaxon which rocked him from the deepest sleep.

He rolled from his hammock onto the floor of the cabin's modest living area. Someone was up on deck. He could hear whispers. It sounded like Spanish. Maybe Portuguese. There were at least three of them. Shit. One he could handle. Two would result in some damage. But three was going to hurt. The door opened and a flashlight poked down at him. *"Vem! Subir!"* It was Portuguese. They wanted him to come up. He must've crossed over into Brazil sometime in the middle of the night. He knew he'd been close. He allowed himself a moment of pride. He'd fucking made it. Thirty days on the water. No outside help or communication other than that time he bribed an official to get through the Panama canal; and he'd made it. After all he'd gone through. *All he'd given up.* No fucking way these punk wannabe pirates were going to ruin it now. It was almost funny that they'd try.

On that last frantic rush to the marina he'd stopped at a Long Beach book store to get some How To Speak Portuguese books and tapes. He'd used the past thirty days to study. He already spoke some Spanish, even if it wasn't a requirement with the LAPD it was a necessity. Portuguese came easy. His favorite of the books was filled with slang and popular swear words.

"*Vai tomar o cue! Filho da puta!*" Stick it in your ass you son of a bitch. He grinned as he tried out his first insult. It worked. The pirates yelled back in a flurry that he had no chance of understanding. Furious, they stormed down the narrow stairs into the tiny living area. They could only fit one at a time - which is exactly what he wanted. He'd once been a champion wrestler. Then there was the stint in the Marines. And of course fifteen years with LAPD. If there was one thing that Frank Ronan did well, it was fight.

The first pirate was in his early twenties. No shirt. Rubber sandals. Skinny. His gun's handle was held together with duct tape. Frank winged a ceramic coffee mug at his face. The pirate fired a shot. It went high. The sound bounced off the fiberglass walls and made their ears ring. The pirate flinched. Frank tackled him around the waist and threw him in an easy hip toss against the wall. It was then a battle of strength for control of the gun. Frank bent the pirate's wrist. Bang. Bang. Bang. Three muffled shots and the pirate was dead.

The second pirate was already on Frank's back. Choking him. Frank reached up and pulled on his head, flipping Pirate Two over and onto the floor. Frank torqued on his neck until he heard a faint crack and the body went limp. Pirate Three was bigger than the others. He swung a metal bar at Frank's back. Somewhere inside him a bone broke.

But he was able to turn and he caught the next swing on the arm. They were now wrestling up close. A quick feint and a duck and Frank had slipped beneath his arm and was now behind him. He drove the Big Pirate into the wall, pinning him there as his free hand searched the countertop for a weapon. He grabbed a fork from the sink and stabbed at the Big Pirate's neck. Over and over. The Big Pirate thrashed but Frank held him face first against the wall and kept stabbing. Finally the man slumped to the floor.

Frank was slick with blood. But victorious. He picked up the pirate's gun and went up onto the deck. As he expected there were no other pirates. Their small motor boat sat empty alongside his 40 foot craft. The glow of the impending dawn was just visible on the horizon. In the other direction, five miles off the starboard, was a shadowy mass that he now knew was the wild, tropical coast of Brazil.

"*Yeaaaaarrrrrhhh!*" He unleashed a primal scream into the yellowing sky. He'd done it. He was free. He was a king. A god. Immortal. Somehow it felt right that this last step had required a blood sacrifice.

His rib had definitely cracked in the struggle. He looked out over the ocean. There were no other vessels in sight but the sun was coming up fast. He wouldn't be alone for long. He climbed back down below deck where he wrapped his ribs tight with a strip of bed sheet. He then dragged the three dead pirates up and threw them overboard. This far out the sharks would get them before they floated to shore. Their left over boat was an issue. As was the horror movie blood that now coated both the lower and upper deck. His main concern was that discovery of either of these two items would result in a deeper search and reveal a self fabricated steel container that was tucked behind a false wall in the hold. The container was air-tight and water proof. He'd welded it himself so that there would be no door or hatch. Sealed inside was $49.5 million in plastic wrapped hundred dollar bills. The total weight of the money and the box was 1200 pounds. His treasure.

By the time he'd finished his coffee and a breakfast of banana and the last of the mahi-mahi that he'd caught yesterday; he had a plan. He was a man of plans. The plans didn't always work as expected, but they bought him time. Time to make the next plan. And then the next. So on and so on. He'd lived his entire life like this, one plan to the next. This current plan however, it was a big one. It was the plan to end all plans.

CHAPTER
TWENTY-NINE

IN BAHIA, time was an abstract concept and it was too late before I realized that my glance had become a gaze. Her bare feet rested on the dash. Her shorts bunched up teasing where the tan on her smooth, softly muscled legs began to transition to a lighter color. Her eyes were hidden behind sunglasses. If she saw me watching her I didn't care.

Jaime Gold had given us his car. It was a generic Ford hatchback. Small, affordable and powered on ethanol. It wasn't going to win any races but it was well maintained and anonymous. We'd left his house in the middle of the night and it was now evening the next day. We hadn't talked much. Taking turns sleeping as the other drove. But when we were both awake the comfort in our silences made it seem as if we'd known each other for months. My mind drifted along with the sway of the palm forest that stretched forever on both sides of the highway. Somewhere out there, not too far off, was the ocean. I could smell it on the breeze. When we stopped for food or gas the air outside of the car was heavy. It took effort to move. Effort to think. Effort to talk. It was easier to just be.

The sailboat that my dad had used to flee his life had been sunk in shallow water. The locals knew of it because it had become a popular haunt for tiger sharks. It wasn't until ten years ago when an American dive tourist explored the site that the boat was identified. Since then it had become a popular tourist attraction leaning heavy on its pirate history.

According to our dive boat guide my dad had been a ruthless outlaw. He'd robbed banks. He'd killed. But he'd also given money to the poor and was considered a folk hero back in the U.S. It was a good story and the guide told it well. I didn't bother to correct him. One hundred and thirty feet beneath the surface the truth was easier to grasp.

I worked my dive from the outside in to the center. The fiberglass body had held up well and there were no major tears or damage that would have caused a wreck. The mast was also intact. But the portals leading to the engine were all smashed open which meant the boat had been scuttled. Next I explored the deck. It too was clean except for a large hole in the middle. The hole was six feet by six feet and based on the edging had been cut with an underwater welding torch.

"He sunk it on purpose," I explained to Marié as the dive boat sped over the water back toward shore.

"But why?" she asked.

"Have you ever seen $50 million all in one place?" I answered. "It's a big 'ol pile. He must have stored it down there and then came back later to haul it up."

"Like a real pirate," she grinned. I could see her writing her story in her head.

"The question is how? He would have cut it out from the top of the deck with an underwater welder. That's a specialized skill. And he would've needed a winch to crank it up to the surface. We're talking a box that weighs over a thousand pounds. He would've needed help."

"With that much money, they must've been people he trusted," she pointed out. "Did he have a contact here?"

I looked up and down the fast approaching coast. There were a couple of small houses set back in the brush but mostly it was a wilderness of palm forest and sand dunes. It was as desolate as it was beautiful. "I don't think so. Honestly, as a kid I never heard him mention Brazil once."

It was a thirty minute boat ride back to the closest town, which was little more than a collection of dive shops and souvenir stands. We ate an early lunch at an outdoor restaurant that operated out of the back of a home cobbled together out of brick and bamboo. The cook was a slow moving, big hipped local woman wrapped in a colorful dress who cooked one dish at a time. When it was ready her husband brought the food out to our plastic table and prepared the plates in front of us. Fresh rice ladled over with shrimp *moqueca*, a yellowish, pasty sauce made from fresh picked yucca root. The dish was alternately sweet and spicy and just as it did with the cook the food commanded our full attention. Once we finished eating the waiter didn't bother to clear our plates. He knew that the spell from his wife's food would keep us rooted in place for the foreseeable future.

"What was it like, after he left?" Marié asked.

"It was quiet," I said, not intending to elaborate.

"No brothers or sisters?"

"Just me and my Mom. She worked so I was alone a lot. Lonely is a better word. The neighbors had a lot of kids and I'd hear them. I remember they were loud. Just yelling and playing all the time. I'd stand at my bedroom window with the blinds closed and listen. Try to pluck a word out of the air and figure out what the excitement was about."

"FBI agent in training," she said. "Did you always want to be a policeman?"

"Always. At first it was to be like my dad. But then... I think it was to show that I wasn't like my dad."

"You said you were married twice. No kids?" she asked.

"Are we going there?" I groaned.

"These questions are purely work related. Remember our deal? You're part of my story too."

For some reason I didn't mind. I wanted to tell her. I wanted her to know.

"Number one lasted barely a year. We were too young. I was too young. Just twenty two. I wanted everything right away. A wife. A kid. A house in the suburbs. Basically, I wanted the life I didn't get growing up."

"That sounds nice. She didn't want it?"

"I think she did. Just not so fast. So we fought and that was it. It's funny, just one fight and we both walked away. When you give up that easy I guess it wasn't meant to be."

"Ok. Boring. Number two?"

"Number two was the opposite. I was thirty. I don't think we ever loved each other. We were just lonely. I didn't really want a family anymore. I just wanted someone to come home to. That one lasted five years. But she wanted more. Kids. The whole thing. And I was never around. One day I realized I'd been working out of town for two weeks straight and hadn't talked to her the entire time. No text. No email. Nothing. It's like I'd forgot about her. When I got home she'd already drawn up the divorce papers. I signed them on the spot. Even more boring."

"No. Not boring. More like... I don't know how to say in English. You look good on the outside but inside it's like all broken. Your dad dies and you're..." She held her hand out level. "It's like nothing happened."

"Damaged goods," I offered.

She smiled, slightly confused, "What does this mean, damaged goods?"

"It means when something with value is broken, but still kinda works."

"Ahh. Damaged goods. I like that. But don't worry," she softened, "women like damaged goods." As soon as she said it she blushed and looked away. When she looked back she'd composed herself. "You and me. This. Us. It seems like we're going in a certain direction, but I just want you to know it's not going there."

"Oh, Ok. That's a relief. I was getting worried I'd have to break your heart."

"Knock it off. I'm serious. I like you, but, you're the story. And this is my job. It's important to me. And the last time I mixed work and a relationship I ended up married, and then shit on for a year in a public divorce. I'd rather not go through that again."

"Don't worry," I said. "Somewhere out there a teenage girl is being held hostage. Finding her is all that matters."

Just like that the mood shifted and the spell of the *muquaca* began to lift.

"Agreed," she said, sitting up straight. "So what's next?"

"Aparecida is the only local connection we have. I bet Dad met her around the time he was hauling the money up from the boat."

"Which means he might have come to shore around here," she said. "You know, we could just ask." She pulled out her phone and opened up her Instagram. "Aparecida's account is still open. I've been scrolling through it. She posted pretty regular. A lot of stuff with her and Leticia. But never your dad." She stopped on a recent photo of Aparecida in Rio at the beach. She then walked back to the kitchen to show it to the old man and his wife. I could see them studying the photo and shaking their head no. She returned to the table and shrugged, "It was worth a try."

"Can I see that?" I asked.

She sat her phone on the table between us and we sat close, breathing each other in as we scrolled through Aparecida's photos. The images showed a mother who doted on her daughter and a daughter who enjoyed the attention. But they all seemed designed to reveal few hard facts about their lives. No dates. No locations.

"Stop. Go back," I said.

She slowly scrolled upward and stopped on a grainy throwback photo of a group of kids posing in front of a school. The post was accompanied by a comment in Portuguese.

"What's it say?" I asked.

Marie translated, "My baby told me today she wanted to be a teacher when she grows up. Just like her Mom. So proud."

I expanded the image. It was a class portrait with Aparecida in the center surrounded by elementary students. She was in her early 20's dressed in a crisp school teacher uniform. She and her students all had big, proud smiles. The photo was taken in front of their school, a one story building that seemed to house only a couple of classes. Despite the modest size it was freshly painted with the name of the town proudly displayed across the front.

"Do you know this place?" I asked.

She shook her head then waved for the waiter, "Oi, Moço." The man sauntered over to our table and she showed him the photo of the schoolhouse. "Do you know this town?" she asked.

"*Sim. Claro,*" he replied. "It's very close. One hour by car."

"*A conta. Por favor,*" she said, asking for the check.

The old man nodded and began to gather the plates. But we were no longer in the same time zone as him. I dropped R$200 on the table and we were out the door by the time he'd wandered back to the kitchen to begin calculating the bill.

CHAPTER
THIRTY

"AAAAAAAIIIEEEEIIIAAAHHHH

"Take me down to the paradise city

"Where the grass is green and the girls are pretty

"Ohhh won't you please take me ho-ome"

"Feliz Ano Novo!" Happy New Year! The cry ricochetted through the penthouse apartment. It was the first minute of 1997 but the D.J. insisted on playing Guns and Roses on a loop as if it were a decade earlier. Frank didn't mind. The song might as well be his anthem. And as every other drunken party-goer seemed to tell him, *"Paradise City, that's Rio, Man! Axel wrote this song about Rio. He loves it here!"*

The penthouse for the night, the DJ, the waiters, the booze and drugs -- the girls. All together the party cost him fifty grand easy. But it was worth it. Twenty stories below was Copacabana beach jammed tight with over a million people come to celebrate New Years Eve. His guests, dressed in white from head to toe per Brazilian tradition and toasting with Dom Pérignon, were crammed against the rooftop balcony to watch the world famous fireworks display. More cheers. A curvy young woman in a flowing white skirt and a strained white bikini top held a plate of cocaine up to his nose. He'd never met her before. He inhaled until he could no longer breathe. The fog from a long day of booze and sun lifted and he was electric once again. He grabbed the woman around her bare waist and they kissed hard and deep. Together they cheered the fireworks. The D.J. cranked the music. More music. More. More. More. Disco lights and fog followed on cue. The rooftop exploded into a throbbing dance floor. The party had just begun.

He was forty five years old. He'd been in Brazil five years now. But what a five years they'd been. Women. Drugs. Food. Surf. Repeat. He'd fucking gorged himself. Five years and a million dollars blown. An impressive feat considering the exchange rate. The backpack of starter cash that he'd taken from the boat was almost empty. But everything was going to plan. He'd been able to set the table. He had a new name, fairly bought from an impoverished family whose patriarch had died of cancer. With that name he now had a bank account. He was also the owner of a chain of failing fast food restaurants which would allow him to launder his money.

It was now time for phase two.

He cursed himself. The party wasn't such a good idea afterall. That fifty grand would've been enough to buy the scavenger ship outright. Now he had to deal with this nosy charter Captain. This smarmy, fake smiling bastard whose belly hung out under his shirt. It had taken almost all day to locate the sunken boat. Frank realized too late that the Captain had been purposely going in circles in order to renegotiate terms. Which meant they were going to be diving in the dark. He hated to dive in the dark.

The welder's name was Alfredo. He was a quiet, dark skinned man in his late 20's who looked like he could swim for hours. "Have you dove in the dark before?" Frank asked. Alfredo just nodded and kept on loading his gear.

"Alfredo's the best. Don't worry," the Captain replied for him.

He wasn't worried about Alfredo. Frank had hired the boat because the Captain had been the only salvage operator who'd agreed to work on a fixed price rather than a commission. But once they hit the open water he hadn't stopped asking about what they'd be hauling up from the wreck. When Frank told him that he was being paid to mind his own business the Captain demanded more money. Frank had no choice but agree. But now the Captain was talking percentages. He wanted half. This got Frank looking around the boat for weapons. He settled on a crate of rusted fishing tools. A filet knife would do the trick. Frank could take the Captain. But he didn't want to play with Alfredo. When the time came he'd need to do it quick.

Frank and Alfredo splashed backward into the water and swam down, down... Frank held the light while Alfredo dragged his tools. The sail boat had drifted two hundred yards from its original site but thankfully the deck was still accessible. Frank marked out a six foot by six foot square near the bow. Alfredo put down his welding mask and sparked his cutting torch. The cut was relatively easy. Once the section of decking was cut free it floated away revealing daddy's precious. A steel container five feet by five feet with a hook on top.

They returned to the surface where they dumped the welding gear in the boat. The boat had a salvage crane that hung off the back and would be able to winch up the cargo and then drop it on the deck. They swam back down to the wreck and attached the winch cable to the hook on the box.

Again, Alfredo did the technical work as Frank carried the light. As the winch began to wind upward they slowly guided the box out of its nest. Once free of the sailboat's hold they grabbed onto the box and took an easy elevator ride up to the surface.

"Cut it open," the captain ordered once the box had been secured. Alfredo nodded and reached for his cutting torch. But Frank was ready. He stepped forward and put a hand on Alfredo's arm. "No, my brother," Frank warned. "It's my box and it stays closed." Alfredo froze. He wasn't a thief. He was a put your head down and do your job kind of guy. But the Captain was his boss and jobs were hard to find.

"Alfredo, I said cut it open," repeated the Captain. Alfredo looked from Frank to the Captain. In that moment of hesitation Frank strode to the tackle box and grabbed the filet knife. That action made Alfredo's mind up for him and Frank turned to find him crouched in a Capoeira stance, one foot forward one foot back, gently rocking his weight between the two.

"This is turning into a pain in my ass," Frank said to himself. He'd seen Capoeira fighters perform for the tourists. Their swooping kicks whipping past their partner's heads in a mock fight that was more dance than combat. In a real fight just one of those kicks would break a jaw. At a minimum it would knock him unconscious. But that was on solid ground. Not on the rolling deck of a boat. As Alfredo's leg tensed for a kick Frank dove for the post leg and punched up with the knife at the same time. He felt the knife draw blood but it was a glancing blow. Alfredo was slick from the ocean and he whirled free to face him. Now Frank was trapped between Alfredo and the Captain. From behind he was hit in the shoulder with what felt like a baseball bat. Simultaneously the blast of a gunshot set his ears ringing. He'd been shot before. He knew that the first shot rarely killed… The second shot punched him in the lower back. This was the dangerous one. The knife dropped from his hand and clattered to the deck. "Fuck that hurts…" He stumbled against his steel money box. He was so close.

"*Mata ele!*" Kill him! Shouted the fat fuck of a Captain. "*Mata! Mata! Mata!*"

Alfredo leaped forward to grab the knife from the deck. Frank didn't have the strength to fight him. Using the steel box to hold himself upright he pulled himself to the railing and fell overboard.

CHAPTER THIRTY-ONE

THE BOY WAS ABOUT SIX. He wore his favorite Teenage Mutant Ninja Turtles tank top. A cloud drifted and the golden light of the southern California afternoon re-appeared, hitting him like a movie spot. His look of deter-mination melted into a smile as he ran and leaped at the rope dangling from the grand magnolia tree in the front yard. He swung high into the air, lifting his legs, allowing his flip-flops to dangle from his toes.

"My boy. My beautiful boy. Forgive me."

The boy looked back as he soared into the sky. The curled ends of his long summer hair floating around his face. His smile a blast of pure love. A tractor beam. Urging... Come with me... Up. Up. Up. Into the glowing sun.

Alfredo held the unconscious man from behind, arms wrapped under his armpits. They'd been floating together like this for most of the night. Now they'd finally caught a current in to shore. Exhausted, he dragged the man out of the crashing white water and onto the sand. He wanted to collapse. But he couldn't. Not just yet. The Captain would be looking for them.

He'd worked for the Captain six months now, it was a steady job and he paid on time. But he was not a good man. He drank. He cursed. Alfredo had also seen him cheat his customers. He would extend their jobs and demand that they pay extra. The customers always paid but rarely returned. When the Captain turned on Alfredo with the gun, it wasn't a surprise. It was this mistrust that saved Alfredo's life. That split second head start allowed him to dive overboard before the Captain could pull the trigger. From beneath the inky surface he easily dodged the contrails of bullets fired from above. He swam deep and far and when he finally came up for air the salvage boat, with its powerful lights sweeping the surface, was a hundred meters in the wrong direction. The Captain knew that he'd survived. He also knew that he could swim. He'd circled the area for over an hour before giving up.

Alfredo relaxed his body and allowed the ocean to take him. Eventually he came upon the man, Francesco, floating on his back, barely alive. Alfredo's first thought was to leave him. The man had been shot and there was blood. There were sharks in this water. They would come. But Alfredo was a good man. A Christian. He'd recently been what the gringo pastor called "born again." Pastor Dan had come from a small place in America called Ohio and had baptized Alfredo in a plastic child's pool behind their simple church. As a boy Alfredo had been raised in the traditions of *Santería*. It was a religion filled with spirits and curses and the worship was a complicated routine of trances, possession and animal sacrifice. In contrast the Christian religion was simple and clean. Its message felt true: "Do good. Help people." As he came up from the pool in the back of the church these were the words that Jesus had spoken to him. The voice had been like the ring of a church bell, so clear and beautiful that he'd broken into tears.

Alfredo pulled the man up the beach and into the cover of the thick coastal brush. The man's shoulder and side were bleeding. He was unconscious but his heart still beat. Barely. It was a miracle that he was alive. It was a miracle that they hadn't been attacked by sharks. Alfredo had to go and find help. But first he dropped to his knees and gave thanks.

The fever had gripped him for three days. The dreams had been the worst part. Ever since L.A. he'd worked hard to cut away that part of his life. If he dwelled on what he'd left behind his insides crumbled. These fever dreams had brought it all back. Now his guts were mush. But as he drank the broth that the old woman brought him, his head cleared and he re-gained control. He could feel himself harden once again. The old woman's black face was wrinkled like the pit of a prune and she had only a few teeth left. A lifetime of sun and wind and poverty had turned her into a caricature. His Portuguese was good by now. He'd studied hard over the past five years. But the accent of these poor northern dune dwellers was a struggle. He needed to get out of here. He needed to get his money back. He crawled to his feet. His injuries had been cleaned and bandaged. He hurt but any infection seemed to have been treated. The gunshot to the lower back is what concerned him the most. Thankfully it seems the bullet went in and out. He'd need to let the tissue heal but as long as there was no infection he'd survive.

He stumbled out the front door of the tiny mud and concrete house and found himself on a slight rise looking out over a checkerboard of white sand dunes. The wind whipped and he had to squint as much against the sand as the sun. The blue sky cut the horizon in half. Far in the distance was the mirror like shimmer of the ocean.

"Welcome to the end of the world." Her voice was hard. She wasn't happy that he was here. But at the same time she was curious about this alien that had fallen from the sky. "Do you speak Portuguese?" she asked as if poking at him with a stick.

"*Sim*," he replied. He'd glimpsed her in the background over the past three days. She was Alfredo's sister. *Cida* they called her. Short for Aparecida. She was younger than her brother, early 20's. But she was smarter. Aware. She understood that Frank's presence put them all in danger. She was dressed in a simple knee length skirt and a collared blouse with short sleeves. Faint sweat marks ringed the armpits. Her skin was lighter than her brother's but dark enough to make the light blue uniform seem like it was floating over her body. It was afternoon and she'd just returned from her work as a teacher in the nearby village. She'd had a long day and a long hot bus ride home but she still put off a contagious energy. She looked him straight in the eye. Daring him. To do what, he wasn't sure.

"Where am I?" he asked. Her answer, a complicated Indian name for the local area, was forgotten by the time she said it. "How far to Salvador?" This is what he needed to know.

"Half a day by car. Faster if you come up by boat," she replied. "And you can't have our boat," she added quickly. "Just so you know." His grin came so quick and big that she had to turn away so he wouldn't see her blush.

"I wouldn't think of it. Your name is Cida, right? I'm Francesco." He offered a hand to shake.

Their first touch sent a jolt from her fingers to her spine and down to her groin. His hand was strong but not cracked and rough like the other men in her life. The mischief in his eyes confirmed her suspicion that he was a bandit of some kind; but his smile... Broad and sincere, it sucked her in and made her want to be part of whatever great, crazy joke he was playing on the world.

Aparecida helped the grandmother serve dinner. The father, Geronimo, was a simple but strong man in his late 50's. Frank tried to explain the history of his name but the man lacked the education to grasp the historical context of the Indian Wars of 1800's America. To him it was just a name. Geronimo fished for a living. Every day he left at dawn and returned at sunset. He sold the catch at the village market an hour away and then brought home any extra for the family's dinner. This is what they ate now. Rice. Black beans. Grilled white fish. It was a light and healthy meal that may not have left him full but gave him strength. He'd need it. They'd all need it for what was to come.

"Does he know where you live?" Frank asked Alfredo.

Alfredo shook his head, "No. I don't think so."

"How does he contact you for work?" Frank hadn't noticed a phone in the house.

"He leaves a message at the pay phone in town," Alfredo replied with a shrug.

Cida sat down to join the conversation. "Then that means he knows where we live. Or at least he can find out." Unlike her brother and father she understood how the world worked. She'd gone to college in Salvador. She took the bus into town every day to teach the children of not only honest, hard working fishermen and construction workers but the occasional drug runner or politician. *"Pai,"* she pleaded. "He's going to come for Alfredo. We need to do something."

Geronimo didn't want to acknowledge that the long honed routine of his life was about to be up-ended, likely forever. "Alfredo did nothing wrong. He's a good boy," he muttered. Then, showing the first sign of a spine, he pointed at Frank, "He's the one they want. He's the bad man."

"He already thinks I'm dead, Sir. I could leave right now and he'll still come for your son. I promise you." Frank was no longer surprised by the naiveté of honest people. He'd seen it everyday as a cop. Or maybe it wasn't just honesty, it was a lack of imagination that doomed people like Geronimo and Alfredo to being victims. But he owed Alfredo his life. He'd do what he could to help the kid. "Do you own a gun?" he asked the father.

Geronimo looked down at his plate. A familiar sense of helplessness descended upon him.

"No. We don't have a gun," Cida answered for the family.

"What about the neighbors? Is there anyone you can trust to help?" Frank asked, already knowing the answer. He'd been outside. There wasn't another house within miles. They were trapped here in the dunes all alone.

"Maybe I can call him? Make a deal…" Alfredo suggested.

"Tell us what was in the box?" Cida demanded. "We have a right to know."

Frank took stock of his situation. Alfredo could fight, but probably wouldn't kill. Geronimo was scared to death. He'd step up when his kids were threatened but this courage would come too late. Aparecida was the one that had potential. He had no doubt that she could kill if she had to. The old woman, well she'd probably hide under the bed and outlive them all. And himself? He was moving better, but… if he was going to survive he'd need to scare these people into action.

"On the first day; he'll cut open the box and find $48 million in cash." He paused to allow the number to sink in. "He won't do anything that first day. The money will scare him. He'll hide. He'll make sure no one is following him. On the second day he'll realize that the money's all his, that no one's coming for it. That's when he'll go out and buy something. Something expensive - but not too expensive. Maybe a car or a motorcycle. Just to make sure that the money is real. It is. This purchase will give him such a rush that he'll then go out and get drunk and laid. In the morning, on the third day, he'll wake up in a cold sweat. Terrified that someone will find out and try to take the money from him. He'll make a list of everyone that could possibly know about it. That list will have one big name at the top." Frank pointed at Alfredo. "On the fourth day he'll find some friends with guns or he'll hire some local tough guys. He'll tell them that Alfredo tried to attack him on the boat and that he needs to be taught a lesson. He'll then call up to that pay phone you mentioned. He'll be charming, say he has some over due pay that he needs to deliver. Whoever answers will give him your location without thinking twice. On the evening of that fourth day they'll travel up from Salvador by boat and in the middle of the night surround your house and kill everyone inside."

Alfredo counted on his hand, "Today's the fourth day."

Frank nodded. Good. He had their attention. They sat in silence. Sweating. Swatting at flies. Frank looked around the simple house, attempting to formulate a strategy. On one wall was a painting of Jesus. On the other wall a photo of Pele. Neither of them would be of any help.

Alfredo suddenly stood up. He gathered his plate and put it in the small sink. He kissed his grandmother on the top of her head. Then he turned to Frank, he'd come to a decision.

"There is someone who can help. Pastor Dan can help us."

"Prayers aren't the kind of help we need, my friend," Frank said.

"Pastor Dan has a gun. I've seen it," Alfredo said.

CHAPTER
THIRTY-TWO

"I THINK YOU MISSED THE TURN," she teased. The patchy, signless roads appeared at random and then disappeared, melting into dead ends or dirt lots; like the one where we'd just arrived. I turned the car around and drove back the way we came until Marié spotted a girl in a threadbare blue and white school uniform. "There! Follow her."

Twenty five years later the school had been expanded with a favela style addition growing out of its side. The paint job had also been updated with a mural of Brazilian soccer legends. The school overflowed with kids, many of them sitting on the floor; but all of them paying close attention to the teacher. Our arrival turned out to be too much for the kids to bear and by the time we got out of the car they'd crowded against the windows to catch a glimpse of the gringo and the former novela star turned journalist. A firm but friendly woman in her 30's came out to investigate. She introduced herself as Juliana and explained that she was the head teacher. Marié showed her Aparecida's Instagram post and Juliana gasped. Of course she remembered Aparecida Ramos, or Teacher Cida, as they called her. She pointed to a chubby girl in the middle row. "That's me! I was, I think eleven when she left."

"Can you tell us *why* she left?" I asked. Marié translated for me.

The teacher thought for a moment and then replied, "All I remember is it was sudden. One day she just didn't show up - and we were all sad but no one told us anything. It took a while to find another teacher. Almost a whole year. Which now that I think about it was strange because Teacher Cida had been super passionate. She was a great teacher. She made us read. That's what I remember most. Something must have happened for her to just quit like that. Why do you ask? Do you know her?"

Marié looked at me. Should she tell her? I shrugged and Marié smartly downplayed recent events. "She moved to Rio. But she recently passed away and we're trying to contact her family. Do you know how we can find them?"

"Oh. I'm so sorry," Juliana said and made a quick sign of the cross. "I don't know her family. But I remember seeing her at church when I was little. I remember because I thought it was funny to see my teacher outside of school, as a real person you know. You should check there. Pastor Dan, he was just starting back then and of course he's still around." She nodded toward me, "And he speaks English too."

Pastor Dan was a "Warrior For God" and if he ever forgot, it was conveniently tattooed in an arc across the top of his chest. His church, *Casa Da Glória*, or House of Glory, had grown from a garage to a sprawling complex. In the center was a warehouse turned chapel where he performed service every evening and three times on Sundays. At fifty seven years old he was still a formidable man. He was African American of medium height and had a thick, stocky build that he'd honed through a passion for power lifting. We found him in his gym, a modest but well equipped space where he was joined by local youth for a daily work out. The clatter and clang of weights battled for supremacy with Pastor Dan's booming voice calling out encouragement.

"Mr. FBI!" he greeted me with a big grin and crushing handshake. "Welcome to Bahia. I heard about your father and poor Aparecida on the news. May they rest in peace. He was a good man. She was a better woman."

"You knew him?" I asked, a little surprised.

"We met. Way back. Twenty years ago, maybe? Obviously he was flawed, as are we all, but from our short experience together I could see his potential for goodness."

"What experience was that?" I pressed.

Pastor Dan was not one to let other people control a conversation. He gave me a tight smile and shifted his focus to Marié. "Marié Alves. It is a pleasure to have you at our humble church. Before you leave, *por favor*, it would be an honor to get a photo for our wall of fame," he said pointing to a wall of photos with minor Brazilian celebrities posing with Pastor Dan. Then, so that she couldn't possibly decline, "It's a little thing but it makes a difference to these kids. They think it's cool to see a celebrity -- what they don't realize is that these visits and photos they de-mystify success. The kids can see that someone like you, a famous actress and now journalist, is a real person. Just like them."

"I'd love to," Marié responded, charmed by his attention. The man had a charisma common with religious figures and politicians. An ability to almost hypnotize with his intense focus.

"Thank you. Bless you. Now, let me change out of these

clothes." His tank top and shorts were stained with sweat and weight lifting chalk. "And I'll meet you for a coffee at our café."

The café was a kiosk with a handful of tables. Each table had pamphlets promoting *Casa da Glória* events. A teenage girl in a "Warrior For God" t-shirt worked the espresso machine. She was serious about her work. Once the drinks were just right she brought them over on a tray. A cappuccino for Marié. Espresso for me. And a big mug emblazoned "Jesus Saves" for Pastor Dan who had changed into his own "Warrior For God" t-shirt and joined us almost immediately.

"I've been in Brazil for 27 years now but I just can't do those little espresso cups," he said holding up his coffee mug. "I like the sip and think that a big American mug gives you. But other than that," he waved a hand indicating his mini-empire, "obviously I'm hooked."

He was stalling. He knew something about my father but was trying to determine if he could trust us. I would need to put him at ease. He was proud of his church. Vanity was the obvious entry. "Tell me about all this. It's impressive. Where did you come from? Why here?"

"Ahh, flattery. One of the devil's greatest drugs," Pastor Dan smiled to let me know he wasn't offended by my opening move. "I'm from Ohio originally. I was an addict. I found god. He sent me here. And I've been doing his work ever since. But is this all for real? Or am I running some kind of con? That's what your suspicious FBI mind is wondering. What you see is built entirely by donations from the U.S. I collect nothing from the people here. The worship. The youth services. There is no charge and no solicitation. But I must admit that at times I do feel like a con man. This life that's been given to me... I often don't feel worthy. But when these feelings come, I throw myself into the work and usually end up with another chapel or another food bank. You get the point."

"This place is amazing. I'd love to come back and do a profile on you and the church," Marié gushed. She had picked up on my strategy.

"We'd love to have you," he grinned, sitting back and sipping from his coffee as if this had been his plan all along. "But please. Enough about me. What can I do for you? It can be isolating up here but I do try to keep up with the news. I thought that the police had closed the case?"

"They closed the case. But they didn't solve the case," I told him.

"Ahh. I see," he replied. And I could tell that he did. He was a street wise Preacher not a naïve do-gooder. He immediately picked up on the implications, "So, their daughter… you think she's still alive?"

"I know she is. I saw her. She's been kidnapped by a delusional white supremacist freak. He tried to kill me." I showed him the stitches on my upper arm. "We think he's holding her and torturing her." I let that revelation eat away at any hesitancy he may have.

"My god. What horrors people can do… I want to help, but I wasn't lying when I told you that this place is run on charity. An appeal to our donors might raise a few thousand toward the ransom but that's about it." He seemed sincere.

"There's no ransom demand."

"Then what does he want?"

"We don't know. Whatever it is, it's linked to my dad. That's why we're here. We're trying to find as many pieces to his life as we can and hopefully one of them will be the missing piece." I watched as Pastor Dan looked out over the church complex. His life's work. I was hit with the feeling that whatever secret he was holding back, it threatened everything he'd built.

Finally Pastor Dan asked, "What do you have so far?"

I laid out what we knew about Dad's later years in Rio as a doting father and husband. I also told him about L.A. and the details regarding the stolen money. I told him that we suspected he purposely sunk his sailboat and then came back at a later date to lift out the bulk of the cash. We showed him the photo of Aparecida at the school and how about five years after my dad would've landed in Brazil she disappeared into his world. Pastor Dan seemed surprised by none of it. "We're running out of time," I appealed. "We know he met Aparecida here. But something else happened. You know. I know you know."

Pastor Dan ran his hand over his closely shaved head. His finger subconsciously lingered on a faint scar that ran from his temple to just above his right ear.

"You need to go to the dunes. If there's anything left... that's where you'll find it."

CHAPTER
THIRTY-THREE

IT TOOK LONGER than usual for the spirit to possess his body. The Priestess was a strong, motherly woman with greying dreadlocks and a flowing white dress and white head wrap. Beads of sweat rolled down her face as she sang. Pleading with the spirits to gift them with their presence. Her drummers had slipped into a trance, their hands moving as if controlled from beyond as they slapped and scraped the drums perched between their legs.

The exact moment of possession was his favorite part. It hit like a long, drawn out musical beat as time slowed and he floated up, up looking down on his body; as if he existed in two places at once. There had been a time when Alfredo had given up the traditions of *Santería* for the easy allure of Christianity. But he had learned the hard way that there were no easy answers. The spirits required work. Life required work. Nothing came for free. Especially salvation.

With experience he had learned to focus his mind during this limbo-like transition and he could often recognize the aura of the visiting spirit as it dropped into his body. But this time there was no recognition. What passed by him now was a violent swirl of dark and red with the horns of a devil. As Alfredo's consciousness slipped into the black void he was hit with a cold shock of fear. This spirit was powerful. More powerful than any he'd seen before.

In order to appease such a deity a sacrifice would be required. A big sacrifice.

CHAPTER
THIRTY-FOUR

THE COASTAL WILDERNESS was an endless stretch of sand dunes and coconut trees and tangled mangrove swamps. While much of the Bahia coast had been taken over by tourists and expensive vacation houses this flood prone area was left for the hard scrabble locals. The road eventually turned to loose sand and we had to leave Gold's car and proceed on foot. I kicked myself for not bringing extra water. Our lone water bottle was almost empty and it had taken over an hour of walking in the heat and sand before we arrived at the remnants of the house.

The house, which had once consisted of three simple rooms, now resembled the ruins of an archeological dig. The roof had caved in years ago. The floor was filled with sand. Small trees and vines grew out of the concrete walls. This had been Aparecida's childhood home.

"What are we looking for?" asked Marié. She'd been a good sport during our hike. Playing the role of intrepid reporter. But she was a city girl and looked to be at the breaking point as she stood beneath a tree, sweaty and dirty and swatting at sand flies.

"I don't know," I confessed. "Maybe just crossing the place off our list."

I walked through the rooms, imagining a childhood in this remote corner of the world. Aparecida had been a teacher. A reader. She must have dreamed of escape. She must have also been capable. Not everyone could adapt from this world to a life in Rio de Janeiro with its TV stars and wealth and organized chaos. Not only adapt, but excel. She would have been the shining light of her family. It's no wonder that my dad had been drawn to her.

The walls of the house were pocked with holes. Bullet marks. Long ago a battle had taken place here. Pastor Dan told us that Aparecida's brother had worked for a dive boat out of Salvador. Maybe he was the one who helped Dad pull up the money... Then they brought it back here... Where he met Aparecida... Word leaked... And they were attacked... The story was coming together. The brother was the key. I needed to find the brother.

"Miles?" Marié called softly, almost a whisper. "We have company."

I stepped out and peered around the door frame. Marié was still beneath the tree. I followed her gaze toward a boy standing in the distance. He was a local, about eight years old. He wore a pair of board shorts and no shirt or shoes. On his face he wore a mask made from a paper plate and tied with string around the back of his head. The eyes were cut out and a crude devil design was drawn on the front. Red horns. Black shadow under the eyes. A tiny black goatee near the chin.

Marié waved for him to come closer, "*Oi rapaz, você mora aqui?*" Hey, kid. Do you live here? The boy didn't move. Marié took a step forward and the boy immediately turned and jogged away. But he didn't run away. He looked over his shoulder and stopped when he saw that we weren't following.

"I think he wants us to follow him," said Marié. She seemed reluctant to play his game but didn't want to be the one to chicken out.

I checked my watch. It was 5:00 pm. We had less than two hours of sunlight. And we still had an hour walk back to the car and had just finished the last of our water. Yet this boy - his appearance wasn't random. He had a purpose. "C'mon. We'll be careful. Just to see what's over the ridge there," I said pointing to a slight hill in the near distance. I then gave the boy a friendly wave and started to follow.

At the top of the hill we paused to catch our breath. We could see out over the ocean. It was a vast blue that seemed to merge with the sky. To complete the effect the waves weren't rolling breakers but rather hundreds of wind whipped white caps cresting and falling like puffy clouds. Down on the beach a couple dozen locals were gathered. They were dressed in all white. The men wore thin shorts and shirts. The women wore flowing dresses and head wraps. Food was laid out beneath a temporary shelter. There was also a larger shelter tucked back from the sand where drummers and dancers could be glimpsed. The sound of the drums was faint, drowned out by the ocean, but I could feel their throbbing pulse in my chest.

"Santería," Marié said. "It's an offering ceremony of some kind. A wedding. Maybe a funeral." Superstition rose up inside her. "We should go back."

I had experience with Santería from a job in the Dominican Republic. The religion was a hold over from the days of slavery, a mash-up of Catholicism and African ritual. The followers believed that we all had a pre-ordained destiny and that the journey toward this destiny was influenced by various spirit guides. A big part of the worship was whipping people into a hypnotic state in which they believed they were "possessed" by one of these spirits. The priest or priestess would then ask the spirit for help in guiding the person toward the right path. According to the practitioners I spoke with, the experience was benign. Almost a type of therapy not too different from a visit with your local shrink. The Dominican case had been tricky. It involved the kidnapping of a local politician by a radical off-shoot of the church. They were convinced that the politician had been possessed by a demon and for over a week they drugged and tortured the man in hopes of driving out the demon. The break in the negotiations came when I consulted a local priestess who was able to identify the evil spirit and give us a little taste of its personality. We then used a drone to plant a microphone on the roof of the kidnapper's safe house and broadcast the demon's disembodied voice. After promising to leave the politician alone our demon then "disappeared." The kidnappers were satisfied that their plan had worked and the politician was released and the kidnappers surrendered. The crazy part was that the politician had been convinced that he really was possessed and he refused to press charges; even after the microphone gag had been revealed.

"Do you see the boy?" I asked Marié. I scanned the beach. Our guide in the paper plate mask had disappeared and there were no children at the gathering. "He wasn't that far ahead," I pointed out. "Maybe he was one of their spirit guides." It was a joke but a quick shiver ran down my spine.

"Not funny," Marié said in a hushed voice.

"They have water down there. We'll get a drink. Say

hello. And then head back. OK?"

She was thirsty and tired. She nodded, yes. But she was nervous. She took my hand as we headed down the gentle slope. It felt good walking beside her like this. Our arms touching. Our thighs brushing against each other. As if we were becoming one.

The Santería followers smiled and waved as we arrived. A shirtless older man used a machete to chop a hole in the top of a chilled coconut and we drank the cool, bitter sweet juice through plastic straws. Marié chatted in Portuguese and occasionally translated. She'd been right, this was a memorial service. She asked about the boy. No one knew him. They assumed he was just a local kid playing around in the dunes. As she talked with the women setting out food I was briefly forgotten and free to move toward the make-shift pavilion of singers and drummers.

The roof was made of logs and palm boughs and held up by tall wooden poles. The ground had been hardened by the feet of dancers who now twirled and swayed to a small group of drummers. The singing was led by the head Priestess, a sturdy woman with grey in her dreadlocks. To the side of the dance floor was a plastic table with a make-shift altar. The table was covered in shells and candles arranged around a framed photo of a woman who I assumed was the deceased. I'd arrived just after the moment of possession. A shirtless black man stood in the middle of the crowd. His head lolled from side to side and his arms and body jerked as if he were a life sized marionette. He alternated between mumbling and shouting. A non-stop stream of nonsensical Portuguese.

He looked familiar. I knew his face. It was the face of his sister.

I pushed through the dancers to the altar and picked up the framed photo. It was a wedding photo. Aparecida in a white gown, laughing and looking out of frame. I could imagine my dad standing next to her, proud of his bride, telling a joke. I was jerked around by the sudden scream of a woman, "*Não! Não! Me deixa!*"

"Marié!" I called. I could see her struggling as she was held back by two women. "Miles! Look out," she screamed.

Two of the drummers grabbed me by the arms. My shoulders strained as they twisted me around to face Aparecida's brother. He was in his fifties but his smooth skin made him look younger. His eyes were bloodshot and darted from side to side. His teeth crooked and yellowed. He screamed the unintelligible scream of the possessed. A fever cry from the depths of Babel. Then his hand whipped up and he threw a red powder into my face. Fire raced up my nose. My tongue grew thick and the dancers holding my arms shoved me forward and I fell... into a silent, bottomless black pit.

CHAPTER
THIRTY-FIVE

FRANK HAD KNOWN guys like Pastor Dan on the streets. A junkie who'd got clean, but had really just traded one high for another. Heroin for religion. And Frank had a rule. Never trust a fucking junkie.

"Where you from, man? I'm from Cleveland. Been down here about two years. Love it, man. Love. It. The people are awesome. So warm. So eager to hear the word, ya know. So where ya from, huh?"

Frank ignored the question and continued to break down the Pastor's gun. It was a .357 Smith and Wesson six shot revolver. An old school cop gun. He'd shot them hundreds of times. It had a good weight and delivered a punch that would put a man on their ass. Most importantly, it had a loud bang that made punks shit their pants. This one was at least fifteen years old and hadn't been cleaned in almost as long. "You shoot this before?"

Dan shrugged, "A couple of times. Out of curiosity. Guns ain't my bag."

"Where'd you get it?"

"Dang, man. I swear you talk like a cop. One of my

parishioners gave it to me. She found it in her son's bedroom and asked me to get rid of it."

Frank had wiped down the pieces with a rag and then snapped it back together. It would shoot. But the barrel needed to be re-bored, there'd be no accuracy at distance. He'd have to get up close. He counted the loose bullets, twelve. He loaded six into the gun and pocketed the other six. All of this he did with a smooth efficiency. He looked up to see Aparecida watching. Just as she'd been watching him for the past four days. He noticed that while her brother and family were all nerves she was cool and composed. "Do you know how to use this?" he asked. She shook her head, no. "Come." He motioned for her to follow him outside. She moved without hesitation. She'd gotten over the need to put up a wall between them. She now wanted what he had to offer.

He held up the gun and handed it to her. The gun scared her. It was heavy and dark, like an object of magic. She took it. Carefully. But trusting. He stepped behind her and pressed his chest against her back. He then reached around and formed her right hand over the gun's handle and brought her left hand up in support.

"See that tree," he said softly in her ear pointing to a coconut tree about 30 yards away. "Keep both eyes open and aim by looking along the top of the barrel."

She did as he said. He remained pressed tight behind her and helped to adjust her arm. He could feel her heart pounding. He could also feel himself grow as her firm curves brushed back against his groin. There was no doubt now that she could feel him. And yet she remained in his grasp. "Now breathe deep." She did. "One more deep breath and as you exhale -- slowly squeeze the trigger." He dropped his hands to her waist and held his head to the side so that the recoil wouldn't cause her to snap her head back and break his nose. She took another deep breath and just as he'd told her; squeezed the trigger. The shock of the bang and recoil caused her to jump and she turned into him, a huge grin on her face. The first time he'd seen her smile. "I did it!" she said. He didn't even bother to look at the tree. With one hand he took the gun and with the other he pulled her head to him and they kissed. It was a short kiss but within it they could both see their future laid out before them. They knew that if they were to survive what was to come they would never be apart.

There were five of them. They wore shorts, t-shirts and flip flops. The oldest was twenty five at the most. The youngest looked about fourteen. He'd yet to use a razor; but he was here to commit murder. The boat Captain had dropped them at the beach and then pulled back out into deep water. Frank was certain that the five would-be killers were Salvador favela kids. A couple of them had likely even killed before. Their lives had been lived fast and hard. He felt a pang of guilt that those lives would end tonight.

The sky was clear of clouds which meant a canopy of stars added to the moon's glow. Frank watched as they checked their weapons. The oldest had an AK-47. The other four had smaller caliber handguns. None of them had extra ammo so whatever was in their clip was their entire load. The oldest had a hand drawn map. He studied it for a long time before looking up and pointing them toward a hill; on the other side would be their target. Before they headed out they each did a huff from a rag of paint. From his hiding spot fifty meters away beneath a blind of coconut boughs Frank could see their eyes pin as the fumes hit the spot. They then gathered in a circle for one final gesture to drum up courage. They put their hands on top of each other and called out, "*Um! Dos! Tres! Morte Negra!*" Black Death. That must be the name of their little band of assassins, he thought. Cute kids.

He followed from a safe distance as they made their way up the sand dunes and through the sparse coconut forest. The house was lit from inside. Through the windows came the TV flicker of the nightly novela. The killers took positions around the house and on the signal of the oldest they opened fire. The windows shattered. The lights were shot out. The TV went silent. They stopped shooting and the oldest called, "Come out! Surrender and we won't shoot!"

No one came out. The house was silent. The oldest ordered the youngest to go look in the window. But the boy shook his head, "No way!" The oldest aimed his gun and unleashed a stream of insults that Frank couldn't understand but had to respect. The youngest reluctantly inched forward and peered inside. "It's empty!" he cried out, sounding relieved.

Frank waited until they'd all gone inside to investigate and then he sprinted up to a window. He took a deep breath and stood up and opened fire. He took out the oldest first and then two others as they started to shoot back. He rolled away and scurried to the opposite side of the house where he again opened fire through the window and finished the last two.

With his gun raised high in front of him he walked around to the front door and carefully entered. The bodies lay motionless on the floor. He kicked away their guns and nudged them with his foot. Once he was confident that all five of the killers were dead he lowered his gun and allowed himself a deep breath. Now came the work. He dragged each body out of the house and lined them up on the ground. He searched their pockets. They each had a small roll of cash. Their pre-payment for the assassination job. He took it for himself. He then stacked their guns in a pile. He'd guessed right regarding the age of the youngest. He was barely a teen. The boy made him think of his son. It had been five years since he left. Miles would be seventeen now. Older than this kid that he'd just killed. The gunshot had entered through the side of the boy's torso, right beneath the armpit. Frank couldn't find an exit wound which meant that the bullet must have ricocheted inside tearing apart the boy's heart, his stomach, his lungs until probably lodging into a rib.

Fuck, he thought to himself and then out loud into the night, "*Fuck!*" The night didn't respond. Nor did the dead boy at his feet. He'd seen other cops after they'd been forced to kill a kid. Their lives were never the same. They either fell into a bottle or they lashed out against the world... or they just faded away. It was at this moment that Frank realized that he was no longer a cop. On paper he hadn't been a cop for a long time, but deep in his soul he thought he'd always be a cop. Now, looking down at the dead body of the boy he'd just shot -- he realized that he'd moved on. No, Frank Ronan the cop was dead. He'd become something else.

Someone had told the killers how to find the house. The hand drawn map in the oldest killer's pocket had only a few landmarks with which to navigate.

One of them was a church.

Never trust a fucking junkie.

CHAPTER
THIRTY-SIX

MARIÉ FINALLY RIPPED free of the women and ran into the dance pavilion. She found Miles laying in the dirt with his eyes fluttered back in his head and his body jerking. Alfredo stood over him muttering a stream of gibberish.

"Make it stop!" she yelled at the Priestess who ignored her and stood back, watching the possession run its course. "Bring him back!" Marié demanded. She ran to grab the Priestess but was restrained by the dancers.

The Priestess put a silencing finger to Marié's lips. "Why are you afraid? He'll come back when he's ready. Look around. No one else is afraid." The Priestess traced her finger around Marié's face, her smooth cheek, down her perfect nose, studying her. "I see… You are afraid for yourself. Afraid of what he may discover about you. Don't worry, the spirit is not here for you tonight."

The fight left Marié's body. She'd experienced Santería ceremonies before. Her mother had consulted with them when her father was diagnosed with cancer. She herself had consulted with them before her first marriage. Each time they'd predicted doom. And each time their predictions had come true. She sagged to the floor and sat and watched. Silently praying to whatever god would listen that Miles be returned to her the same man that had left. A good man. A brave man. Maybe the kind of man she could love.

The boy in the paper plate mask was back. It felt good to see him again. I had been so lonely. How long had I been here? Weeks? Days? The beach was empty. Where had everyone gone? And it was so quiet. Even the ocean had been muted. All I could hear was the squeak of the white sand beneath my feet. The boy led me a short distance and then turned inland where we soon came to a picket fence surrounding a small cemetery. The squeak of the sand was replaced by the chunk of a shovel digging into the earth.

The boy had disappeared again. Crazy kid. There was now a man digging a hole. I recognized him. It was Aparecida's brother. Somehow I knew that his name was Alfredo.

"Hello?" I called to him. He didn't seem to hear me. "*Tudo bem? Boa tarde.*" I'd picked up at least this greeting over the last week. He continued to ignore me. Intent on his work. Laid out in front of him was a line of shallow graves. As I moved closer I saw that each grave held a dead body looking up at the sky. I recognized the bodies. Some of them. The first one was my dad's old partner. His throat was slit. His pants were around his ankles. Then there was my dad. And Aparecida. Their bodies were hacked and bloodied and their faces stitched together with coroner thread. I also recognized Paulo Heinrik with his cut throat and the bib of blood staining his white dress shirt. There were others I didn't recognize. They looked like locals. Brazilians. All of them had died violent deaths. Three of them were young men wearing shorts. Their bodies seemed slick with sea water and blood. There was another group of even younger men who were dressed in T-shirts and shorts and flip flops. They had all been shot. One of this group was just a teen. His smooth, round face frozen in surprise. The last body was a large bellied middle aged man. He had died more peacefully than the others. One simple gunshot between the eyes. At the end of the row was an empty grave which Alfredo had just finished digging.

Alfredo finally turned to me and smiled, "You are Francesco's son?" Even though he spoke Portuguese I understood him completely.

"Yes. And you're Alfredo."

"Yes. I am Alfredo."

"Who are they?" I said motioning to the dead bodies.

"They are the cursed," he said matter of factly.

"The cursed? What do you mean?" But as soon as I asked I realized that I already knew the answer. The money was the curse. All of these people had been touched by the stolen money. "Who is this for?" I asked pointing to the empty grave.

"The next one," he replied and I realized that the shovel in Alfredo's hand had turned into a gun.

"Wait..."

He smiled and swiftly raised the gun to the side of his head and fired. His body fell back, landing in its grave.

"No!" I gasped.

Suddenly the earth let out a groan and my legs gave out as the ground lifted and began to roll -- unfurling like a wave toward the horizon. Then just as suddenly as it started, it stopped. The picket fence boundary had disappeared and the cemetery was no longer contained. I was standing in the midst of an endless plain filled with freshly dug holes. Empty graves.

Thousands of them.

CHAPTER
THIRTY-SEVEN

FRANK GATHERED the guns into a pillow case and threw it over his shoulder and headed for town. He left behind the five dead bodies on the ground in front of the house. He'd already told Alfredo that the family would need to move. They were upset but he'd promised to buy them a new house. A real house. A goddamn mansion if they wanted. They believed him. They'd taken their most important belongings and were now huddled with Pastor Dan in his make-shift church.

The "*Casa da Glória*" evangelical church had been a garage in its former life. Dan had done a good job of cleaning it up. The exterior was painted a bright white and he'd installed a huge sign over the front door that was lit with a spot-light. Frank didn't knock. He slipped in quietly just in case Dan had turned the family against him. Aparecida saw him first. She rushed to give him a hug. The others were kneeled on the floor with hands clasped and deep in prayer. They jumped to their feet. Awash in relief.

"It's done. But he'll be sending more," Frank told them and dropped the bag of guns on the floor. "Everybody take one." Alfredo and Aparecida moved to pick a handgun. So did Pastor Dan. "Not you," Frank said and grabbed Dan by the arm, shoving him back into a plastic chair. "This look familiar?" Frank said, holding up the hand drawn map.

"No. What is it?" he scrambled.

"It's the map you gave them. You told them where to find us."

"Wait. Hold on," Pastor Dan scrambled. "I didn't know what they were going to do! They called the church and asked for Alfredo. He said he was his boss. I just gave them directions!"

"Then why didn't you tell us when you discovered the truth?" Frank asked.

"I was scared, all right? Man, I can't get involved in this shit. I'm trying to start something here. I can't... I just can't do this."

"So you thought the best plan would be to let them kill me?" Frank pulled his gun and jammed it into Dan's forehead. "Stop making me state the fucking obvious!"

"OK! OK! He offered me money! But I changed my mind! I didn't tell him anything. I swear. We're all alive. You caught them, right? No harm no foul, brother."

"*Mentira. Você e um mentiroso.*" You're a liar. Alfredo didn't understand their English but as soon as he picked up the discarded map from the floor he realized what had happened.

He looked from Dan to the wooden cross dominating the wall behind him. His new found belief dropped out of his body as if someone had pulled the plug from a drain. In a flash he raised his freshly claimed hand gun, a black metal 9mm.

"No!" cried Frank and he dove to knock down Alfredo's arm as he fired.

Dan crumpled to the ground. But he was still alive. The shot had grazed the side of his head. He groaned and sat

THE RIO AFFAIR   163

up, clutching his bloody scalp. Alfredo moved to finish the job but Frank wrapped him in a bear hug and talked him down, "When we're done you can do what you want. But right now we need him. He's a sucker. We need a sucker."

Salvador Bahia was an old city whose smiles and fresh paint and constant thrum of music served to cover up its dark history as the center of the Brazilian slave trade. The port was no longer filled with human cargo and slaver auctions -- it was now a jumbled clockwork of cruise ships and cranes loading and unloading shipping containers bound for all corners of the earth. But there was still a touch of the old world along the edges as local fishing boats flit amidst the goliaths. It was here, at the intersection of the old and the new that Gilberto Santos ran a modest salvage boat operation. He kept his boat docked near a warehouse that he owned at the northern edge of the waterfront. He also owned a small apartment nearby but he'd slept on the floor of the warehouse for the past four days. Next to his money. After returning in the night with the steel box he'd paid some boys to drag it inside and then kicked them out and locked all the doors before cutting a hole in the top with a welding torch. The amount of cash scared the hell out of him. He'd initially assumed it was drug money. Then he was convinced it was fake. But after changing a handful of bills at the bank he realized it was real. It was then that he allowed himself to imagine the possibilities. A house on the beach. A yacht. Oh, he'd have so many women. But first he needed to get rid of that damn bible thumping diver. Get rid of Alfredo and the money would be his, no strings attached. He'd be the richest man in all of Salvador.

He'd returned from dropping off the boys a few hours

earlier. Being away from his money had been stressful. But now he was back. He sat in the dark, staring at the steel box and cradling an AK-47 that he'd just purchased from a cousin who worked for the local police. At his side were six thin envelopes of cash. Five were the final payment for the boys. One was for the gringo pastor who was right now driving them back to Salvador. They were late. The pastor had called around midnight and said they'd hit the road right away. It was already dawn and they still hadn't arrived. He got up and fixed a pot of coffee. Where the hell were they?!

Finally there was a knock at the door. He snatched the AK and peered out the door's peep-hole. It was the gringo pastor. What's his name...? Something ridiculous to match that goofy grin; Pastor Dan. He was alone. Gilberto set the gun against the wall and slipped outside to talk with him.

"Where are the boys?" he asked. His paranoia rose as he scanned the empty dock.

Pastor Dan pointed off to the road. "There in my car. Passed out. They got drunk and then made me stop so they could screw *putas* on the way home." He then pointed at the blood tinged bandage wrapped around his forehead like a headband. "One of the little shits took a shot at me when I tried to drag them out of the place."

Gilberto relaxed. "Sounds about right. I knew I shouldn't have paid them up front."

"Help me get them out of the car? I need to get back. I have a church service this afternoon. Please, I can't deal with them anymore. One even threw up in the back seat. It's a fucking mess."

Gilberto laughed, "Yeah. Yeah. Just a minute." He pulled out his keys to lock the newly installed locks on the warehouse door. As soon as he turned away Pastor Dan pulled a gun from the back of his pants and jammed it into Gilberto's back.

"Open the door. Or I blow you to hell and take the keys myself," Dan ordered.

Gilberto whirled around and smiled. This scrawny preacher wasn't like the other gringo. Hell, he didn't even have his finger on the trigger. "You don't have the balls. Go ahead. Do it! Let's go! Shoot! Blow a hole in me you fucking pussy!"

Pastor Dan gave up and turned to run. Gilberto pounced. Fast and cat-like despite his size. They hit the ground and wrestled for control of the gun when Frank appeared behind them.

"Might as well get up. It's not loaded," Frank said, pulling his own gun. "But this one is. And I do have the balls to use it."

Gilberto scrambled to his feet with the gun in hand. "No. You're dead! I saw you drown!" He aimed at Frank and fired. The gun clicked empty. Click. Click. Click. "*Merde.*" He turned to run -- but Alfredo and Aparecida, both armed and looking bad to the bone, stepped out from the side of the building. Gilberto glanced in the opposite direction toward the road and Dan's car.

"Your boys are dead," Frank said. He kicked the warehouse keys toward Gilberto. "Now open up. We'll talk inside. Who knows, maybe we can make a deal."

CHAPTER
THIRTY-EIGHT

MARIÉ SAID that I'd only been out for about twenty minutes but I was exhausted. We sat under the coconut trees and I devoured a plate of sliced fruit offered by the women. Mango, oranges, cantaloupe, chilled coconut water. The dream was still vivid in my mind. Who were the empty graves for? Me? Leticia? No. If there were any god or justice in the universe Leticia had to survive. Gregor Heinrik? For sure him. If I was going to die for this damned curse I was determined to bring him along with me.

The Santería ceremony had ended. The spent followers gathered their belongings and quietly walked off in various directions. I saw Alfredo watching me from a distance. I pulled myself to my feet and approached.

"Alfredo?"

He nodded, "Sim."

"My name is Miles. I believe you knew my father." I spoke in English but unlike in the dream world we didn't speak the same language. He just nodded and smiled. He was a lean, densely muscled man who carried himself with simple dignity. In his eyes I could see wisdom. Not the type that you're born with; rather, the type that is earned through years of hard luck. Marié introduced herself and translated.

He replied in Portuguese, "Yes. Your father was my friend. He was not a good man. But he was a good friend."

I don't know if it was the haze of vulnerability left over from the ceremony or the surreal disconnect from the real world that Bahia provided - or maybe I'd just stopped being angry; but his words, words that rang so true that they hurt, burst a dam inside of me and a lifetime of grief and loss roiled to the surface. The feeling was one of panic as tears and then sobs took over my body. Desperate for a place to hide I latched onto Marié and buried my face in her shoulder. Her thin arms held me together.

Almost as suddenly as it had come the emotion faded and I was left feeling lighter than I had in years. Euphoric. Both Marié and Alfredo's eyes were red and wet in sympathy. These two people, both of whom I'd really just met, were the closest thing I had to family. Was I really that alone in the world? It was a feeling of being unmoored. A feeling that had never bothered me until right now. But then I realized that I wasn't alone. My father had given me a sister. She was a part of me that extended beyond myself. She was also a part of Alfredo.

"Did you know his daughter?" I asked as I recovered.

"*Sim*," Alfredo smiled. "I met her one time. I went to visit in Rio when she was just a little girl. She was full of smiles. And always laughing. Francesco gave her everything."

"She's still alive," I said. "I saw her."

"I know. I can still feel her," he replied and touched his chest. "But you must go now. The police found your car. They'll be here soon."

"How do you know?" I asked. I was still in a fog from the Santería ceremony.

"Text message," he said with a grin as he held up his cell phone. But then the smile disappeared and he spit in the sand. "That son of a bitch Pastor Dan tipped them off."

Night landed as Marie and I walked along the beach. But the faint glow of the ocean lit the way and after a short trek we arrived at a small bed and breakfast style hotel called a *posada*. Alfredo had directed us here. He knew the owner and assured that we'd be safe. The roads leading from the beach were all being watched and it was pointless going after Pastor Dan until morning. Tomorrow was Sunday. That would be the time to hit.

The posada was owned by a middle aged couple trying to make an honest living in a remote world. The wife ran the office and cooked. The husband maintained the colorful beachfront cabanas and grounds. They didn't seem to recognize Marié and didn't ask questions. They welcomed cash. Our room was a simple one room structure with a hammock on the front porch looking out over the ocean. The bedding was a clean white sheet. There was no need for blankets. Nor did we need air conditioning as the windows were aimed to funnel the ocean breeze.

There was also no need for words. Over the course of the past days we'd been hurtling toward this point in our minds. During our silent walk along the beach she'd taken my hand letting me know that things had changed since she'd tried to draw a line between us during lunch. Now, in the faint light of the bedside lamp she pulled her shirt off over her head and then dropped her shorts to the floor. She stood there, looking at me, unashamed and unafraid, simply presenting herself. Her light tan contrasting with the white skin of her breasts. I stepped forward and took her face in my hands and we kissed. Our lips barely touching. I could feel her tremble. Or maybe that was me. "Mmm. You taste good," she whispered.

She took my hand and led me into the bathroom. Under the warm water of the shower we washed away the sweat and sand and explored each other's bodies. With our hands first. And then our mouths. Then, unable to wait we made love against the cool tile wall. Both of us coming to the finish almost immediately. And then laughing. And then kissing and rushing to the bed to do it all over again; but this time slower, savoring the experience as if we both knew our time together had a finite end.

She was propped on her elbow. The sheet rested just below her naked hip. She slowly traced her finger down the side of my body. Circling around the dried stitches from the cut on my shoulder.

"After my dad died, I was in a how you say, in a cloud?"

"In a fog," I corrected.

"I was in a fog. All the time. And then one day a photo of him came up on my phone and I just lost it. I was in the supermarket and I started to cry. I was shaking and this old lady came up and held me. Then when it was over it was like the sun had come out. I was back to normal. Better than normal. I actually felt this power. Like my life had just begun."

We both fell quiet. Perhaps a little nervous at how easy this had been. How well not only our bodies fit together.

"What do you want?" I asked.

"What do you mean?" she said. Wary.

"Have you ever heard of a black swan?"

"A swan is like a duck, right? But isn't it white?"

"Not always. Every once in a while there's a black one. But really it's a metaphor. It means something rare. Unexpected. In a negotiation the black swan is what we call finding the true motive. The one that people have buried deep down inside. Once you've found this hidden desire, their true price, that's when the real negotiation begins."

"Are we negotiating now?"

"No. You've already won," I grinned. "Now we're just talking."

"Good to know," she smiled back. "Hmm. What do I want? I guess, I want to do something important. When people see me now all they see is this character from a TV show. In their minds I'm going to be stuck forever as a teenager. I want to be a real person with real things to contribute."

"You want respect," I offered.

"I guess so. I mean, yes. I want respect," she said, owning the idea. "What about you? What do you want?"

"I want us to stay here like this. We can build our own posada. Have beautiful children and grow old and happy like Jaime Gold."

"Mmm. Sounds nice. But that's a fantasy," she pointed out. "Try harder."

"You're really going to make me go there?" I groaned.

"Yes. It's an order."

I turned and looked out the open window. Outside, it was pitch dark. The rolling crash of the ocean muffled any intrusion from the real world.

"What I want is for none of this to have ever happened. I want my dad to do the right thing thirty years ago and turn in the money and stay home and be a real man. Be a real dad."

"But that doesn't count. It's impossible. He's gone."

"That's the thing about black swans," I said, realizing it

myself for the first time, "Sometimes you search your whole life and never find one."

I could see her eyes start to well up. I reached over and brushed a tear away. "I'm not that pitiful am I?"

She didn't reply. Instead she slid her smooth thigh over mine and reached down to place me inside of her. Then we made love again. With a sudden need to empty ourselves into each other. Afterward, we lay spent and entwined drifting on the fantasy I'd drawn in the air. I'm not sure how much time passed like that, but I was eventually pulled back to the real world by the sound of her sleep. I carefully rolled out of bed and walked outside.

The sun hadn't come up yet but it was no longer pitch black. I took out Leticia's photo. Every time I looked at her I saw him, more and more. Marié was wrong. My dad wasn't gone. He was still alive inside my sister. But unlike him I wasn't going to run away.

CHAPTER
THIRTY-NINE

THE BLOOD DRAINED from his broken nose down the back of his throat and made him gag. He hawked up as much of it as he could and spit in the gringo's face.

Gilberto Santos had lived a life of greed. Since he was a boy growing up in the favelas of Salvador he'd stole and conned and fought for every scrap he ever had. This desperate need to constantly fill his pockets had left no room for family or friends. When he needed a woman it was easier to pay for her. The one love of his life, if he could call it love, was his salvage boat company. The original boat had been won in a card game over a decade ago. He may have cheated to win that first boat but he'd worked hard to turn her into a successful company. Now this gringo pirate bastard wanted to take it all away. Well, he can fuck himself. And have a face full of bloody phlegm for his troubles.

Frank had been part of enough interrogations not to be phased by a spit in the face. Hell, it was a sign of progress. The last rebellion of a beaten man. The important thing was not to react. Simply wipe yourself clean and smile. As if the end were inevitable. And it was. Gilberto Santos had held out for an hour. He'd been stripped naked and tied to a chair and beaten across the face and torso with a phone book. All he had to do was sign over ownership of his boat and warehouse and this would all go away.

"Sign the paper, *Gordo*," Frank repeated for the hundredth time. "It's a fair price."

"Go fuck yourself," Gilberto groaned.

Frank sighed and picked up the phone book again. It was splotchy with blood. He searched for a clean surface to grip. He cracked his neck, then lined up his swing like a pinch hitter for the Dodgers and...

"*Não*. Enough." Gilberto Santos broke. Sobs rippled through his body. Piss dripped onto the floor as he went limp from exhaustion and relief. Frank placed a pen in the man's hand and using the phone book as a hard surface Gilberto signed the ownership deed for his company, handing over his life's work.

"That's a good boy," Frank said. "Be happy. You're doing a good thing." Frank folded the paper in half and, making sure that Gilberto could see, he handed it to Alfredo who stood against the wall. "Congratulations, Son. It's all yours."

It had been a dizzying few days for the young man. His boss had tried to kill him. He'd pulled a dead man from the ocean. He'd survived an assassination attempt. He'd lost his religion. Now he was the owner of his own business. Just as he'd been re-born in that kiddie pool behind the church he'd been re-born again today in this warehouse. His naiveté had been washed away and he was ready to accept his place in the real world. The world of men who got shit done.

"Oh, Pastor Dan!" Frank sang. "You're up, my friend."

Dan had watched the interrogation from a corner. He'd tried to pray. But mostly he just stared in awe at the violence being unleashed. He'd seen shit go down in the streets of Cleveland but this was a different level. This was clinical. A professional beating. Now it was his turn. "I told you, I'm sorry! I won't tell anyone! I swear!"

"I'm not going to hurt you, Pastor Dan," Frank said, loose and easy. He was in a groove. He had his money back. He was untouchable again. A resident of Olympus. On his way across the warehouse floor he walked past the steel money chest. He ran his finger along the side, relishing in its touch. Then he came to Aparecida who had in the past 24 hours completed her transformation from backwater school teacher into a goddess of war. A black Athena. She took his breath away. He stopped and kissed her. Claiming her. She kissed him back accepting his claim. Finally he made it to Dan who crouched against the wall with his head in his hands. "Look at me," Frank said. Dan looked up to see Frank holding his pistol out, butt first. "Take it," he ordered.

Dan reluctantly obeyed. He'd shot guns before and could tell by the weight that it was loaded. For a second he imagined shooting Frank and then taking the money for himself. But a glance over at Aparecida and Alfredo disavowed him of that idea. "What do you want me to do?" he asked, terrified of the answer.

"You're going to kill him," Frank said, nodding to the blubbering prisoner.

"I can't... C'mon, man. I'm a man of god. Don't make me do this."

"Don't worry about that. God wants you to kill him. Believe me. I know this."

"You don't know that!"

"Oh, I know. I know because from this moment on *I am your god*." With that he grabbed Dan by the ear and drug his whimpering carcass to the center of the warehouse. They stopped directly in front of the barely conscious Gilberto Santos. "I assume this will be the first man you've killed?"

Dan had lost the power of speech. He just nodded, yes.

"I recommend you do it fast. One shot. Right between the eyes."

Dan raised the gun and aimed. "I can't," he moaned and let his arm drop.

"You can," Frank said as he stepped close and raised Dan's arm again. "It's easy. Like letting go of a balloon." Then he leaned into Dan's ear and barked, "*Do it!*"

Bang. The gun fired.

Gilberto's head snapped back and then lolled to the side, a red circle appeared in the center of his forehead. Dan stared wide-eyed at what he'd done. Click. Click. Click. He turned to see Aparecida snapping photos with a little yellow disposable camera: Pastor Dan with the gun. Pastor Dan with the gun and the dead body of Gilberto Santos. Pastor Dan crumpling to his knees in horror at what he's done.

"Congratulations. You've been re-born," Frank said, taking back the gun. "From now on, when you pray... you pray to me."

CHAPTER
FORTY

THEY SAY that religion is a cash business; and based on the overflow crowd at the *Casa da Glória*, business was booming. Pastor Dan was in great form. The speakers outside the church blared his sermon throughout the small town. *"We are poor! But we are NOT hungry! That is because we are fulfilled. Why?! Because we are God's chosen! Not the rich man... Nooo! The rich man will enter heaven when a camel walks through the head of a needle. I didn't say that. Jesus Christ the Lord said that!"*

Alfredo had been waiting at the *posada* when we woke up. After a quick breakfast we drove into town to catch Pastor Dan's first service of the day. There would be three of them. Each one filling the converted warehouse to capacity and touching nearly every person in the town. The town that, according to Alfredo, he now ran like his personal fiefdom. He owned the police. Supplementing their salaries with donations. He owned the Mayor as well. No one was elected without the support of his followers. All of this had been made possible by the deal he'd made with my dad. My dad would allow him to live, no thrive, and in exchange Pastor Dan and his church would launder his money.

According to Alfredo it took five years to run the remaining forty eight million dollars through the church coffers. The church eventually had accounts in dozens of banks in cities all over Brazil. Alfredo, Frank and Aparecida made hundreds of deliveries depositing bags of cash in the various branches. The banks rarely asked questions but when they did the explanation was simple: The money came from wealthy American churches eager to save the souls of poor, desperate Brazilians. Once all of the money was flowing through the banking system Frank and Aparecida left to start a new life in Rio. Alfredo remained behind to run his salvage boat. They'd offered him enough money to never work again but he declined. He owed Frank for saving his family but the money was dirty. He was intent on earning his own way. He was no longer a Christian but he still believed that you reaped your after-life.

"What are we looking for?" Marié asked as we sat across from the church compound.

"What am I looking for," I replied. Alfredo had informed us that the Rio Police had put a bounty on my head, R$50,000 for information leading to my arrest. Thankfully Marié wasn't on their radar yet. "You're staying here. Keep the car running and don't get yourself arrested. Because if I go down, I'm counting on you to finish this. Leticia's counting on you. Please don't fight me on this."

"All right. All right. So, what are *you* looking for?"

"Financial transactions. Bank accounts. Wire transfers. Anything connected to Rio or my dad," I replied. "But this is a smash and grab job. There won't be enough time to read things in there."

Alfredo knocked on the car window. It was his car. He'd given it to us. It was a new Peugeot compact with tinted windows and a powerful turbo charged 2.5L engine. It would outrun anything that the local police would be driving. He'd also drawn us an escape route to the main highway. I should have been more suspicious about why he was so concerned with our escape.

As I moved to leave the car Marié grabbed my hand, "Don't get caught. I don't think I can do this by myself." I could see real panic in her eyes.

"You can. Because that's who you are. I knew that from the time I saw your first news segment," I assured her. Her panic thawed and her eyes began to fill with emotion. I leaned over and kissed her. "For good luck." And before things got out of hand I turned and I followed Alfredo across the street. Her taste lingered in my mouth. I could taste something else. Violence. It was in the air, like the metallic tang that comes before an electric shock. There was about to be violence. In the daylight. With witnesses.

The church service had just started. Pastor Dan would speak for forty five minutes and then take a break and the music would kick in. If things went to plan we'd be long gone by then. The front gate of the church's property was watched by two security guards. But their job was mostly symbolic. Alfredo and I, dressed in "Warrior For God" t-shirts that we'd bought on the street, smiled at the guards and were waved right through.

Once inside the property Alfredo and I split up. I moved along the inner wall to a one story building that housed the administrative offices. The row of doors were locked and dark inside. One was secured with a heavy padlock. That would be Dan's office. I didn't have the tools to pick the lock but the door's hinges were rusted from the humid air. If I put my weight into it I would be able to break it open. But it would make noise. A lot. I would have to wait for Alfredo's distraction. Thirty yards away was the coffee kiosk where Marié and I had sat yesterday afternoon. Was it really just yesterday? Since I arrived in Brazil every day had been a lifetime. A young Security Guard was flirting with the Barista girl. She enjoyed the attention but she was also a good church going girl and kept trying to re-focus him on the wall mounted TV and the live broadcast of Pastor Dan's soul saving.

Alfredo had refused to tell me his plan but he'd promised a distraction. He'd better hurry, the Security Guard had just clocked me loitering outside the office door. He stood to approach when the Barista pointed to the TV and called out, "*Olha!*" Look! On the TV screen we all watched as Alfredo walked down the middle of the church aisle and stopped directly in front of the podium. The service came to a halt.

"My Brother," Pastor Dan said with a broad grin. He was wary, but couldn't afford to cede control. "My friends, this man you see before you was one of my original flock. He'd lost his way but now he has returned. Praise Jesus!" The nervous energy in the church exploded in relief. "Praise Jesus!" Pastor Dan addressed Alfredo again, "Welcome home, my brother. Are you here to save your soul?"

"No. I'm here to take yours." Alfredo reached behind him and pulled a gun from the back of his pants. Dan had guessed that Alfredo was unhinged. He was ready and as Alfredo made his move Dan sprinted. The first shot shattered the wooden pulpit. The second shot hit Dan in the shoulder. The third shot hit him in the chest. Dan fell to his side, unable to breathe. Unable to move. "*Não... Por favor...*" he gasped. Alfredo ignored the pleas and as he moved forward he fired into Dan's body. Over and over. When he was satisfied that Dan was dead he turned and waved the gun at the horrified congregation. Shock exploded into panic as a hundred people fought to squeeze through the narrow entrance.

I watched the TV monitor in disbelief. But the flood of

people fleeing the main church jerked me back to my senses. Alfredo had killed for me. No. Not for me, for Leticia. I looked over to the coffee kiosk. It was empty. The Security Guard and Barista had split. I turned and slammed my shoulder into the office door. It gave on the first attempt.

It was dark inside. The lone window had been painted over to provide privacy. I pulled out a small flashlight that Alfredo had provided and took in the space. It was a simple office. Just a desk and two chairs for visitors. There was only one file cabinet. I pulled it open and ripped through the files. Church memberships. Sermons. Promotional material. Nothing helpful. Fuck. The screams from outside continued. I still had time. I turned to the desk. It was empty. But there was a locked drawer. I yanked on it. It wouldn't budge. I kicked and kicked. Still it wouldn't open. Finally I flipped the heavy desk over. The bottom of the drawer was made of flimsy balsa wood and it gave way with one more kick. Inside the drawer I hit the jackpot: A laptop and a handful of USB pen drives.

Another gunshot cut through the screams.

Time was up. Police would be on their way. With the USB drives in my pocket and the laptop under my shirt I slipped out of the office. I risked a glance at the TV monitor. Alfredo lay on the ground in a pool of blood. He'd shot himself.

"No..." I groaned. But there was nothing to be done except honor his death. I tucked my head and jogged across the grounds joining the panicked stream of people running out of the gates.

CHAPTER
FORTY-ONE

THE CAR WAS RUNNING when I arrived and we were moving by the time I'd closed the door. Marié drove like she was in a heist movie and as police swarmed the church Alfredo's map delivered us in the opposite direction, through the town and onto the highway leading south to Rio. It was only then that I realized how scared she was as she continued to peg the gas to the floor.

"Easy. Slow down. We made it," I said and put my hand over hers.

She snapped out of her trance and let up on the gas. She looked over at me.

"Are you OK?" I asked.

"I'm OK. Are you OK?"

"I'm OK," I grinned. "Do you want to know what happened?"

"I already know. I could hear the people as they came out," she replied.

"That's right. I forgot you spoke Portuguese." It was a nervous joke. One that we instantly forgot as we hit traffic and then slowed to a stop behind a line of cars. Far in front I could see flashing police lights.

"It's a blitz," she said. She quickly scanned behind us for an escape route but there were already cars behind us and the highway was a straight line with no off roads. We were trapped. "They're probably looking for drugs. They do these all the time. They wouldn't have had time to set this up just for us," she tried to assure me. "Climb through the backseat into the trunk. If it's just me, they probably won't look too hard."

"What if they do?" I asked. "They can't take us."

She clenched the steering wheel. "I'll figure something out."

For some reason I believed her. I moved to climb into the backseat.

"Hey, you forgot something," she said.

"What?"

She leaned in and gave me a quick kiss. "You didn't wish me good luck."

"Good luck. And if that doesn't work drive like hell," I said as I lowered the back seat and climbed into the trunk. We arrived at the roadblock moments later. I could hear a dog padding around the car. She was right. They were looking for drugs. I tried to listen as she rolled down her window and spoke with the officer. I couldn't understand what they were saying but she was putting on a performance. He quickly lost the gruff cop voice and actually sounded like he was apologizing for the inconvenience. I then heard the window close and she began to pull away.

"We did it!" she whispered.

But then a hand slapped the back panel of the car. "*Para!*" Stop!

Shit. Don't stop! Go! I wanted to yell. But I held back. Let her handle it... She slowly braked and rolled down her window. I could hear the Officer ask her a question and then the door opened and she climbed out of the car.

An eternity passed.

And then I could hear her climb back in the car and call out a friendly, "*Tchau!*" And we were speeding along the highway again.

"You can come out now," she called.

I scrambled out of my hiding place and back up to the front seat. She had a big smile on her face. "Don't you want to know what happened?" she finally asked.

"Naw. I heard," I replied.

"Oh yeah. I forgot you spoke Portuguese."

"Of course I want to know! Tell me!"

"He wanted a selfie to show his wife. She's a big fan." And she let out a scream of delight and pounded on the steering wheel. "Yes! We did it! We really did it!"

"No, you did it," I grinned. "That was awesome." It was a little victory. Worth celebrating. But we still had a long way to go. The next step would be to access the laptop and the pen drives. Jaime Gold had offered his help. I was willing to bet that the Mossad could handle Pastor Dan's passwords. I would also need to contact Special Agent In Charge Peter Wills. How many days had passed? I'd lost track. I'd need to extend my vacation.

We fell into a comfortable silence and stared ahead as the road opened before us, stretching in a razor sharp line to the horizon. We'd escaped from Bahia. Two more graves had been filled.

So many to go.

PART THREE
THE HORROR. THE HORROR

CHAPTER
FORTY-TWO

THE SUBMARINE BREACHED off the coast and the small crew scrambled up the ladder and onto the narrow observation deck. A half kilometer away, across the black of the ocean, they could see the glimmering lights of Rio. The men burst into laughs as they inhaled the tropical night air. They'd made it!

In 1945 Rio de Janeiro was already a thriving beach city famous the world over. Before the war had reached its zenith German tourists and even German military had been welcomed with open arms by a certain class. The wealthy landowners were sympathetic to the Nazi cause and were even known to throw rallies in support. But as the war grew Brazil's government began to see the movement as a threat and stamped out any public Nazi support. In private however, there were still pockets where German refugees could find sanctuary with no questions asked. Gregor's favorite part of the family story was how his great grandfather, Gustof Heinrik, had taken a life boat from the submarine to Copacabana beach and then, like a conquering general, walked right into the Copacabana Palace Hotel and had a drink to commemorate his arrival.

Along with its standard crew the submarine held three officers including Gustof. In the hold was a treasure in gold bars. The wealth would be used to fund their new utopia. Gunther had also brought a second treasure. His journals. His life's work. Gregor never met his great grandfather, the man had been gunned down in a café by a coward Jew assassin before Gregor was born. But Gregor felt like he knew him. He'd spent much of his childhood in the secret library that Gustof had built on the family's farm. These days when Gregor made his pilgrimages they were done in secret. He avoided the family. His relatives had grown soft. They'd inter-married with locals and spawned half breed children who then went on to breed even more carelessly than their parents. His own generation was an embarrassment. They were so clueless that not one of them had noticed when he'd returned to clean out the library. The journals and files, which had been transported from Germany, were now stored in his own climate controlled reading room. It was here, surrounded by the spirit of his ancestor, that he prepared to carry on the family's legacy. His great grandfather had named his farm *der Garten*, The Garden, and its true crop was never intended to be soybeans or sugar cane; no, Gunther Heinrik had a much grander vision. One that Gregor intended to honor.

The original Greta had been a failure. Looking back on it now Gregor saw that he'd been clumsy. Childish. Years ago he'd gone back and rectified the mistake. Intent on her being his first - he'd tracked her to a São Paulo nightclub. He fumed as she danced like a whore. As strange men groped her ass. Gripped her waist. It made him nauseous. He didn't approach her there, in public, rather he waited for the Sleeping Beauty pill in her drink to take effect. He then steered her by the elbow out of the club and into his car. They'd drove through the night and as dawn rose over *der*

Garten he carried her into a barren field where he laid her in the dirt and butchered her like a hog. The rush was as unexpected as it was overwhelming. He'd barely got his pants open before gushing into the bloody dirt. The swirl of white and red as his seed absorbed into the earth was an image he'd never forget.

Now a new Greta would soon take her place in his personal pantheon. How many had there been? Most were a blur. Did one remember all of the spiders one crushed? He was a predator. He hunted. He fed. But this Greta, Greta 2.0, he had to admit she was special. She was not just a meal. She had a purpose. Thanks to her the garden would soon be all his to do with as he pleased.

The dress was more conservative than she would have chosen for herself. The stiff fabric ran down her thigh to just below the knee. It was an expensive dress. This she recognized. It was the kind that actresses pretending to be high powered businesswomen wore in the novelas. She liked how it made her stand up straight and made her feel older. Like a grown woman. She hadn't been allowed to look at herself in the mirror but she trusted His opinion and he'd told her that she looked perfect. *Perfeito*. The compliment had sent a shiver up her arm.

He'd finally revealed his face to her the day before. It was a ceremonial moment. She'd cried. He wasn't expecting that kind of reaction. She cried and wrapped her arms around his neck in an embrace. He summoned all of his self control not to recoil in disgust. He then peeled her off and assured her that she was not going back in the box. She had proven herself during the battle at the *sítio*.

But now it was time for her to prove herself again.

She was struck by how his hand sweat. Was he nervous? They exited the apartment and descended in the elevator. She wore black out sunglasses but they didn't wrap around the sides so she was able to take in glimpses of her surroundings. They were in a tall apartment building. They must have been in the penthouse because the elevator ride was long and didn't stop once to pick up other passengers. She'd heard of fancy penthouse apartments having their own private elevator. Once they arrived in the garage he led her by the hand to his car. This time he placed her in the front seat. He gently helped her step up into the Porsche SUV and then leaned over to fasten her seat belt. She could tell from how the car moved, jerking as it wound through narrow streets that they were somewhere in Rio. "Where are we?" she asked. He didn't reply. Instead he turned up the car's stereo. It was classical music. Not the kind of relaxing classical music that she'd heard at the dentist or piping through the speakers at the shopping mall, but deep and intense. It reminded her of the music that she would hear in a movie when the hero was setting out to battle the bad guy.

"You can take the glasses off now," he told her. They'd arrived in front of the bank. He studied her as she blinked and took in her surroundings. Allowing her the freedom of sight was a big step. Her first reaction was critical. If she failed this step then they'd have to return to the apartment and begin again.

She looked out the window at the busy street. She knew this place. They were on the main avenue that ran through Ipanema and Leblon. She had a friend from school who lived near here. She couldn't remember the exact street - maybe she could look her up on Instagram and send her a message. But as soon as the thought appeared she stuffed it deep down in her belly. She couldn't afford to entertain hope. Hope hurt. She looked over at the Man. He was watching her intently. She smiled and asked, "Is this the place?"

"Yes, my dear," he replied. He was pleased. She hadn't reached for the door handle. Her first reaction was to look directly at him. She was ready. "Do you remember your instructions?" he asked.

She took a breath and recited the instructions that they'd been practicing all morning, "I go to the front desk and tell them I want to open my safety deposit box. They'll give me a form and then I'll write out the number of the box. Then I'll go to a room where they'll check my fingerprints. Once that's done I'll be left alone with a metal box. I'll open the box and take out a computer drive. Then I'll leave through the front door and return straight to the car and give it to you."

"Good girl." He handed her a small piece of paper folded in half. She opened the paper to reveal the number of the safety deposit box written in neat, careful handwriting. "Can you read it?" he asked. She nodded yes. He smiled and reached over and unlocked her seat belt. "You're going to make me very proud, Greta."

CHAPTER
FORTY-THREE

"COME, we'll talk out on the water." Jaime Gold woke me at dawn ready with the Mossad's digital forensic report. They'd been able to gain remote access to the laptop and had spent the night digging into every corner of Pastor Dan's on-line world. The house was silent as I slipped out of the guest room. Marié still slept, her tan limbs tangled in the cool sheets. Our long drive from Bahia had been uneventful but exhausting. When we'd arrived late in the night Jaime greeted us with food and showers and we'd fallen asleep upon lying down in the soft bed. Now he led me outside and down to the beach where two surfboards were waiting. They were 9' longboards which seemed to get a decent amount of use.

"I assume you can paddle one of these?" he asked. Then, without waiting for an answer he picked a board up under his arm and waded into the water. The waves were gentle, waist high but they broke long. I followed and together we paddled out through the white water and into the calm rolling ocean. At eighty years old Jaime was still wiry and strong. He reminded me of an Indian yogi as he sat on his board bobbing in the water. "I don't catch as many waves as I used to, but I still paddle five kilometers a day," he said and gave me a little bicep flex to prove it. Eighty year olds are allowed to brag as much as they want I realized.

"Thanks again for your help," I said. "I owe you a car by the way."

"Forget about it. It was stolen. I have a valet vest and whenever I need a new car I just go to the nightclubs in Buzios," he said, referring to the luxury resort town about a half hour down the coast.

"Surfer. Car thief. Spy. How do I get in on this retirement plan?" I asked, more than half serious.

He laughed out loud. The sound was absorbed by the water and the morning fog. But he quickly turned pensive, as if my observation had reminded him of the cost of this idyllic life. I noticed that when pressed into a corner he subconsciously rubbed a scar on the inside of his forearm. He followed my gaze and pulled his hand away from his arm. But it was too late. He grinned, acknowledging that his tell had been busted. He held up his arm for me to see. "Tracking chip. They put it in about five years ago. Too many secrets. Wouldn't want the old goat wandering out of the pasture."

"Nice pasture, tho."

"That it is," he replied.

The ocean lapped against our surfboards and a faint breeze gave me a chill. I reached down and pushed my hand through the inky water to prevent our boards from floating away from each other.

"Did we have any luck with the laptop?" I asked, ready to get down to business.

"You did good," he replied. "The USB drives were mostly promotional church stuff. Although one of them had a spreadsheet detailing the money that he'd been paying to the local police and politicians. This was interesting but it didn't offer any links to your dad. Or Heinrik. The team then worked through the computer's history and emails. This led to his bank accounts. As you suspected his financing didn't come from American donations. Paulo Heinrik was using him as a laundromat to clean money for his clients. It's the same system that your dad created years ago. It seems once your dad got his money out he handed the funnel over to Heinrik. The way it works is the dirty cash is deposited into one of the church's bank accounts around the country. It's then paid out in the form of a charitable donation. The official description says that the money is going to pay for the construction of a school or an orphanage. But in reality the cash is going back into someone's pocket. Minus a small fee for Pastor Dan and his Warriors For God."

"Alfredo said my dad finished cleaning his money years ago. That would have been before any digital trail or online banking."

"Which still leaves us with the question: where's your dad's money? What we do know is that he didn't go through all that trouble just to bury it in the ground again."

"So we're back were we started?" I said, frustrated.

"We're never back were we started," he replied. He had the answer. He was just going to make me earn it.

"All right. I'll play. If I had fifty million burning a hole in my pocket what would I do? Buy property? No, that's too permanent. I'm a fugitive, it needs to be liquid… Park it in the bank? Too boring. My dad was a gambler. He needed risk. The stock market?"

Jaime nodded, "Aside from Casa da Glória's *charitable* giving it also paid a small portion into a private hedge fund based out of São Paulo called *Magnolia Investimentos*. The hedge fund's firewall is top-of-the-line so the boys weren't able to pull any names or account numbers; but it was incorporated 20 years ago, which would line up with your dad's time-line."

Magnolia. The word rolled over me like a wave. And then, as if on cue the sun broke free from the horizon and spilled out over the ocean surface.

"It's him," I said. "When I was a kid we had a Magnolia tree in the front yard. He hung a rope from the branches and I'd swing on it… When I got older he'd make me climb the rope in order to toughen up my grip for wrestling. That tree, it was like part of the family."

It was a good memory. One of the few.

"I think you need to go to São Paulo. Go shake the tree. See what falls out."

"Do you trust her?" I looked down at her sleeping form and tried to replay every single exchange. Until now I hadn't questioned her motives. But as Jaime and I had walked back to the house he'd planted the seed of doubt. "Do you trust her?"

"Why?" I asked.

He didn't answer. Just kept walking. Did he know something? Of course he did. The man was a bottomless pit of secrets. "I just want to make sure that you ask the question," he finally replied.

He was right. I knew almost nothing about her. But I realized I'd told her everything. About myself. About my past. It had felt good to share. Like sinking into a warm bath. But it was reckless.

I lifted her phone from the bedside table and took it outside. Over the last five days I'd seen her use it only a handful of times but by force of habit I'd watched as she entered her security code. It took me three attempts and the phone and her secrets were laid open for me. A quick search confirmed that she hadn't made any out-going communications. Her e-mails, phone calls, text messages and WhatsApp messages were all in-coming. All were in Portuguese. And all seemed to be work or social. It was a relief. But as I clicked the screen off I noticed that the plastic phone case was mis-aligned. I peeled it away and there it was. A dime sized tracker stuck to the phone's metallic back. This wasn't a sophisticated device like Jamie Gold had in his arm; but it was still not the kind of thing that you bought in a corner electronics store. I ran through the players that would have had access to her phone. Royce? David Barry?

"It was Detective Amalero," she said from the doorway. Her sheet wrapped around her like a shield. "He threatened my mother. I was going to tell you... And then, things kind of happened. And it was too late. I didn't tell him anything."

"He's just been following us," I said.

"I didn't have a choice. I swear, I wanted to tell you," she said, her voice cracking. "What should I do?" She was scared. Scared of being caught in something beyond her control. Scared of losing something she really wanted. "Please, say something," she pleaded.

It took all my strength not to wrap her in my arms. She held power over me. I imagined Amalero holding a gun to her head. The image generated a jolt of rage. I wanted to tell her to wait here. That I'd come back and we'd live happily ever after in that little house on the beach. That we'd have beautiful children. She'd teach them to read and write and they'd act out little plays for us to applaud. I'd teach them to surf. That we'd watch the sunsets in a hammock. That we'd grow old and make love every day until we died. I wanted to tell her all of these things.

But I didn't.

"Keep him on a string. Let him follow you," I said and returned her phone.

"You're leaving?" The crack in her voice was gone. She'd hardened to reality.

I had to leave her behind. Where I was going I couldn't afford to be weak. I placed my fantasy in a vault and locked the door. Maybe I'd come back for it. Maybe not. But at least it was there. Safe from reality. "I'm already gone," I said and walked out and got into Alfredo's car and drove -- thinking of nothing but the road ahead.

Dad would've been proud.

CHAPTER
FORTY-FOUR

LETICIA LOVED to play the choose-the-line game with her mother at the supermarket check-out. Usually the goal was to pick which line would be the fastest. But today she tried to pick the slowest. Anything to grant herself an extra moment of freedom. The bank lobby was crowded and the other customers were all looking at their phones, lost in their own little bubbles. She reached for her own phone but realized that she didn't have one. She hadn't looked at a phone since... since the night that He took her. Suddenly she was hit by the smell of butchered pigs and she gagged.

"Are you Ok?" the woman behind her asked.

Leticia pulled herself together. "Yes. I'm fine." She had a job to do. Do the job and then He would be happy. Or would he? She realized that she didn't know what would happen after she returned to him. Would he let her go? Even if he did let her go, *where* would she go? Were her parents really dead? Or were they out there looking for her right now? Or, would he put her back in the box?! Panic rose from her belly and into her throat making it hard to breathe. She scanned the bank lobby. There were security guards at the doors. Could she ask one of them for help? Or would they just laugh at her? She didn't look like she was kidnapped. She was walking around free. Maybe she could run away on her own? But there was only one entrance and he was waiting outside. Then she spotted the elevators. There was a "down" button. That meant there was a parking garage below the building.

"You're next, sweetheart," the woman behind her said, nodding toward the teller window.

Leticia made her decision. She stepped out of line and bolted for the elevators. She pushed the down arrow and waited. Staring at the blinking light, pleading for it to hurry. Ding. The door opened and she darted inside and pushed the close door button. But as the door closed a hand reached in to hold it open.

It wasn't him.

It was just another man. He shot her a dirty look and held the door open as more people streamed into the elevator. Finally the door closed. She clenched her fists as the elevator gears jerked and they slowly moved down, down, down... and rocked to a stop. The door opened onto the first level of the parking garage. She pushed her way out as the doors closed behind her.

She was alone. The valet parking stand was located to her right. Straight ahead were rows of parked cars. To the left was the concrete curve of the ramp leading up and out of the garage. A glint of sunlight peeked around the corner. Be calm. You're so close. The elevator dinged open behind her. She whirled to see a man pushing to exit from the back of the crowd.

She took off sprinting up the ramp. Ahead she could see the bright blue sky. The heels of her shoes clacked and skid on the cement. The ramp was longer and steeper than it looked. Her breath came in gasps. Her leg muscles burned. This was the most exercise she'd done in almost two weeks and her body was failing her. She had to stop or she'd pass out from the blood pounding behind her eyes. She hunkered into an alcove and waited to catch her breath. She listened. No one was following. Relief flushed her with energy and she took on the final ten meters and emerged onto the sidewalk.

She walked fast. She screwed up the courage to look behind her. Still no one. She couldn't believe it. She was really free! A black Porsche SUV was parked at the corner. It couldn't be Him. He'd told her to meet on the opposite side of the building. Or had she gotten turned around inside the garage? No. It had to be just another car. She put her head down and walked past. Behind her she heard a car door open and close. Oh god! Run! But her legs were drained after the ramp. She fell to her knees. He loomed over her. As he picked her up into his arms she felt a needle prick on the side of her neck. She tried to fight him. But her punch failed to connect. Her hand wouldn't do what it was told. Then her head rolled back and she saw his face. His angry face. It was the last thing she would see for a long time.

CHAPTER
FORTY-FIVE

WHY DIDN'T he kill me? The question rattled around in my head as I made the four hour drive to São Paulo. There was no good answer. He was not a sloppy man. Despite his methods I had to admit he worked with a purpose. Did he know who I was? He must have. His father would have told him. Right before he slit his throat. Maybe he assumed that I'd die in that box? No, if he wanted me dead I'd be dead. He wanted me to survive. The question is why?

I'd studied psychopathic behavior at the FBI training center in Quantico, but I'd only met a true psychopath one other time. It had been during a prison riot in Texas. The prisoners had taken over a wing and were holding three guards hostage. After a week long stand off I was called to negotiate their release. It was pointless. The leader of the up-rising was a twenty nine year old MS-13 hitman. He was serving life for killing a foster family who'd had the audacity of taking in the orphaned child of a rival gang member. I met with him through bullet proof glass in the prison visiting room and before I could make my opening offer he hauled up one of the guards and stabbed him through the eye with a shiv. It took a few seconds to get over my shock but when I forced myself to face the situation in front of me I realized his weakness. His Black Swan. He wanted an audience. I had a choice. I could walk away and deny him that audience, which would mean that the two remaining guards would be killed. Or, I could turn off the mic hidden inside my shirt and make a deal with the devil.

I walked out of the prison with one guard alive. In exchange I had agreed to watch as the hitman cut off the remaining guard's genitals and stuffed them down his throat until he choked to death.

What did Gregor Heinrik want from me? As my instructor at Quantico put it, "In the mind of a psychopath the only difference between masturbation and a masterpiece is an audience."

São Paulo, Brazil, the most populous city in South America, is an ungodly sprawl of high rises and favelas that stretches from horizon to horizon. Without the distracting natural beauty of Rio de Janeiro the city is able to get down to business and serves as the financial heart of not only the country but the entire continent. *Magnolia Investimentos* operated out of an office on the ninth floor of the Safra Building. The building was thin and tall and made up of vertical lines that looked like the bars of an old fashioned bank teller. The bright copper color added to the effect and made the building pop from the drab concrete and steel that stretched in every direction. Flowing in and out of the building were an army of financial workers sweating the summer heat in their suits and business dresses. It was smart to hide a slush fund like Magnolia inside the office building of one of the largest investment banks in the country. It gave my dad's fund an air of legitimacy. It also provided security. Cameras lined the periphery and I'd already spotted a clockwork of plainclothes guards working the sidewalk.

From my window seat in a café one block away I considered my options. For the first time I truly felt like a fugitive. I couldn't call Special Agent Wills for help. He would be forced to report any contact. I couldn't risk involving Marié. And Jaime Gold had been a big help but I'd left Marié at his house which meant he was now compromised. I could trust Royce Mirza; but the Rio police knew we were close. They'd be watching him. I was truly alone. During the drive I'd taken stock of my situation. Jaime Gold was able to give me R$1000 in cash. R$300 of which I'd used to buy a pre-paid cellphone. He also provided me with a Sig Saur sub compact handgun which I had strapped to my ankle. Gas from Rio to São Paulo, and food, had cost me another R$300. Money would soon be a problem.

The long drive had also given me time to consider *Magnolia Investimentos*. The fund's assets and their investor list were all confidential. All I had was their address and a hunch. If the fund had been controlled by my dad -- upon his death the assets would fall to his legal heir. Which in Brazil would be Leticia Silva. This must be Heinrik's play. Manipulate Leticia in order to give him control of the fund. But how? I needed to find out how the fund worked. I needed to find out who ran the day to day. Who traded the money? Where was the money held? But these Brazilians and their security. It was almost a fetish. I wouldn't be able to force my way into the office. But if they really were connected to my dad, they might be curious. I decided to just go up and ring the doorbell.

I stashed the Sig Sauer in the car and walked into the building's lobby. As I expected armed guards and a metal detector denied interlopers like me access to the elevators. I walked up to the reception desk and told them the truth, "*Magnolia Investimentos por favor. Meu nome é Miles Ronan.*"

The desk clerk was a no nonsense young man in a uniform, he searched down the list of companies and shook his head, "*Descupla, Senhor. Magnolia não ta aqui.*" He noticed that I didn't understand and placed a call for help. A few minutes later the building manager, a sharply dressed woman with a harried smile came from a back office. She explained in broken English that Magnolia Investimentos had ended their lease. "How long ago?" I asked.

"One month ago," she replied.

"Did they leave a new address? Or a phone number?" I asked.

She'd anticipated the question and handed me a business card for *Samuel Martes*, President of Magnolia Investimentos. "I believe the phone number still works. At least you can try to leave a message."

I walked out of the building and back to the car. I used the pre-paid cellphone to call the number on the card. The call went straight to voice mail. There was no greeting only a short beep. I left a Hail Mary message, "Hi, this is Miles Ronan. Please call me back at this number. I'd like to speak with you about my father, Frank Ronan. Or as you may know him, Francesco Silva."

I then pulled the car out and allowed myself to get lost in the city's dense traffic. São Paulo was more organized than Rio and the people seemed to have more purpose. But it lacked the magic and mystery. As I drove I continued to work through the cold hard facts of the case. My father had been killed thirteen days ago. Magnolia Investimentos had been shut down thirty days ago. Was there a connection? If Paulo Heinrik had been arguing with my dad and suddenly my dad looked like he was going to cut him off... Maybe

Paulo did order the hit? Or had Gregor been operating on his own? Still too many questions.

I had become hopelessly lost and was about to pull up a map when the phone buzzed. A text message came through from a blocked phone number. It read: "Let's talk." And provided the address of a city park.

The botanical gardens were surrounded by a high stone wall and required a paid admission. Once inside it was a maze of gardens and ponds. Tourists, school children and families wandered the paths while monkeys could be seen darting along the tree tops. The lush tropical green rose up all around and blocked the chaos and noise of the city. I sent a follow up text, "I'm here." The reply came immediately, "Go to the *castleinha*."

I followed the map deep into the park to a small wooden castle that doubled as a children's playhouse. Sitting at a picnic table was a man in slacks and expensive running shoes with a baseball cap pulled low. A private security guard stood nearby. He moved to intercept me but the man at the table waved him off. Samuel Martes looked every bit of his fifty one years. He was overweight and pale and balding and had dark circles under his eyes. On his wrist was a Patek Phillippe which he adjusted when he grew nervous. "You have his ears," he said and visibly relaxed. He held out a soft hand to shake, "Samuel Martes. I worked with your father. My condolences."

In every negotiation there is a power differential. Usually this means that one party has the power to inflict pain; either physical or financial. But the reality is that there is a more significant power. That would be the knowledge differential. The ability to identify an opponent's deepest, darkest secrets. Their true motive. I knew nothing about Martes or his connection to my father but clearly I made him nervous; I needed to play it cool until he revealed why I had power over him.

"Did you know him well?" I asked.

"You want to know if I knew what he was -- Yes, I did. In theory at least. But I didn't know the details. His real name, Frank, I just learned a few days ago from the news."

"Your English is very good," I said. "You've lived in the U.S.?"

"Yes. I studied there. Columbia. After I graduated I worked a few years on Wall Street before returning home."

I allowed an uncomfortable silence to build. He looked around. Other than his security detail the only people in the area where a handful of kids playing in the castle and a couple of nannies dressed in white uniforms gossiping in Portuguese.

"Do you have a family?" I asked.

"I do," he said without elaborating.

"I'm not interested in the money," I assured him. Softening him up for the hard hook. "As long as you can help me find my father's daughter -- I'll walk away and no one needs to know a thing about your connection to him."

"Oh god," he sighed.

There it was. The reason for his anxiety. Now I needed to place it out on the table for both of us to see. "I know you're not a criminal. But you did business with one; and if anyone ever found out you'd be ruined," I said.

"Oh, I don't know about that. This is Brazil. The stigma you Americans apply to shame is not quite the same down here," he said as he adjusted his watch. He'd done a good job of covering but he'd used the word, not me: shame. He was a man who valued his status as a legitimate business-man. He wasn't like the corrupt politicians or money launderers or crooked cops. No, he went to an important school in America. He was an upstanding member of society. My existence threatened that standing. He took a deep breath and unburdened himself in a confession of sorts. I'd seen it hundreds of times. The need to explain. The need to be seen as a good person.

"I'd just like to start by telling you that in the beginning, I didn't know anything about your father. I should have known. It was all too good to be true. But he offered me my dream job. A chance to run my own fund. It would have taken years to get to that place in my previous firm. So I quit and came to work for him."

"When did you learn the truth?" I asked. I was sympathetic. I could see my father sucking him in and never letting him go.

"Right away. The money was coming from churches and failing restaurants. It was clearly being laundered. But Agent Ronan there's a reason your dad hired me. Without being arrogant, I'm very good at what I do. We quickly began to make a lot of money. Legitimate money. And your dad sat back and gave me complete control. I always planned to leave; but he made it too easy to stay and before long it was too late to leave."

"So why shut down the fund now?" I asked.

"Your dad was sick. Cancer. Two months ago he came and told me to sell everything.

He said that he wanted to hand the money over to his kids when he was gone. It took about six weeks to unload all of our positions and then once we were completely liquid we walked away. To be honest it was a relief."

"So he told you about me?" I said, surprised.

"He said he wanted to make sure his kids were taken care of. Plural. At the time I thought he'd just mis-spoke but... he must have been thinking of you too."

"What did you do with the money?"

"As we divested each position the cash went directly into Bitcoin. I tried to talk him out of it, but he'd become obsessed with digital currencies. Which now makes sense. They're anonymous. Portable. Easily transferable anywhere in the world. But having everything in one place scared me."

"How much money are we talking about?" I asked.

"On the last day of closing, the fund was valued at $1.2 billion. U.S. dollars. Minus my percentage your dad's take was close to $900 million. The asset class fluctuates quite a bit as you may know. But based on Bitcoin's value today that position is close to a billion."

He waited for me to register the number.

"A *billion* dollars?" I had to say it out loud otherwise it felt fake. Leticia's life would mean nothing in the face of a billion dollars.

"I told you. I'm very good at my job." Martes wasn't bragging. It felt like an apology.

"Where does Paulo Heinrik come in?"

"He was your dad's lawyer. I assume he would have been in charge of the will and handing over the Bitcoin wallet after your dad died."

"How does that work?"

"Bitcoin is stored in an on-line account called a digital wallet. The wallet can only be accessed with an encrypted password. So you'll need two codes to access the money. The digital wallet code and the password, then no matter who you are -- you have access. Simple as that. But if you lose either the code for the wallet or the password, then the money's gone."

"Where's the wallet now?" I asked. A bad feeling was starting to form.

"Your dad would have put it somewhere safe. He

wouldn't have trusted Heinrik. He didn't trust anyone. Probably a safe deposit box. And probably in your sister's name considering that you aren't a Brazilian citizen and wouldn't be allowed to open an account."

"Would Paulo Heinrik have been in charge of helping Leticia access the box?"

"Probably. Heinrik would be in charge of the will, so he'd be the one to inform your sister, and maybe you, of the existence of the safety deposit box. I'm guessing that whoever killed your dad is now using her for this purpose. And I promise you, I'm not involved. Your dad already made me very rich. Besides, your dad scared me. There was a darkness to him. I would have never crossed him. I swear."

I noticed that he struggled to look me in the eye. But it wasn't because he was lying. He seemed truthful. It was because I intimidated him. He considered me an extension of my father. An avenging angel. "Where's the safety deposit box?" I demanded, allowing my voice to drop into a growl. I would become the thing he feared.

"I don't know. I would guess in Rio. He never left the city. When we met I had to go to him," he said.

"Paulo Heinrik's son is the killer. He's holding my sister hostage and she's dead the moment he gets what he wants. Which means I need to get there first. If I don't -- I swear I will hunt down everyone that's ever touched that money and I will make them pay."

Martes took a deep breath and offered his best guess, "Check HSBC Bank in Ipanema. That's where Francesco would've gone. It's secure. Local. And he knew them. Please, I have a family... I didn't have to answer your call. If there was anything I could do, I'd do it." He was genuinely scared. Ten days ago he thought he'd won the game. And now there were dark, unpredictable forces circling his little kingdom.

"My car is out of gas and the police will be looking for it soon. So what you can do for me is give me your car. Then you're free," I said.

"My daughter's waiting at school. I need to pick her up," he said. He really didn't want any more entanglements.

"Give me your fucking key!" I barked. The security detail looked over and my hand dropped to my ankle holster.

"Ok. Ok. Relax." He quickly pulled out the key fob for his brand new Range Rover.

"You can buy a new one," I said. "But do it fast. Dad's money has a habit of getting people killed."

CHAPTER
FORTY-SIX

SHE TOOK a shower and composed herself. She then ate a quick breakfast of melon, cheese, fresh baked bread and orange juice. Jaime Gold was pleasant, as usual. But he didn't offer any information and she didn't press. Marié told herself that it was good that Miles had left. At first she'd been rocked with embarrassment. And regret. But she quickly hardened. She'd been foolish to get involved with him. He was the story. Her first instinct had been correct. She needed distance. Now she was free to check on her mother and deal with Detective Amalero and get back to work. Yeah, it was good that he left.

She took a bus from the coast up the mountain to Teresopolis where she retrieved her car from the hospital parking lot and then drove back down to Rio. It was just after lunch when she arrived at her apartment building in the neighborhood of *Laranjeras*, a maze of old Rio buildings nestled at the base of *Corcovado*. She parked in the deep basement garage and rushed up to her fourth floor apartment to check on her mother.

Teresa Alves was only in her mid 60's but was already a frail woman. Marié was her only daughter. Her only family.

And as such was a constant source of both pride and anxiety. Marié had warned her that she'd be out of touch for a few days but still, the absence had been difficult. She hadn't bathed. She had barely eaten. She'd slept only in fits. The police detective had been kind enough to check on her but his last visit had left her more anxious than relieved. He'd been gruff, frustrated that Marié hadn't called, and Teresa came away with the feeling that his previous concern had been an act. But now her daughter had returned and all was right with the world. Teresa quickly set about making them a late lunch of rice and beans with grilled chicken and vegetables. It was her go-to meal when she was too nervous to be overly creative.

Marié saw that her mother hadn't done well in her absence. Even though she was an adult she'd rarely spent this much time away from her. "I met someone, Mamãe," she said as she toyed with her lunch. She hoped that the news of a potential new man in her life would calm her mother's nerves. Teresa nodded and smiled. This was good news. She wanted grandchildren before she was too old to enjoy them.

"Is it the American?" she said.

"The detective told you? He was here again wasn't he?" Marié simmered. That son of a bitch had promised to leave her mother alone.

"*Querida,* be careful. This detective knew things about you. Things he shouldn't know."

"What things? What did he say to you?" Marié asked, alarms ringing in her head.

"He knew that you went to Bahia with the American." It was an accusation. As if it were her fault that Amarelo was following her. She was right. It was her fault. But now that she no longer knew where Miles was going, there was nothing more that she could offer. She stood up from the table and went into the bathroom where she cracked open her phone case and took out the GPS chip. She set it on the floor and smashed it with her shoe. She then flushed the remains down the toilet. She had almost removed the chip a dozen times over the past few days but each time something held her back. She now realized what it was. She'd been scared to commit herself to the story. Hell, if she were honest with herself she'd been afraid to commit to being a journalist. But now she no longer wanted a way out. Not only was she one hundred percent in the game, she was tired of losing.

"It's a good start," he said. The short script that she'd spent the last three hours writing had been returned covered in red edits. "But lose the corruption angle. It's too abstract." Her producer could see her formulating a string of objections. "Hey, I'm with you. It's the root of all evil. But it's a problem with no easy solution. The audience wants problems that can be solved. Good vs Evil. And you have that here. You just need to build out your bad guy. I'm not scared yet. Make me piss my pants. That's what gets you the lead." He gave her a wink and left her alone to come to the realization that he was right.

She spent the next two hours on a deep dive into the world of Gregor Heinrik. First she searched for his school in the small alpine town where he grew up. He seemed to have been an average student. Even his futbol efforts were mediocre. All in all a forgettable childhood. Then as an adult no marriages. No social media accounts. No photos with friends. No accomplishments or awards. He was a blank. She needed something to put up on the screen and shake people out of their complacency. Something that said, look at this! This is the manifestation of the evil eating away at our society. But Gregor Heinrik had become much like the sins he represented, an invisible, faceless monster.

No one is born a monster she said to herself. She wasn't sure if she believed that, but it sounded nice. She did a broad search for news stories related to his hometown. One story jumped out. Around the time Gregor would have been in law school a young local woman named Greta Shefer had disappeared. The story tells how she'd gone out to a nightclub with friends but never returned home. A search ensued but she was never found. Unlike Gregor, Greta had been a popular and active teenager. Several photos popped up from her teenage years. Marié scrolled through the images and came to a sudden stop on a high school class photo. A chill ran down her neck: Gregor Heinrik and Greta Schefer had been in the same class.

It was late when Marié finally returned home. Her mother had fallen asleep on the sofa in front of the TV. Her novela was long over. Marié had half expected to find Detective Amalero waiting but it looked like he'd given up on her. It was a relief. Marié woke her mother and helped her to bed. She then went into her own room and began to pack a bag for her flight to Santa Catarina first thing in the morning.

CHAPTER
FORTY-SEVEN

THE RANGE ROVER had been lined with bullet proof metal and the windows were thick shatter proof glass. Yet the leather seats fit like a silk robe. It was a beautiful, lethal machine. Perfect for hunting monsters. There were no police on the highways of Brazil. The speed limit was enforced via cameras placed at twenty or thirty kilometer intervals like digital speed bumps. The result was a mad race from one camera post to the next. But the speeding tickets for the Range Rover were going to Samuel Martes so I had no reason to slow down and I was already approaching Rio having shaved an hour off the four hour trip.

It was night when I parked across from the HSBC branch in Ipanema. The bank was located on a busy street in the lobby of a ten story office building. It was after business hours and an armed guard stood outside the front door. The front windows and entrance had been secured with roll down steel security doors. Cameras were posted on each corner making it impossible to approach without being recorded. But I'd come to learn that these precautions were standard in Brazil. And this bank branch looked like a regular commercial bank that probably had thousands of customers through its doors every day. My optimism began to fade. This was hardly the ultra secure, top secret, movie villain vault I'd built up in my mind. The safety deposit box was a good theory. But still, just a theory. I couldn't afford to sit here and wait for Heinrik and Leticia to show up. Besides, it had been seven days since I'd seen them at the ranch house in Teresopolis. They could have already emptied the box. In which case Leticia would already be dead. I needed to keep moving.

Capitão Royce Mirza clocked the Range Rover with São Paulo plates upon exiting the police headquarters. High end vehicles like that were rare in Rio. Not only did the import taxes double their original cost but they were a magnet for car jackers. Only an arrogant prick or a gringo who didn't know better would drive in Rio at night in a car like that. When the Range Rover called even more attention to itself by flashing its lights he knew that it must be the gringo. He gave a quick nod and walked to his car and drove slow out of the lot leading the Range Rover through sparse night streets to the northern end of Copacabana beach, an area called *Leme,* which was quiet, dark and came to a dead end. He parked on the beach side of the street and walked to a nearby kiosk with plastic tables. The kiosk was winding down business for the night but the owner was happy for a last gasp customer. Royce sat down at a table with a view of the street coming into the dead end and ordered two draft beers and lit up a cigarette.

"Dude, you are so cool. I want to come back as you in my next life," I said as I walked up and took the seat across from him.

"You'll get your chance sooner than you might want, driving around in that thing - like some dickhead playboy from São Paulo." He wasn't joking. He handed me a glass of beer. We sat and drank and enjoyed the warm night breeze coming off the ocean and the Bossa Nova coming from the tiny speaker perched in the kiosk.

"You're not going to arrest me?" I finally asked.

"Haven't decided yet."

"What's the reward up to?"

"Not much. That Rover's worth more than you. After the first day the excitement died down. It's like they're waiting for something. I wouldn't be surprised if Amalero is on your tail now, just waiting for you to lead them to the money. Where's your girlfriend?"

"Marie is actually one of the good ones. When this is all over she could be an ally for you," I said, hoping that the non-answer would deflect his curiosity. But it didn't.

"Is she in the Rover? Are you bugged?"

"Knock it off, man. I left her behind. I'm on my own. I can't do this if I have to worry about her being taken down by assholes like you all the time."

In a flash he grabbed my wrist and bent my arm behind my back and slammed me flat over the table as he frisked through my shirt and pants and my hair. Satisfied he released my arm and returned to his beer. Resentment rose off him like steam.

I gathered myself and sat back down. "Fucker. You almost broke my arm."

"What do you want from me?" he said.

He was right. I did want to use him again. And it wouldn't be an easy ask. I would need to deploy some negotiator Jedi mind tricks. The first step was to calm my own mind. Stop thinking about me. Start thinking about him. He was pissed and had put up a wall between us. If I was going to get anything from him I'd need to break through his defenses. This was easier than it seemed. A simple apology often worked like magic.

"Hey. I'm sorry for dragging you into this mess. You went way beyond letting me into the crime scene. And then giving me info on the case… and then getting me out of that jam at Paulo Heinrik's office. You must have had to eat a lot of shit. I owe you and you have every right to walk away right now." I then waited for the magic to take hold. The key to this technique was silence. No matter how awkward it got you had to wait for the other person to speak first. If you could get them to acknowledge the apology that you've just dropped in their lap; their natural reaction is almost always to offer something in return.

Royce's body slowly relaxed and he took a deep breath, exhaling a week's worth of being pissed off. Finally he grinned. Deep down he knew he'd been played, but it didn't matter. He had what he wanted. His efforts had been acknowledged. Now he could get back to the fun of being a highly trained bad ass.

"All right. What do you need, faggot?" he asked.

I leaned in and wiped the smile off his face, "I need to rob a bank."

CHAPTER
FORTY-EIGHT

DETECTIVE AMALERO HAD HAD a long day. Before he got out of his car and went up the stone steps into the Mayor's mansion he tapped out the final crumbs of cocaine from a square baggie onto the screen of his I-phone and inhaled it in two quick bursts. He wiped up the remaining dust with his finger and rubbed it into his gums. He barely felt the effect. He'd been awake since last night when the GPS ping had returned from Bahia and come to a stop at the old Jew's beach house. He'd been aware enough to drag himself out of bed and race from the city just in time to slip a second GPS tracker under the bumper of the Peugeot. He had then lost Miles when he switched cars in São Paulo. But he'd gotten lucky when he spotted an off duty São Paulo police officer working private security at the botanical gardens. He'd once bailed the guy out of trouble when he'd gotten drunk in Rio. The guy owed Amalero for saving his marriage. But Amalero would tell Mayor Pesado none of this - the Mayor trusted him here in his home in the middle of the night because Amalero brought him results; not explanations.

"This Samuel Martes, is he going to become a problem?"

asked the Mayor. He was still dressed in his slacks and button down shirt. He'd been up sorting public works proposals when Amalero called. Finding new ways to skim from these government construction projects was the reason that he had remained in power so long.

"Samuel Martes' problem causing days are over," replied Amalero. "Sadly, after I talked with him he choose to end his own life."

"That is sad. Convenient. But sad," Pesado smiled.

"And will *that* become a problem?" Pesado asked. Too many times he'd tied up a loose end only to end up with more loose ends.

"Not for us," Amalero assured him.

Pesado absorbed Amalero's confidence then nodded, "Good. Good. Now tell me how this Bitcoin thing works."

Amalero went on to explain how Frank Ronan had moved close to one billion dollars into digital currency and stashed the keys to the account in a safety deposit box in his daughter's name.

"I think Frank Ronan is my new hero," Pesado grinned. "From now on, no one goes in or out of that bank without us knowing about it."

CHAPTER
FORTY-NINE

THE UNIFORM HAD fit him as a teen and he'd spent hours in front of the mirror in his bedroom. Saluting. Standing at attention. Even sitting at his desk and doing his homework became a heightened experience while draped in the stiff, grey fabric. As he grew into manhood he'd needed to have it altered. This process had been delicate. Rather than bring it to a respected tailor he brought it to a seamstress who worked out of a favela in São Paulo. An overweight woman with missing teeth whose days were spent in a closet-like room dumbly churning through an inexhaustible pile of mending. The woman couldn't read and he was sure that she was ignorant of the Nazi insignias. Even so, he'd refused to leave the garments. Instead he paid her to put aside her other work and he sat and waited until she'd finished with the alterations.

Greta's reaction at seeing him in his uniform caused him to swell with pride. After her failed practice run at the bank in São Paulo he'd returned her to the box for a short reminder lesson. His great grandfather's notes explained that it was important for the subject to test their boundaries before placing them in a critical situation. The exercise had been designed so that he could yank on her leash.

He now stood over her clad in his black leather boots and straight jacket and creased wool slacks. Upon removing her blindfold he'd expected shock or fear or even hate. But no, she'd made no reaction at all. Her eyes were dead. Despite himself, his mouth formed into the slightest of grins. He'd done it. He'd carved out her soul. She'd become a zombie. Tomorrow morning would be her final performance. And then, if all went well, they would finally be joined by her holy release.

CHAPTER
FIFTY

THE BANK'S security was deceptively tight. There was only one entrance and an armed guard sat both outside and inside. The tellers sat behind bullet proof glass and the vault room was located at the rear of the bank accessed through a series of security doors. And of course cameras covered every inch of the floor and back room and half a block in every direction from the entrance. If either Heinrik or Leticia had been here they would have been caught on camera.

"There are many ways to rob a bank," Royce said. "But this, unfortunately, is the most effective." The bank manager's hand trembled as he looked at the blurry photo of a man in dark sunglasses standing outside the gated entrance of a preschool.

Royce had just explained that I was an FBI consultant called in to help catch a gang of bank robbers who were planning to kidnap his toddler son and force him to open the bank's vault.

"I want to be clear," Royce continued, "there is no danger to your son. We've contacted the school and they're keeping him inside until you arrive. But we believe that this team has been casing you and your bank for at least a week. It would be a big help if we could have access to your security footage."

"*Claro.*" Of course. "Whatever you need," he stammered. He was about forty and had the confident manner of a man who was good at his job. But he was rattled by the thought of his son being kidnapped. This is why he hadn't noticed that the blurry "bank robber" in the photo was actually Royce. Before he could get a closer look I pulled the photo away and stood up, signaling that we had no time to waste.

The manager led Royce and I into the video room and ordered the tech to provide us with anything we needed. He then excused himself to call his wife and check on his son.

The night passed in a blink. The last thing she remembered was the Man injecting a shot into her arm. She'd grown used to the shots. They'd become a welcome friend. They not only put her to sleep but gave her beautiful, magical dreams. She woke up lying on a blanket on the floor of the windowless room. She broke into tears. It was such relief not to wake up inside of the box.

He'd helped her to dress in the fancy businesswoman outfit in silence. He then escorted her out of the penthouse and down the elevator and into the SUV all without uttering a word. When he removed the dark sunglasses they were parked on the busy avenue in front of the bank.

"Good morning, Greta," he said.

"Good morning."

"Today is redemption day. Do you know what that means?"

The question forced her to focus. She'd experienced a tingle of excitement at being out in the street again. But she quickly snuffed it out. She would need to focus. "It means I have a second chance."

"Correct. Do not fail me, Greta. This *will* be your last chance."

She sat up straight. "I will be good. I promise." And she meant it.

"This is who we're looking for," I said and showed him my photo of Leticia posing in front of the Christo. Thiago was in charge of the bank's security room. He was a pleasant, skinny young man who was happy to have some excitement. The last action he'd seen was a month ago when he'd caught one of the tellers skimming from the till. But Leticia's photo was underwhelming. "I thought that this was a gang. That they even kidnapped someone. I hate kidnappers. I have a cousin who was kidnapped. They cut off his finger and mailed it to my Aunt and Uncle. Can you believe that?"

Royce assured him that the gang we were tracking was appropriately vicious and that the teenage girl was being forced to work as their scout under the threat of death.

"Oh, that's cool," he replied.

"How long will this take?" Royce asked.

"Depends. How far back do you want to go?"

"Eight days," I said. It had now been eight days since Gregor had taken Leticia from the sítio.

"The cameras run twenty four hours a day but we can fast forward through most of it. We should be able to get through it in a couple hours. Less if one of you takes another monitor."

"I'm on it," I said. I could tell Royce was uneasy. He kept looking out the window toward where the Manager was making a call from his office.

"Who the hell is he calling?" Royce muttered.

"Relax. He's just checking on his kid."

Suddenly Royce's phone buzzed. He looked at the caller I.D. "Shit." He answered the phone and even though he spoke in Portuguese I knew that it was trouble. When he hung up he explained that a car jacking ring had just hit a delivery truck on the outskirts of town. "You're on your own, Brother. Work fast. Because I guarantee that manager just called to confirm our story. I'm giving you fifteen minutes before this place is swarming with people that really don't like you."

<hr>

She felt like an imposter. It was her photo on the passport but the name, Leticia Silva, felt unfamiliar. She knew deep down that it was her real name but like a shirt that she'd grown out of it no longer fit. The bank teller confirmed her identity and called over the bank's Assistant Manager to lead her back to the safety deposit vault.

The Assistant Manager was a serious woman in her late thirties. When they arrived at the vault she had one last security check to perform. She ordered Leticia to place her thumb on an electronic fingerprint pad. The pad blinked green confirming her identity. The Assistant Manager nodded in approval and walked to a wall of tiny metal doors and pulled out a long, thin safety deposit box. "Follow me, please," she said and led her out of the vault into a small room that resembled a department store changing booth. "For your own privacy I suggest you lock this room from the inside." She then pointed to an old fashioned phone attached to the wall. "If you need assistance just pick up that phone and I'll be called." With that, the Assistant Manager turned and walked out, leaving her alone with the metal box.

She quickly moved to lock the door. In another life the small, windowless space would have made her panic; but now it was a comfort. The room felt so safe. So quiet. She wondered how long she could stay here without triggering the Man's anger. She was tempted to lie on the floor and curl herself into a ball. But at the same time the metal box called to her. What was inside? Why was it so important? She picked the box up. It was light. Finally she opened the lid. Inside were two items. A thumb sized USB computer drive and a thin, white envelope. The envelope was sealed but the name *Leticia* was written on the outside in a scrawling style that gave her a shiver of excitement. It was her father's handwriting.

The Man had said nothing about an envelope. He was only concerned with the computer drive. She traced her finger over the letters. *L-e-t-i-c-i-a*. She could hear her father's voice. "Leticia, baby. I love you more than anything in the world." This is what he'd whisper in her ear every night before she went to bed. She came to a decision. This envelope was hers. She slid her finger under the lip, lifting the envelope open. Inside was a photograph.

Twenty minutes of fast forward scrolling and she still hadn't appeared on the video. I was about to give up hope. I peeked out the window and clocked the Bank Manager who was now waiting by the front door of the bank. Shit. The Rio Police were on their way.

"*Aqui. Acho que esta ela…*" Here. I think it's her.

I whirled back to the monitor. The young woman frozen on screen was dressed in a formal but stylish business dress. At first glance the woman seemed too old, but when the camera zoomed in I realized that she wasn't a woman. She was a nervous teenager.

"Let it play," I said.

Thiago didn't understand English but understood what I meant. He let the video play as Leticia walked up to the Teller, showed her passport and was then led to the safety deposit vault. The footage followed her into the vault but ended when she went into the private viewing room. He fast forwarded the footage. She was inside for a long time. At least twenty minutes. What was she doing in there? She finally emerged and with her head down she hustled fast out of the bank and into the street where another camera angle captured her as she climbed into the passenger side of a black Porsche SUV parked in front of the bank. The Security Guard stopped the footage as the Porsche drove off screen.

"When was this?" I demanded. The Security Guard didn't understand. "*Que dia!? Que hora?! Quando*?!" I pointed at a calender on the wall. The Security Guard zoomed in on the time stamp.

"*Dois dias atrás*." Two days ago.

She sat on the bank floor and stared at the photo she'd taken from the envelope. The faded image was of her dad standing with a young boy at the beach. It was like discovering a door leading to a secret world. This secret world version of her dad had a full head of hair and looked strong and proud. And he had a son. The boy was beautiful. He had wavy brown hair that fell in curls over his ears and was missing a tooth. The two of them had identical smiles. Identical sparkling blue eyes. They were shirtless with wetsuits peeled down to their waists and both posed with their arms held high as they flexed their biceps. On the back side of the photo there was writing. Again, she recognized her dad's scrawling penmanship. It read simply, *"Miles' first wave."*

Miles... this must be the boy's name... her father's son... which meant that he was her brother... She had a brother! Did he know about her? Maybe he was looking for her? Maybe he was coming to save her?!

A knock on the door jerked her out of her fantasy. "Is everything OK?" the Assistant Manager asked through the door.

"Almost done," she answered.

She needed a plan. She scanned the room and found a courtesy pen attached to the table. She composed herself, gathered her thoughts and wrote out a note on the back of the envelope. She took one last look at the photo, memorizing the details. Memorizing the face of her long lost brother. She then locked the photo and envelope back inside the safe deposit box.

"Espera. Wait... Stop!" The Bank Manager tried to grab my arm as I walked out but I did a quick arm drag and slid by him. He yelled for the outside Security Guard and I took off running down the street. As I turned the corner I looked back and was surprised to find no one giving chase. The police hadn't arrived yet. I slowed to a walk and pulled out my burner phone and dialed Royce. The call went straight to voice mail. "Hey, Man. I saw her. She was there. But we're two days behind. Call me." As I left the message I darted across the street toward the Range Rover.

The small Brazilian manufactured GMC compact hit me just below the knees and I was scooped into the air. On pure instinct I used the car's momentum and landed on my feet. But as I took my first step pain exploded from my knee to my hip and I crumpled to the ground.

"Mr. FBI, you should be more careful about where you walk." The thick accent was familiar. I rolled onto my side and looked up at my old friend Detective Amalero lighting another cigarette.

"Please... We have to find her... He's going to kill her..." I gasped in pain.

"I'm sorry, Gringo mother fucker. I don't speak English," he said. And with a wave two of his men jumped to secure my hands with zip ties and dragged me screaming into the back seat of the car.

CHAPTER
FIFTY-ONE

UNLIKE IN RIO or São Paulo people here lived out in the open, unafraid of their neighbors. It made Marié nervous. The flight from Rio had been two hours long and she'd driven another one hour through farm lands and then up into the mountains of Santa Catarina where she found the village. She'd half expected a surreal alternate world of Nazi soldiers patrolling the streets and tall, blond towns-people looming in the doorways. But the town's Bavarian façade was quite charming. A gimmick to attract tourists. And the locals were big smiled Brazilians, not Aryan boogie men.

Greta Shefer's parents lived in a one story house tucked behind a waist high brick wall. Marié had been wary of approaching them about their daughter but to her surprise they were eager to talk.

"There was never a ransom call. So the police never took us seriously," Roberto Shefer said. He was a serious man who had grown into a bitter man.

"I don't understand. She's been missing for twelve years. What did they think happened to her?" Marié asked.

"They said she ran away," said his wife Lorena. "But she

was twenty two years old! She didn't need to run away. If she wanted to leave she could have just left. Do you know what they told us? They said that she was obsessed with America and hired someone to take her north to the U.S. It's ridiculous. We're not poor. She could have gone to America anytime she wanted!"

"Did you have the feeling that she was running from something. Or someone?" Marié asked.

The couple glanced at each other.

"No. But she should have been," Roberto said.

Lorena put a calming hand on his arm. "Greta was a special girl. She had a... a light about her. Ever since she was a baby, people loved her. She was always popular. This made her too trusting sometimes. Even after the Heinrik boy came into the picture."

"Do you think he was involved?" Marié asked.

"We don't think. We know," Roberto snapped.

"We can't prove it," Lorena cautioned.

"That monster killed our daughter. Everyone knows it. They're just too scared to do anything," Roberto said. He was defiant in his opinion, daring Marié to challenge him.

"I believe you. That's why I'm here," she replied.

His body un-tensed and his eyes welled up with tears.

"It's been a long time since anyone has been willing to listen," Lorena said, clutching her husband's hand.

"I want to bring this monster down," Marié assured them. "If you help me understand what happened I promise your daughter's story will get told," Marié said.

For the next thirty minutes Lorena told the story of Gregor Heinrik's obsession with their teenage daughter. The most striking part was how despite his frightening behavior Greta took pity on him and refused to let her parents involve the police. Once Greta went away to college in São Paulo her parents assumed that the threat had passed. But then one day she stopped returning their calls. They contacted her roommates but they hadn't heard from her either. That's when Roberto and Lorena called the police. The police traced her movements back to a nightclub. A bouncer remembered seeing her leave with a man. The man had been tall and well built but he'd been wearing a hat and there were no security cameras. According to the bouncer they seemed to be friends. There was no sign of a kidnapping. No sign of a struggle. No ransom demand. And most importantly no dead body. Roberto and Lorena begged the police to look into Gregor's whereabouts on the night of her disappearance, but they refused. They then pressed the Heinrik family to help. That's when the trouble began.

The Heinrik family turned the town against the Shefers. No one wanted the media to dig into their past. They were a tourist destination now. The only good to come from their efforts was that Paulo Heinrik and his son Gregor were banished from the community. The Heinrik family owned a massive farming complex in the area but Paulo and Gregor were forced to take a buy-out by the cousins and told to leave and never come back.

"That farm is worth a lot of money," said Roberto. "If he hadn't been guilty there's no way they'd have taken that deal. The word going around town now is that a big international company is looking to buy the whole thing."

"When Greta was a girl we brought her to a birthday party at the farm," Lorena said. "Gregor and Greta weren't friends but they were classmates. He was a quiet kid. Never smiled. Never looked you in the eye. But that day at the family's farm he was different. He smiled and talked and just had so much fun. I didn't even recognize him at first. I asked the family cook, who is that boy? And when she told me it was Gregor I was shocked. She told me that the farm was the only place where he ever smiled. For some reason he just loved the place."

"Do you know why it was so special to him?"

"No. I only know that it's been taken away from him. And that makes me happy."

Marié came to a dead end. On her phone's map the farm spread through the region like a tumor. Over a hundred kilometers of forest had been cleared and re-purposed as an industrial sized agricultural operation that thanks to the year round growing season and low labor costs generated massive profits. An overgrown dirt road led to the original 1940's farmstead but it was blocked by a rusted barbed wired fence. If she wanted to pursue the lead she'd have to go on foot.

On the flight this morning she'd felt silly about coming all this way on a hunch. But the conversation with the Shefers confirmed her suspicions. Gregor's story was bigger than Miles' sister. But she needed proof. Like her producer said, she needed to scare people. The farmhouse was important to Gregor, she needed to find out why.

She parked her car off the side of the road and waited. Every few minutes a farm truck drove past, but the farm was like a small city and the workers were too busy to give her a second look. She sucked up her courage and climbed through the fence and headed on foot up the road.

After a ten minute walk she came to a stone farmhouse tucked amidst a tangle of pine trees. The windows had been boarded up and the roof shingles were falling off. The stone was made of old fashioned hand cut blocks and the wooden eaves had been carved in rounded swoops. It reminded her of etchings from a book of fairy tales that she read when she was a girl. She half expected a wolf dressed as a grandmother to poke her head out the door. But the door was sealed. No one had been inside in a long time. There was nothing here. She stepped back and took some pictures with her phone. The afternoon sun cast shadows and she was able to give them a nice spooky vibe that would play well with her origins of a serial killer theme.

As she started back to the main road she spotted the crumbling remains of a barn in the distance. She checked her phone, she still had twenty minutes before she needed to get on the road back to the airport. As she arrived at the barn she noticed that the grass had been worn down more than at the main house. Someone had been here recently.

"*Hola? Oi?* Anyone here?" she called out.

A scuffling noise came from inside.

"Who's there?" she called.

An orange fox burst from the door and bolted across the field into the high grass. "*Meu Deus...*" she gasped. Then she laughed and scolded herself.

The barn's roof was still intact but the front door hung to the side allowing easy access. The interior was empty except for forgotten hay bales and a pile of scrap lumber. It was dark. She turned on her phone's flashlight. She could now see that someone had been working with the lumber. Fresh sawdust was on the floor. There was also a box of tools. A chisel. A saw. And a large shovel propped against the wall. She bent over to inspect the pile of discarded wood. One of the broken pieces seemed to be an aborted effort. She sifted through the scrap and found a matching piece. Each piece was about the length of her arm and one end was cut like a spike while the other end had a rounded top. When held together they resembled a thin gravestone.

And carved into the center were the spiral lines of a *swastika*.

She dropped the wood as if she'd been burned. She wanted to run - but she forced herself to take deep breaths. She reminded herself that this was why she'd become a journalist. She had a responsibility. She re-arranged the wood pieces and laid them on the ground and took a photo. The flash lit up the barn and beneath the pile of discarded wood she saw a spot of color. She aimed her light to reveal a discarded dress. It was a thin, casual summer dress torn at the shoulder as if it had been ripped off. Dark stains ran down the front. Blood? She tried to find some sign that it may have belonged to Leticia. The size was about right, but was it her style? She realized that she didn't know much about Leticia. She scolded herself. When she got back to her office she needed to draw up a full profile. Despite what her producer said this was Leticia's story too.

Marié snapped a few more photos. She then hustled out of the barn. The sun had gone down more than she expected. She tried to cut through the field but lost sight of the road in the tall grass. A dog barked in the distance. She froze and then dropped low in the grass and tried to listen. But all she could hear was the pounding of her heart. The dog barked again. Closer this time. Someone was walking through the grass. A man. The steps were strong. Heavy. She could also hear the panting of a dog.

She pulled out her phone. She needed to call someone and let them know where she was. Just in case. But who? Miles had disappeared. Detective Amalero? No, she couldn't trust him. Maybe Capitão Mirza? She pulled up his name in her contacts and sent him a text with a screenshot of her GPS map and the barn photos she'd just taken. She then peered through the grass, trying to find the road. That's when she saw them… handmade wooden grave markers jutting from the earth. Each one was about half a meter tall and had subtle markings. Some had Nazi icons but others were more artistic with flowers painted on them to blend in with the field. Some were green to match the grass. Some were black, like a slash of evil. It was as if each had their own personality. Their own story. There were dozens. The field's true crop was not hay or soy or rice; it was death.

The terror propelled her to her feet and she ran! There! The road! Her car was waiting where she left it! She could make it! She risked a look over her shoulder... A tall, powerfully built man watched her from across the field. He held a German Shepard on a leash. For some reason he wasn't chasing. She slowed and came to a stop. The grey light of the dying sun cast his face in shadow.

"People know where I am!" she shouted. A cold chill ran through her body as he failed to respond. He stared back. Silent. Calculating. She should run. She knew she should run. But here he was... right in front of her... the antagonist of her story and this might be the only chance she'd ever get... "Where's Greta Shefer?! Where's Leticia Silva?!" she called. "What did you do with them?!" She expected anger. Or a denial. But he offered nothing. As if she were nothing. Then suddenly...

"*Fass,*" he whispered in German and unsnapped the leash from dog's collar. The dog sprang into the air and shot across the field.

She RAN.

But it was futile.

The dog leaped onto Marié's back dragging her screaming to the ground.

CHAPTER
FIFTY-TWO

THE FIRST TIME he met Paulo Heinrik was in a meeting here in his small consulate office. Back then Heinrik was just another local lawyer trying to get a visa approved for a wealthy but legally compromised client. Deputy Consul David Barry wasn't impressed. Why did a Rio de Janeiro State Representative, twice convicted of embezzlement, deserve a vacation in Miami? And for god's sake, the lawyer even admitted that his client was hoping to buy a condo there. During the last ten years the number of Brazilians parking their stolen money in Florida condos had sky rocketed. Barry was about to deny the application when Heinrik slid an envelope of cash across the table.

The brazenness of the offer was probably the reason that it worked. Barry had never taken a bribe before. He'd never been offered a bribe before. Sure, he'd allowed people to buy him meals. He'd accepted small trinkets and gifts. But never as a quid pro quo. Paulo Heinrik's envelope of cash was so in his face. So blatant. So shocking. That Barry didn't know how to respond. And the longer that he stared at the money on his desk the longer it began to feel like it belonged to him. It wasn't a large sum, a few thousand Reals, but enough to be useful.

In retrospect he blamed his wife. They'd been married for twenty years and slowly but surely she'd grown bored with him. He couldn't remember the last time they'd had sex. He'd grown tired of begging and two weeks earlier had given in to temptation and slept with a prostitute. Ever since, he'd thought of nothing else. He was desperate to call the girl again, she'd even given him her number; but money was an issue. He lived off a government salary and cash withdrawals from their joint bank account would be noticed by his wife. This envelope sitting in front of him was freedom. A month of sex. No begging required. It was something he deserved.

Over the next three years Heinrik delivered him many such envelopes and he'd gone on to develop a dangerous addiction. A shameful addiction. One that threatened not only his marriage but his career. He'd hire one girl for lunch and another for dinner. On the weekends he'd visit a brothel and have three at the same time. He was obsessed. But not delusional. He knew that it would all come crashing down. So when Heinrik offered him a chance to help steal Frank Ronan's fortune; he looked into the mirror and saw a loser with nothing to lose.

He'd done his part. He'd pulled the levers to get Miles to come and identify the body. He'd then teased the Mayor so that his men would keep Miles on a string. It was Paulo Heinrik who had made a mess of things by thinking that he could control his psychopath of a son. Now Barry was at the mercy of an insane person. He considered ending it all. Or ditching his life and making a run for it. But he didn't have the courage for either option. Thankfully the text he'd just received from the Mayor meant he wouldn't have to test himself. They had Miles Ronan in custody.

And Miles Ronan was the key to everything.

CHAPTER
FIFTY-THREE

I WAS BEING HELD in a windowless room deep inside the Rio central police station. Paint flaked off the walls and the cement floor was stained with blood and urine. I wondered if this was the same room where they'd beaten the confession out of the handy man. So far my only torture was the fact that they were ignoring me. I banged on the door until my hands were bruised. Demanded a phone call. Demanded to speak to a lawyer. Demanded that they get off their ass and rescue my sister. But nothing. Drained, I sat down against the wall and my lack of sleep caught up with me.

I woke up to the smell of food. David Barry entered with arms full of take-out. "I wasn't sure what you ate. I thought maybe you were a vegetarian, being from California. Vegetarian's not easy here. So I settled on pizza. Calabresa or heart of palm? They're both amazing," he said laying the two boxes out on the interrogation table. "How are you doing? They didn't hurt you did they?"

"I'm fine. Hungry..." I sat down at the table and dug into the food. As I ate I looked toward the door half considering an escape. He noticed.

"You're not under arrest, but you're also not free to go. That said, I do have good news." He took a deep breath for his big announcement, "Gregor Heinrik has made contact."

"Contact with who?"

"Detective Amalero. The detective's been reaching out the past several days with a phone number he found in the father's phone. Yesterday Gregor finally replied."

"What did he want?"

"He made a ransom demand."

It was so unexpected that I almost laughed. "Why would he do that? He's already won."

But Barry wasn't joking. If this was true then Leticia might still be alive. All of the pain and doubt of the last week was forgotten. A ransom call meant that there was something that he wanted. It meant that there was a deal to be made. It meant that he'd just stepped into my world.

Detective Amalero placed his phone in the middle of the table and played back the message. The voice was electronically altered and spoke in Portuguese, which Barry translated for me. "*I have the girl. Tell her brother that if he wants to see her alive he must give me the password. I'll call this number again in one hour and if he doesn't have it - she loses a finger. Then an ear. And then a nose. Tell him that the pain she's experienced up until now will be a fond memory.*"

"How long has it been?" I demanded.

"Fifty minutes," Amalero replied without checking his watch. It was an expensive watch. I couldn't afford a watch like that on my salary.

"Then you should've brought this to me forty nine minutes ago. Play it again," I said.

He bristled but played the message again. This time I

listened past the words trying to pick up ambient noise. No luck. The message had been typed out and generated by a computer program.

"Do you know this password he's talking about?" Amalero asked. His English was better than he'd let on.

"I have no idea," I said.

Barry and Amalero shared a concerned look.

"He already has the contents of the safe deposit box. What does he need a password for?" I asked.

"Watch here," Amalero said and pulled up a video on his phone. It was the bank security video of Leticia exiting the safety deposit room. He froze the video and then pinch and zoomed on Leticia's hand. She was holding a black, rectangular metal case. A USB pen drive.

"We think that pen drive contains a digital Bitcoin wallet," Barry offered. "In order to access the wallet he'll need a password."

"And the password wasn't in the safety deposit box?"

"Apparently not," said Barry. "From what I understand Bitcoin wallets and the passwords are generally stored in separate places. It looks like your dad set things up so that both you and your sister would have to be present in order to access the account. Your sister had control of the deposit box -- and the hard drive. Which means you'd control the password."

"Sorry, boys. I haven't heard from my dad in thirty years. Heinrik should know that."

"After you were detained, Detective Amalero returned to the bank and was given access to the box. He found this inside," Barry said and nodded to Amalero who handed me a photograph.

The photo was a grainy photo of me and Dad posing on the beach. I didn't remember the photo - but I remembered the moment. The inscription on the back was in dad's hand writing. I couldn't believe that I remembered what his hand writing looked like after all these years. But there it was, *"Miles' first wave."* What he didn't write, what he didn't have to write, was what happened after the photo had been taken. After we'd rinsed the salt water off under the beach showers - and we stowed the boards in the back of his pick up truck - and he'd taken a pocket knife from his glove box and led me down to a retainer wall looking out over the water. When I went back home for Mom's funeral I'd gone out to the beach and was surprised that it was still there, *VB 6/28/91,* carved deep into the cement. Venice Beach June 28, 1991. The time and place of my first wave. A moment that existed only for the two of us. One that we sealed with a handshake and a solemn vow to never forget. Our secret code.

"It's a clue, right?" Barry asked.

"Yeah. It's a clue," I replied. I then turned to Amalero and asked, "Was there anything else in the box?"

Amalero thought about the answer longer than necessary and before he could come up with a good lie, his phone rang.

CHAPTER
FIFTY-FOUR

I'VE BEEN on hundreds of ransom calls and every time I'm hit with nerves. My palms sweat. My heart races. But this time felt different. This would be the first time that I had a personal stake in the outcome. A new emotion entered the mix: fear. The call came at the exact time as promised. This was a good sign. It meant that Heinrik was motivated and reliable. I next needed to find out if he could speak English because I knew that I couldn't trust Amalero or Barry to translate.

"This is Miles Ronan. Who am I speaking with?" I said before Amalero could speak up.

"Do you have the password?" The voice was digitally created. Flat, monotone, masculine but the voice of a machine without the inflection that is so helpful in negotiations. There was a slight delay before his replies as he typed into the computer program.

"Can I call you Gregor?"

"No. No names. Do you have the password?"

"I'm sorry, how can we have a conversation unless you have a name? Is there something I can call you?"

"You can call me Frederick. Do you have the password?"

The reply came quicker than expected. Another good sign. He was eager to work with me. "Hi Frederick. I don't have the password. Yet. But I'm close to figuring it out. The problem is that I'm really nervous about my sister. It would help me concentrate if I had proof that she was still alive."

"She's alive. For now," said the voice.

"That's great news, Frederick. But how can I trust you? I need proof."

The phone dinged. A text message arrived from a blocked number. It was a photo of Leticia standing against a white wall holding today's "O Mundo" newspaper. The photo was staged so he probably took it earlier today anticipating the need for proof of life. In the photo she looked straight into the camera. She didn't smile. She wore the same clothes that she'd worn in the bank security video. They looked like they'd been slept in for the past three days. Her coffee colored skin was gaunt and unhealthy. She had dark circles under her eyes. Her hair was a tangle that hung down past her shoulders. But she was alive.

"Did you get the picture?"

"Yes. Thank you, Frederick. But photos can be faked. I need to talk to her." I let the demand hover. Ten seconds passed without a reply. Then twenty. I could see Barry grow nervous. I held out a hand warning him to remain calm.

Finally, after thirty seconds of silence the voice returned, "You can ask her a question. I'll tell you her answer."

I hit mute on the phone and looked to Barry and Amalero, "I've never met her. She probably doesn't even know I exist."

"Stop stalling. She's alive," Amalero said.

"I know she's alive. But every time we make him do something out of his comfort zone, he reveals something about himself." I couldn't let Amalero rattle me. I had to think of a good question. One that wouldn't be wasted. One that would help me learn something. The only thing we had in common was our dad. I still held the photograph of me and Dad in my hand. I turned off the phone's mute and said, "Hello, Frederick? Are you still there?"

"What is your question?" the voice said.

"There was a photo in the safety deposit box. Ask her who was in the photo?"

The phone line went dead. I immediately noted the time on the clock. We then waited.

Amalero smoked. Barry tapped his fingers on the table. I ran through the conversation so far. The only detail that stood out was the name. Frederick. The name had significance. A common alias would have been something like José or Roberto. But Frederick was not a Brazilian name. Why did he associate himself with this name? He was a Nazi. That was the legacy that he clung to. Maybe Frederick Nitzche? The Ubermensch. That's it. He considered himself a superman. A human god. Which meant he was arrogant. He felt, no he believed, he was superior to me. Before I could come up with an angle on this insight the phone buzzed. I checked the clock. Three minutes had passed. This meant that Leticia was not in the room with him. But she was close.

"Hello, Frederick," I answered.

"The photo was her father and you. Her brother," said the voice.

Her brother… She knew who I was. The realization filled me with energy. I took a deep breath and drained the emotion from my voice before continuing.

"OK. Thank you, Frederick," I said.

"No more games. I want the password or she loses a finger."

His first mistake. An empty threat. Cutting off a finger was a visual act. He'd have to risk a photo or a video and he'd already shown that he wasn't willing to risk making visual contact. I now needed to let him feel like he was winning; without giving him a win. "Ok. Please don't hurt her. I'll give you the password. But I can't do that until Leticia is with me. Is there a safe place that we can meet?"

"*Marina Piratas.* Be at the end of the pier in one hour," he said and immediately hung up.

I looked to Barry and Amalero, "Do you know where that is?"

"I do," said Barry. "It's a yacht club in *Angra Dos Reis*. But it's a two hour drive. We'll never make it."

"The number's blocked. We can't call back," I said. "What if we drive fast?"

"It's too far," said Amalero. "We wait here and he will call back and you will give him the password. No more of your games."

"Until my sister is safe, no one gets the password," I said. "No one."

I grabbed another slice of pizza and leaned back in my chair to wait for them to come up with a solution.

"We could take a helicopter?" offered Barry.

CHAPTER
FIFTY-FIVE

THE BULLET HAD SKIMMED across the back of his shoulder and now his entire shirt was soaked. How long had he been here? Even though silver duct tape covered his eyes he knew it was late. The night breeze had died but the morning heat hadn't yet arrived and the favela was quiet except for the sounds of sleep, more intimate here than in his air conditioned apartment building. His shoulder hurt but the throbbing in his head was his main concern. It meant that he was dehydrated. He needed fluids.

He tested his movement. His hands were bound in front of him with duct tape. His ankles as well. They hadn't covered his mouth. They were probably worried that he'd suffocate. This was good. It meant they wanted to keep him alive. He was able to loosen the duct tape over his eyes which gave him a sliver of vision. He could see that he was on the floor of a small favela living room. Across from him a shirtless boy of about twelve slept sitting up on a ragged couch. A chrome .45 pistol bigger than his forearm lay across his lap. If he jerked in his sleep he'd blast his skinny leg off.

"*Agua,*" he moaned. The boy barely stirred. Royce called

out again, "*Água.*" This time the boy jerked awake and fumbled to aim the gun at Royce. But Royce was harmless. Tied up and crusted in his own dried blood. "*Por favor, rapaz. Agua.*" The boy looked out the front window at his older partners to make sure they were passed out; then he brought a plastic water bottle over to Royce and poured it into his mouth. Royce gulped, trying to catch as much as he could before it ran onto the floor. When the bottle was empty he thanked the boy, "*Obrigado.*" He then laid back down and passed out.

When he woke again he heard voices arguing. The sun was already hot and he could smell scrambled eggs and fresh bread. The sleep and the water had cleared the fog from his mind. He could hear four of them including the boy. He guessed the other three were in their mid twenties. From what he remembered they knew how to handle themselves. They were arguing about what to do with him. The most popular option seemed to be kill him and dump his body in a rival favela. He'd been missing for a day and a night. The gang was right to be scared. BOPE would be tearing the city apart by now.

He used his teeth to rip open the duct tape around his wrists. Then he unwrapped his ankles. Once free, he crawled on his hands and knees to the wall by the front door. He needed a weapon. All four of them were armed. The boy had the revolver. The other three wore AK's over their shoulders. Royce let out a low groan as if he'd just woken up.

"*Betinho*, go check him out," the boss said to the kid.

The kid, eager to impress, strolled into the living room with his gun dangling at his side. Capitão Royce Mirza of the famed Rio de Janeiro BOPE force took less than three seconds to disarm the boy and drop him to the floor with a strike to his neck, disabling his vocal cords for the foreseeable future. Mirza then stepped out the door and fired off five shots. Two of the gang members were dead before they could unstrap their weapons. The third was hit in the stomach. He fell to the ground and tried to crawl away. Royce kicked him over onto his back and knelt beside his head.

"Who sent you?" he demanded.

"You shot me... Oh god! It hurts!" the young man blubbered. He was in his late twenties, with red hair and bloodshot eyes.

Mirza pressed the barrel of the gun into the young man's cheek. "Who sent you to grab me?!"

"I don't know his name! He's a cop! But we didn't know you were BOPE. Please, we didn't know! We never would have done it!"

Mirza wasn't surprised. Only a cop would have his personal phone number. The call that pulled him away from Miles and the bank had claimed that his men were waiting for him in a parking lot near the airport. When he arrived at the lot he was knocked down with a shot across the back as soon as he stepped out of his car. The gang had then descended on him, punching and kicking until he lost consciousness. But when they got him locked up in their hideout they must have seen his BOPE tattoo and whatever plans they'd originally imagined had gone out the window.

"Tell me everything," Mirza demanded.

"The cop said to make you disappear for two days. After that we could let you go."

"Why two days? What was he doing?"

"I don't know!" he cried, clutching his blood soaked stomach.

Mirza pressed the gun into the man's wound. "Why two days?! Why did he want me to disappear?!"

"He didn't say!!"

"What did he pay you?" Mirza demanded, at least this the punk would know.

"Nothing. He just said no more protection money for Pesado," he groaned. He was fading. Suddenly he went into shock and started to convulse. Mirza put him out of his misery with a single shot to the head. He had what he needed. It was well known to him that the Rio Police collected protection money from the favela drug gangs which was then funneled up to the mayor's office. And it wasn't a coincidence that the only cop with the authority to speak for Pesado was the same cop who had been hunting Miles.

Detective Amalero wanted Mirza out of the way. This was easy to understand. But why did he need him gone for two days? This wasn't a random number. They were planning something.

Mirza walked to the ledge of the rooftop. He was perched high on a steep cliff that looked out over the ocean. Below him was an endless maze of favela houses. Already he could see locals pointing him out. A gunshot popped in the distance. He dropped to a knee and searched his pocket for his cellphone. Miraculously it was still there. But the battery had long since died. He cursed and stuffed the kid's revolver in the back of his pants. It was going to be a long walk home.

CHAPTER
FIFTY-SIX

"HE'LL TRY to give us a new set of instructions when we arrive," I said. I had to yell over the sound of the helicopter. "These will move us to a new location where he'll be in control of the setting. The key is to delay. Throw up road-blocks. We want to make him change his plan until he no longer has the advantage. But he needs to agree to each change. He can't feel like he's being forced into a corner. That's when he's most likely to do something unpredictable."

"Like hurt our hostage," Barry nodded along.

"That's right," I said. At least Barry pretended that I was in charge of the negotiations. Detective Amalero didn't bother with make-believe. I'd hoped to draw him into an argument on tactics; which would give me a better idea of his next move. But he sat up front with the pilot and didn't look back once the entire ride.

Looking down from the helicopter I could see why Gregor chose this place for his last stand. *Angra dos Reis* was a constellation of islands located in southern Rio de Janeiro state. The islands, hundreds of them, ranged in size from kilometers to meters. From above it looked like a giant pinball machine with sleek white boats flitting between the curved coastlines. Once we were out there on the water, where I was sure he was leading us, we'd be at his mercy.

We landed at a helicopter pad on top of a yacht club. From there it was a short sprint down to the pier at *Marina Piratas*. The dock was crowded with tourists loading up their families for day trips on the water. As we pushed our way to the end of the dock the one hour countdown hit zero and Amalero's phone buzzed.

"32," read the text message. Barry pointed to the numbers written on the dock next to each boat, "It's a boat berth." Both Amalero and Barry moved down the pier to berth #32 where a small fishing boat was moored. The boat had a windshield in front of the cockpit but no roof and a rusted sport fishing chair at the rear. The keys were in the ignition.

I grabbed Amalero by the arm and begged, "You're walking us into a trap. Let's at least charter our own boat. Text him back. Tell him that there's an engine problem."

He shrugged me off and shot a look to Barry, "Deal with him."

"You're starting to grow tedious, Agent Ronan," Barry warned.

"David, if Heinrik controls the exchange we're in his hands," I explained. "And I guarantee none of us walks out of this alive."

"I did warn you," Barry sighed as he pulled a compact Glock revolver from his jacket and let it hang at his side. "One of the Marines at the Consul gave me this. I barely know how to use it. So if you struggle, there's a good chance it goes off all by itself."

"Just get in the fucking boat, Gringo!" Amalero called out as he started up the engine.

I sat in the bow of the boat with one arm handcuffed to a railing. Each bump caused the steel cuffs to dig into my wrist. But at least the view was nice. Islands dotted with expensive vacation homes and paradise cove beaches passed on each side. At times it felt like I could reach out and touch them. In the beginning the boat traffic was heavy and we had to endure the friendly waves and honks of the various pleasure cruisers. We were now far enough from the main islands that we could each be alone with our thoughts.

Barry sat across from me with his sunglasses on and his head tilted back to catch the rays. It seemed like he'd already checked out of his old life and begun a new chapter as an ex-pat pirate. It was a transition that had happened too suddenly to have been sudden.

"Why the charade, earlier? Why not just drag me out here kicking and screaming?"

"We had to wait for Heinrik to make contact. And I figured we'd at least take a shot at getting you to cough up the password," he replied.

"How long have you been working with him?"

"I've never met the son. My relationship was with his father," he replied. "This would have all been a lot easier if he were still around. But it is what it is, my friend. If everyone plays their part then everyone will get what they want - and no one gets hurt. That includes the girl."

He seemed so sure of himself. As if the deal was already complete. But he was mistaken. Heinrik was a psychopath. He was incapable of compromise.

"You Forrest Gumped your way into this didn't you? I'll bet Paulo Heinrik had been working on this since he learned that my dad had cancer. First he pushed my dad toward Daniel Gonsalves who taught him about Bitcoin and lured him into moving his money. Then he probably helped dad set up the safe deposit box, promising to make sure that Leticia would be given the account after he died. But I'm sure Dad didn't trust him completely; so he held back the password, he made sure that I had to be there with Leticia in order to access the money. That's why they argued... I was the wrinkle in his plan. And then the murders. That was Paulo's big mistake. He couldn't trust anyone other than his son, but his son went too far. It was too flashy. Too suspicious. That's why he had to bring you in. He needed someone to manage the gringo FBI Agent. Keep me busy until they were able to brainwash Leticia into opening the deposit box. You did good. I've been chasing my tail since I got here. And now the big finale, use Leticia as leverage to get me to hand over the password. The detective here seems like a late addition. Maybe when you realized you wouldn't be able to control Gregor Heinrik on your own you decided to bring in some local muscle?"

Barry gave my breakdown a golf clap. "Well, you *are* the FBI Agent."

"And you're a State Department employee. You'll never get away with this."

"Was a State employee. I turned in my resignation yesterday. Besides, Detective Amalero is only the tip of the spear. He has powerful benefactors who have already smoothed the way for my retirement here in Brazil."

"What about my dad? Did you know him too?" I asked.

"No. We never met. But I have to say I envy the man."

"He was murdered in his sleep."

"Yeah, but he had a nice run until then," Barry grinned.

"The boat's here," called Amalero. He pointed ahead to a sleek 38' Bayliner cabin cruiser sitting in the water 200 meters ahead. There were no other boats in sight and the closest island was almost a kilometer off the starboard. It was a good spot. There would be no witnesses. Amalero slowed the throttle and we made our approach.

Gregor Heinrik in the daylight was still an intimidating figure. He wore a wide brimmed straw hat, mid thigh shorts and no shirt. The sun glinted off his oiled body as if he were a living statue. The shadow of the hat hid his eyes which made his smile feel as artificial as the rest of him. Amalero tied the fishing boat alongside the Bayliner and we climbed up the ladder.

"My friends!" Gregor called. "Welcome aboard!" As each of us stepped on deck he greeted us with a handshake and a one armed bro embrace. "Detective Amalero, it's a pleasure amigo. Mr. Barry, very good to see you. My father spoke highly of you. It seems his trust was well placed. And finally, Agent Ronan. I hope you don't take any of this personally. It is, how do you Americans say? Just business."

He held his hand out waiting for me to accept his apology. Waiting to embrace. As if the events of the past week had been a spirited barter session at the local market. I'd heard the tone before. Charming but forced. A psychopath's mimicry of sincere conversation. The danger would occur when this rehearsed pattern was disrupted. When he faced an unexpected moment. This is when the façade would fall and he'd lash out with violence. Like a child flinging their toys across the room. Images flashed through my mind. A brown skinned teenage girl wearing a leather mask. The roof of a steel box illuminated by a cellphone glow. Gregor's grey eyed gaze as I crumpled helpless at his feet in the grass. I pushed down my revulsion and anger and took his hand. "Of course. Just business."

"Excellent! Excellent!" he grinned. "And I have a surprise for you. In appreciation of your sacrifice I'm going to give you one million out of my share. For you and your sister to do with as you please. After-all, it is your inheritance."

"That's very generous," said Barry. "Isn't that generous, Agent Ronan?"

"Where is she now?" I asked.

"She's close. We'll get to her soon enough. Right now, let's get settled in. Come. Come." He led us to the secondary deck where a table was waiting in the shade with two laptops. "Both computers are brand new. Never been used. You'll be able to set up your own accounts and after we make the transfers we can throw them overboard. And the wi-fi of course is satellite and completely secure." He was proud of his plan. "But first, a toast!" He walked to a wet bar where a bottle of champagne sat on ice. He popped the cork. The bang made us all flinch just a little. "No guns. I promise!" he laughed. He'd transformed from the Cheshire Cat to the Madhatter. He poured four glasses and handed them out.

"What should we toast?" asked Barry.

"We shall toast the man who made this all possible," Gregor said, suddenly serious. He held up his glass and looked directly at me, "To Frank Ronan."

"To Frank Ronan," agreed Barry and Amalero. They followed Gregor's lead and took long drinks.

I stared at the golden liquid bubbling in my hand. It was time to take away his toys. "Frank Ronan would've thrown this in your face and then jammed the glass through your eye into your brain," I said and sat the glass down on the table untouched.

"Come now. You have to drink!" Gregor said. The insult didn't bother him. He was upset that I wasn't following orders.

"Miles. Don't..." warned Barry.

"I want to see Leticia. Now," I said.

Gregor stepped over to me and stood an inch from my chest so that I had to look up to make eye contact. "It's bad luck to make a toast and not drink," he warned. I could see the vein in his neck pulse as he contained his anger. It was time to push him over the edge.

"Get the fuck off me." I slammed both hands into his chest. It was like shoving a tree. I flashed back again to the night at the sítio when I'd failed to wrestle him to the ground.

"You're disappointing me, Agent Ronan," he said in a low, barely controlled voice.

"Milesssshhh just take a drinnnk," said Barry stumbling against the side of the railing. Behind him Detective Amalero pressed his hand against his head, trying to steady himself. Unlike Barry he recognized that something was wrong. "*Filho da puta,*" he mumbled and tried to pull a gun from the back of his pants. His fingers failed him and the gun clatter to the deck; followed by Amalero. I looked at my champagne glass on the counter. A thin layer of powder had settled at the bottom. I whirled back toward Gregor just in time to see his fist jackhammer into the side of my chin.

CHAPTER
FIFTY-SEVEN

THE BLINDFOLD BLOCKED out the sun. But she was so thirsty. The gag in her mouth had become soaked with ocean water. Her dad had taught her about the ocean. About reading the swells. About feeling the current. About calming her mind. She also knew that she came from a line of fishermen on her mother's side. Her grandfather had lived his life on the ocean. Her uncle, who she'd met only once, also made his living on the water. This lineage gave her confidence. She would survive this ordeal. Just as she'd survived the others.

Then she heard the approaching whine of the fishing boat engine. The sound made her so giddy with hope that she nearly capsized. She re-focused her mind on the movement of the water. Anticipating the up and down swell. Knowing that it progressed from smaller to larger and then back down again in a predictable pattern. Count the waves. Trust the water. Calm your mind. Count the waves. Trust the water. Calm your mind.

The fishing boat had brought her savior. She just had to survive long enough to be saved.

CHAPTER
FIFTY-EIGHT

I WAS OUT ONLY a few seconds but it was long enough for Gregor to cuff my arms around the pole that held up the roof of the lower deck. He was crouched on his haunches watching me as I came back to consciousness.

"Have you ever seen a shark feed?" he asked.

A fog hovered around the edge of my vision giving his face a halo. Making him look like a mad angel of death.

"They don't chew their food. They rip it into pieces small enough to swallow whole," he continued.

"A shark -- is that what you think of yourself?" I mumbled.

"Of course not. Sharks are dumb fish. Like your friends." He stood up to reveal Barry and Amalero laid out on the deck behind him. They were unconscious but still breathing. As my vision cleared I could see that he held a machete in his hand. It had a hard black plastic handle and a dark steel blade whose color lightened along the razor sharp edge. He stepped between the bodies and with an easy backhand flick cut both of their throats. The cuts severed their jugular arteries along with half of their windpipes. The smell of blood and discharged gas from their stomaches caused me to gag. Gregor was unaffected.

"Sharks don't actually like to eat humans. They prefer fish. So I'm sure they'll enjoy these two," he smiled over his little joke.

"Psychopaths can't process humor. How long have you been rehearsing that one?"

He ignored my dig and focused on dragging the bodies to the rear of the deck. "Every summer when I was a boy my dad would bring me shark fishing. He thought it built character to face down monsters. My job was to make the chum." Gregor gave the blade a little twirl and went to work chopping into the carcasses. It was the matter of fact work of an experienced butcher. "The key to a good chum isn't just the ingredients, it's the motion in the water. The sharks don't just respond to the smell. They also respond to the vibrations. The flailing. So when we threw the chum overboard I'd be forced to jump in as well. To splash around in the bloody water until the fins began to appear. He and his friends would sit in the boat and laugh as I begged for them to pull me out. And you thought your father was bad. But we shouldn't complain. We are the men that they made us. Do you think your father was proud of you? Of what you've become? My father wasn't proud of me. He was scared of me. That's why I had to kill him. He was weak. He was never going to carry on the legacy that we'd been granted. He would always just talk. Talk. Talk.Talk."

He then picked up a shovel and flung the human chum over the side of the boat.

"But you and I, we are the same. I can see it in your eyes. I can smell the fear on you, but you're not weak. You can look the monster in the eye." He stepped closer as if to study me. "I think us humans, we think too much. That's why our fear is so much different than the baser creatures. It overwhelms most people. Some of my... my projects - just die of fear. It's the strangest thing."

"I hate to ruin your fun but if you feed me to the sharks you'll never get the password," I said. It took all of my training to keep my voice from cracking.

"You misunderstand. The chum isn't for you." He reached down and pulled me to my feet and pointed out over the water. That's when I saw her. The red trail of human chum floated in a lazy curve away from the boat toward a brown skinned teenage girl sitting on a paddle board. Her wrists were bound to the paddle board's oar which rested across the back of her shoulders like a crucifix. Her mouth was gagged and a blindfold was tied around her eyes. With each rise and dip of the swell she wobbled and fought to regain her balance. It was only a matter of time before she tired and fell off the board. Or until a shark ripped her off.

"Are we ready to do business, Agent Ronan?" Gregor smiled. He was now the Cheshire Cat and Mad Hatter all in one. "Here is the deal: You will give me the password and I will give you the fishing boat so you may rescue your sister."

I went numb. Overwhelmed by his madness. "Ok. I'll give it to you. I'll give you anything you want."

He took a small key from a pocket in his shorts. He then uncuffed my hands from the pole and re-cuffed them in front of me and motioned for me to head up the short steps to the upper deck where the laptops were waiting. My thoughts turned to potential weapons. Both Amalero's and Barry's guns had been thrown overboard. Gregor had only a machete that I could see. I could try to overpower him, but I'd already failed at that. I could dive overboard and take the fishing boat and try to save Leticia; but the bigger boat would run me down within minutes. I could also refuse to give him the password - it's doubtful that he'd let Leticia die as long as she could be used as leverage; but now that he had me in hand he could simply torture her until I surrendered. I was in a box. And a negotiation can't be won from inside a box. Which meant that I had one path: find a way out of the box.

"Is the offer for one million still on the table?" I asked, stalling for time as I slowly climbed the stairs.

"Of course, I'm a man of my word."

"That's good to hear. I should warn you, the other two mentioned that they had another partner. Someone that was connected in Rio. I'm worried that he's going to come after us now."

"Mayor Pesado is a coward. He's also broke. His enemies will put him in prison as soon as he can no longer buy their protection. He won't be a problem for long."

Bruno Pesado, the Mayor of Rio. The enemy of my enemy. A potential ally. But only if I could get out of here. We arrived at the table.

"Write down the password," he said pointing to a notepad next to the laptops.

A USB pen drive was plugged into one of the laptops. I assumed that this was the external bitcoin wallet. I glanced out over the water. Leticia was still upright on the paddleboard. The trail of red chum circled around her legs. I held up my cuffed hands, "How can I write like this?"

"You're stalling," he said.

"I want this over with more than you. C'mon, *Frederick*, you've won. Besides, you're not going to be able to read my handwriting," I said with a grin, desperately gambling everything on the hubris of the ubermensch.

He smiled his fake smile as he calculated my options. Then, confident in his physical superiority, he set the machete down far out of my reach and used the key to unlock one of the cuffs. As soon as my wrist was free I kicked the laptop and sent it skittering across the deck. He grabbed at the precious pen drive and I spun and leaped over the rail, screaming...

"Leticia!"

I hit the water hard. As I dove down my wet clothes cinched around me like cellophane. I tried to get my bearings. There... the dark shadow of the boat's hull. I dove. Down down down. Hoping that I'd have enough air. Hoping that the monster took the bait. That he'd stand at the rail waiting for me to swim toward the girl sitting out on the paddleboard while instead I went the opposite direction. But my lungs were already on fire. I made it beneath the sharp crease at the bottom of the hull. Halfway there. I crawled up up up. A second shadow appeared above me. The fishing boat. I kicked. I dug. Leticia and the monster were no longer in my thoughts. I needed to breathe. I shot up out of the water and gulped for air. Shhh. Too loud. I pulled myself up the ladder at the rear of the fishing boat and as I scrambled to the driver's seat; I saw him.

"You're making me angry," he called down in his flat voice. "You can't outrun me in that junk. It doesn't even have enough gas to make it back to the marina."

I ignored him and reached for the keys dangling from the ignition. The boat started with a rattle and I jammed the throttle. The bow lifted into the air as the rotors dug into the water and the mooring rope held the boat fast to the Cruiser. Finally, just as the motor began to smoke the wood railing tore off and the fishing boat lurched free. I steered away in a big arc and as I swung the boat back around toward Leticia and the paddleboard I heard the big cruiser engines roar to life.

I could see her now. It would be our second meeting and

she still hadn't laid eyes on me. The first time she'd been masked and swinging a knife at the edge of the jungle. This time she was blindfolded and shivering in the middle of the ocean. I glanced back. The Cruiser started to move toward us in a slow turn. I had just enough time to dive in and cut her free and pull her back into the fishing boat. But it would be pointless. The cruiser would slam into us seconds later. I wanted to call out to her. Assure her. Give her the strength to hang on just a little longer. Another hour. Another day. Another week. As long as it took. But I didn't. Instead I gunned the throttle and whipped the boat at a ninety degree angle spinning off a hard wake that slammed the side of the paddle board knocking her into the water.

One minute. The paddle tied across her shoulders would keep her from sinking but in her weakened state and with a gag in her mouth she'd struggle to keep her head out of the water. I figured she had less than sixty seconds before she drowned. Unless he turned back. I could hear the cruiser gaining on me. But he couldn't have us both. By the time he slammed into the fishing boat and drug me out of the wreckage she'd be dead. No. He had to turn back. He had to save her... she was the key to the password... without her I'd never give it up... she was worth a billion dollars! I looked over my shoulder. The cruiser's bow grew as it came closer and closer.

"Turn back!! Go save her!" I screamed into the wind.

The cruiser was almost on top of me when finally its engine shifted down and it veered off.

"*Aaaarhhh!*"

I screamed and screamed and screamed. Not stopping until I beached the fishing boat on the sand of a small island cove dotted with sailboats. I'd escaped his box. Now it was time to build a box of my own.

PART FOUR
THE BLACK SWAN

CHAPTER
FIFTY-NINE

THE GERMAN SHEPHERD was well trained. It stood over her tracking her every move.

"You're trespassing," said the man. The statement was a question.

The man was a security guard and not the mad scion of a Nazi murder factory. The sudden relief made her laugh out loud. "I'm a journalist," she said. "I got lost. Can you please call your dog off."

"*Aus*," he said in German. The dog returned to the man's side. He was a tall white man in his early forties. His hair was buzz cut short and he carried himself like a former soldier. "Sit up slowly and put your hands over your head," he ordered.

She complied, using the time to concoct a story.

"What are you really doing here?" he asked.

"I was lost. I swear. And then I saw that house over there on google maps and I figured I'd go and see if there was anyone who could help me."

He wasn't impressed. "I'm going to search you now. Don't move," he said. As he approached the dog stayed at his hip. He ran his hands down Marié's arms and torso and patted down each leg all the way to the ankles. It was a cold, professional effort. He came away with her cellphone and car keys. "I'm going to need the access code for your phone."

"Forget it," she said. "I'm not under arrest and you're not the police."

"The code. Or you don't get the phone back *and* I call the police."

She looked up at the sun setting in the distance. The air had begun to cool. If she fought she'd be trapped here for a long time. As she considered her options he grabbed her by the chin and held the phone up to her face. The recognition app kicked in and the phone lit up in his hand.

"Stay here," he said and walked toward the road as the dog stood guard.

She watched as he scrolled through her phone and then made a call on his own phone to report her presence. It was a quick call. Whoever was on the other end didn't waste time in making decisions. The security guard returned to where she was kneeled and returned her phone and keys.

"You can go. But if you're seen on the property again you'll be arrested."

"Who did you call?"

"The boss."

"Who's that? I'd like to speak with them. I'm doing a story on the Heinrik family."

"They have no comment."

"Oh, are you their spokesman?"

"Like I said, you're free to go. The offer expires in ten seconds."

She probably could've made her flight back to Rio but after discovering that the security guard had deleted the photos of the barn and field she decided to stick around and make a nuisance of herself. The small hotel was a collection of chalets arranged around a pool and spa. The hotel's restaurant catered to romantic couples and the lights were low. Marié was able to sit in the shadows at the bar and be alone without being alone. She nursed a glass of red wine and thought of Miles. He needed to know what she'd found. What if Leticia was beneath one of those markers out in the field? She had his email address. But as she tried to compose an email her fingers began to shake. She deleted the draft. Then she remembered Capitaõ Royce Mirza. She'd sent him the photos before she'd panicked. She called up their chat. The photos were there. The text message had gone through. But there was no reply. She called his phone number. It went directly to voice mail. She left a message letting him know that she was OK but she'd found something and they needed to talk.

"How was the wine?" The bartender was young for the job but did it well. She looked at her empty glass. She didn't remember drinking it.

"Good. I think."

"Another?"

"Yes, please." She watched as he made a perfect pour. "Are you from around here?" she asked.

"I was born and raised here. This is my parents' hotel," he said with a sense of pride.

"It's a beautiful place. I have a question."

"What do you want to know? I'm at your service," he grinned.

"Today on my way here I was a little lost and I drove by this big farm outside of town what's that place all about?"

"My dear, we don't talk about that place," he said. Then

with a dramatic look over his shoulder to make sure no one was listening he beckoned her close and whispered, "They grow soybeans."

"Soybeans?" she replied. "Sounds serious."

"It's our community's dark secret."

"Well, that and the whole Nazi thing," she said.

His eyebrows rose and he put his hand to his mouth. "Oh my god, girl, you are naughty."

Marié had guessed right. He was an ally. "I'll bet the Heinrik family hasn't made life easy for you."

"You're fishing. Be careful, darling. The water is dark and deep in these parts."

"And if I were fishing... where would I go to catch the monsters?"

He gave her a look to let her know that he was no longer playing, "Why would you want to do something like that?"

"It's my job," she said and slid a business card across the bar. It read: *Marié Alves / Jornalista / O Mundo Report.* "I'm going to nail these racist, homophobic bastards. Expose all their secrets. So they can't hurt anyone ever again. If you're able to help, I promise I can keep your identity a secret."

He bit his lip. She could see him cataloguing a lifetime of insults and abuse and weighing his desire for revenge against his need for self preservation. But any cooperation she was going to wring from him evaporated when a balding middle aged man in a suit took the seat next to her. The Bartender slid Marié's card into his pocket and greeted the man, *"Senhor Perriera.* Welcome back, sir. Would you like your usual?"

"That would be perfect. *Obrigado, Ronaldinha,"* the man said using the feminine form of the nickname, Ronaldinho. The bartender turned to fix the drink but Marié knew by the way he'd absorbed the insult that their conversation wasn't finished. The man smiled at Marié. He had an agenda. "The duck is excellent here. As good as you can find in the restaurants you have in Rio."

She nodded and refused to take the bait. He offered a fat, hairy hand to shake. "Tomas Perreria. I'm a lawyer. I represent the Heinrik Family Farms."

"Word travels fast," she said.

"Concern travels fast. They're not used to being targeted by journalists. My clients would like to know the subject of your story. And if possible, even help. What would you say to an interview?"

"I'd say, yes. Who will I be interviewing?"

"Senhor Anton Heinrik is the farm's chief executive. He's willing to make himself available to you. We just need a little information first, such as -- the subject of your story?"

The bartender delivered Perreria's drink. Johnnie Walker on the rocks. He swirled the glass without taking his eyes from Marié. The ice clicked. Marking the time that it took for her to consider her answer. She doubted that there would ever be an interview. But she'd play along.

"I'm doing a story on the lawyer, Paulo Heinrik. I'm sure you've heard he was recently found dead?"

"Yes. Tragic. The family was saddened to hear about that. I believe the police called it a home invasion? Rio is such a violent place. It's much safer here. But the Paulo branch of the family hasn't been connected to the business for many years. Their percentage of the farms were bought out over a decade ago. So it seems there wouldn't be much reason for an interview."

"I was hoping to find more background info. Childhood. Formative years. That kind of stuff," she said.

He stopped twirling the glass and took a drink. His first. He savored it. "You can buy this same whiskey in Rio, or anywhere really, but it doesn't taste the same. It's the ice.

The water around here is special. Rio has beautiful women. We have water."

"So, tomorrow morning? Interview? Where should I meet him?"

"Tomorrow is a full day. Mr. Heinrik would like to schedule something for next week. I understand if you can't wait around here that long. He's happy to do the interview over the phone."

"I see. Unfortunately I have a deadline. I'll need to have this done before then."

He took a long, slow drink and when the glass was empty placed his hand over Marié's hand. It was warm and wet. "I'm going to do you a favor. I'll give your producer a call. Let him know that we'd like to participate. I'm sure he'll give you more time. Besides, since poor Paulo is already dead there's no real rush, is there?" With that statement he considered his business concluded and placed cash on the bar. "*Ronaldinha*, thanks for the drink. It's great to see the hotel doing well. My best to your parents. And you Senhora Alves, a pleasure. It's not often one gets to enjoy two of Brazil's treasures at the same time. A girl from Rio and a whiskey on the rocks from the mountains of Santa Catarina. Be good you two."

She watched as he left the restaurant as if exiting a stage. "I feel like I should applaud," she said.

Ronaldo gave her a polite smile but the easy banter from before was gone. "Be careful. He's even more dangerous than he seems."

"He said they'd be willing to talk, but not until next week. Why the delay? If they're willing to talk, why not right now? Is something happening here in the next few days?" she asked.

"I don't know. But Perreria was here maybe three weeks ago. He had dinner with an old gringo. Really old, but sharp up here," he pointed to his head. "He had Perreria kissing his ass. You don't see that very often."

"American?"

"He had an accent but didn't look American. Maybe from Europe?"

"Did you hear what they were talking about?"

"It seemed like business. They had business papers with them. I think he stayed here at the hotel. Let me see if I can find his name." He turned to the computer behind the bar and called up the guest registry and scrolled down through the last two weeks.

But Marié already knew who it was. By the time the bartender turned and gave her the name she was already working on her next question, why had Jaime Gold been meeting with the Heinrik family lawyer? And more importantly, why had he kept it a secret?

CHAPTER
SIXTY

ANTONIO HAD BEEN WAITING for the message all evening. When it finally came he could picture Ronaldo's long fingers cradling the phone and his front teeth, white and straight gently biting down on his juicy lower lip as he composed the invitation: *"Room 29. Hurry."*

He parked along the road a half kilometer away and pulled up his thin hoodie as he hustled through the hotel's back gate and zig zagged along the winding pathways. He had the property memorized by now. He and Ronaldo's affair had been conducted here, in empty rooms, late at night, their proclamations muffled in the thick pillows and fresh linen. He'd forever associate hotel rooms with Ronaldo. Whenever he traveled and stepped into a new room he half expected Ronaldo's strong, lean arms to wrap around him from behind and a gasping whisper in his neck, *"Finalmente."* But tonight there was no embrace. Ronaldo stood across the room and peered out the window blinds.

"Did anyone see you?" Ronaldo asked.

"Of course not. Ronaldo? *Tudo bem?*" Is everything OK?

"Sim, Querido," he said with a faint smile and nodded

toward a young woman sitting at the small hotel room table.

Antonio jumped. He hadn't noticed her when he entered. The lights were low. She was very pretty. Striking even. So much so that he considered the possibility that Ronaldo wanted to include her in their evening session. The few times he'd been with a girl had been awkward and forced; but never had they been this attractive.

"Hello, Antonio," she said. "It's nice to meet you. My name is--"

"Marié Alves," he finished for her. As soon as she spoke he'd recognized her as the actress turned journalist. "What is this, Ronaldo?" he asked.

"Marié is a guest at the hotel. She's working on a story and, and I thought you might be able to help her," Ronaldo explained and then apologized, "I'm sorry, but it seems like an important story. Otherwise I wouldn't have called."

"A story about what?" he asked. But deep down he knew and he began to back toward the door.

Marié, sensing that she was about to lose him, stood and motioned for him to come and sit on the end of the bed. "Please Antonio, it's not about you. I'm doing a story on your cousin, Gregor Heinrik. And was hoping you could give me some insights... anything about him and his connection with the family property."

"I'm not involved with the farms. Ronaldo, you know that," he complained.

"But you know things, Antonio. You talk to everyone," Ronaldo chided.

"Antonio, can I show you something?" Maria said. She pulled out her phone.

Antonio was almost at the door when he succumbed to his curiosity. He sat down next to Marié as she showed him photos: The field of grave markers. The Nazi symbol carved on a wooden marker. The torn and muddied dress.

"Do you recognize this place?" she asked.

"It looks like the farm... out past the old family house. No one goes out there anymore... What are those?" he asked pointing to the grave markers.

"Graves," Marie said. "I think your cousin Gregor Heinrik has been killing girls and burying them out there."

Antonio stared hard at the photos. Flipping back and forth between them.

"You don't seem surprised," Marié noted.

"I'm not." He handed the phone back. "I'd be more surprised if he wasn't doing something like that."

"Gregor kidnapped a fifteen year old girl in Rio about two weeks ago. I think he still has her. None of the graves I saw out there were fresh. So she might still be alive. If I could ask you some questions... Off the record, if you prefer... It might help save her life."

Antonio looked to Ronaldo for help. He clenched his arms around his thin body. Terrified. A twenty year old boy going on ten.

"This is your chance, Antonio. All the time you talk about how you want to stop these people. They've been making you miserable for your whole life. They've been making this whole town miserable. You can end them. Just picture their fucking faces when they turn on the TV and all their dirty, racist secrets are exposed to the world," Ronaldo said, his voice rising. The next part was hard for him to say but he meant it, "If you don't do this, Antonio... I don't want to talk to you again."

"Ronaldo..."

"I'm serious. If I wanted to fuck a pussy -- then I'd fuck her," he said pointing at Marié.

"Ok! Ok. Ok. I'll do it," Antonio said.

Marié smiled. She'd chosen the right ally. She'd have to remember to talk to her producer about offering Ronaldo a job.

CHAPTER
SIXTY-ONE

THE WALK down the favela had been more embarrassing than dangerous and he had to restrain himself from chasing down every insult or rock thrown his way. When he'd arrived at the base of the hill he must have looked like a mad man. Sweat and filth from the night before. Blood splatter on his shirt from the killing this morning. He had to pull his badge and step into the middle of the street to stop a taxi. From there it was a jerky crawl through mid day traffic. He'd tried to borrow the driver's power charger to plug in his dead phone but the man's knock-off device didn't match. He was forced to sit back and let the city pass in silence. His thoughts turned to his family. His wife and daughter. This job was their burden as well. They had to wake up in the morning or go to bed at night never knowing when he'd come home. Then when he did arrive they couldn't ask him about his day. It was an unspoken agreement that he lived in two worlds. Their world. And the Other. Royce was growing tired of living in the Other. The more he saw of it the more he realized that it was not a place. It was a thing. A giant, morphing, parasitic beast. Sucking away at his soul.

As he opened the door to his apartment the smell of fresh rice and boiling black beans wrapped him in their familiar hug. His wife stepped out of the kitchen and smiled. It was a smile of relief. He was home. She moved to him but he held up his hand and said, "Shower first."

She nodded and examined his clothes. "The shirt in the trash." Then added, "Your boss called. He said you weren't answering your phone."

"It died. Plug in for me?" he asked, handing her the phone and then heading for the bathroom.

His wife was five years younger than him and had never once complained about his hours or his moods or the violent nightmares. She'd lost her father when she was a teen. Gunned down by a drug gang. She married a cop with her eyes wide open. Not because she wanted protection, but because she wanted to be a part of the solution. She cooked for him. She made a home for him. She tended his wounds. And every day she sent him back out filled with the fire necessary to hunt down the animals who would create more widows and orphans. But something had shifted within her in the last few weeks. It took a visit to her friend's astrologist in order to completely understand. The woman had read her chart and announced that her need for revenge had been sated. She was ready for her husband to step away from the wars and become a regular man.

He emerged from the shower and sat at the small kitchen table in his boxer briefs. A new bandage was taped over his shoulder. His tan, muscled back bent over the plate of rice, beans, sweet potatoes and beef and she could see the life flow back into him as he inhaled the food. He finally looked up at her. He tried to smile but the effort seemed too much and he gave up. Instead he unplugged his phone from the wall and went outside on the patio, closing the glass door behind him. She'd wanted to talk to him about what the woman had said. She'd even rehearsed her speech. But today wasn't the day. As she gathered the dishes she promised herself, "Tomorrow. I'll do it tomorrow."

Royce scrolled through his messages. His men were worried. Then there were the two calls from the journalist, Marié Alves. The big one though was his commander, the Chief of the BOPE battalion. This one needed to be addressed right away.

"Hi, Chief. It's me," he said. "I'm alive."

The pause on the other end of the line was relief not anger.

"I'm on my way in," Royce said.

"Don't," said the Chief. "There's an arrest warrant out on you."

"What? Why? Is this a joke?"

"They want to charge you for aiding and abetting a fugitive. Your FBI buddy."

Royce leaned against the wall. "Who's they?" he asked.

"It's coming from the top. Pesado," the Chief replied. "He's probably just throwing a tantrum. Rio Police don't have the balls to arrest you; but it's best you stay home until this FBI case goes away."

"Do we know where he is now?" Royce asked.

"Amalero has him. As far as I'm concerned they can keep him. And you will survive to fight another day. Understood?"

Royce understood. He understood that Special Agent Miles Ronan was being sacrificed to the beast.

"Starting now you're on vacation. That's an order," the Chief said. The line went dead before Royce could object.

Royce clenched the phone, tempted to hurl it off the balcony onto the freeway below. But he didn't. For years now he'd raged at the beast and it had absorbed his blows.

Laughing and morphing and growing stronger. He suddenly realized that the way of the BOPE was futile. If he was going to cut off the beast's head he was going to need this flimsy piece of plastic. This weapon of modernity.

"I was born here! Amongst you! I was raised here! Amongst you! The color of our skin is nothing! We are brown and black and white but we are all of the same mother... and that mother is Brazil!" he bellowed. The crowd, thrilled by the novelty of one of their own possibly becoming president, erupted in cheers.

"*Pe-sa-do! Pe-sa-do! Pe-sa-do!*"

Bruno Pesado stood at the microphone and pumped a fist in the air. He'd been speaking for an hour and his shirt was soaked with sweat. He could easily go for another hour. Today was a big day for him. That's why he'd chosen to come here, his home town of *Duque de Caxias,* to announce his candidacy. *Caxias,* a suburb of Rio, was a drab, disorganized sprawl of box like houses and garbage strewn streets. To outsiders it was barely discernible from a favela. Amazingly, thanks to a coastal oil refinery located within its boundaries, it was one of the wealthiest cities in Brazil. The tax revenue should have transformed it into a thriving, modern metropolis. An industrial compliment to the beauty of Rio. Instead, the fire hose of tax money was funneled off into an impenetrable maze of shell companies and construction projects set up by a revolving cast of politicians. The city was left with barely functioning public services and a crumbling infrastructure which flooded the streets with garbage and sewage whenever it rained.

Pesado's career had begun in *Caxias*. City council. Vice Mayor. This was his proving ground. By the time he was in his early thirties he'd skimmed a war chest of cash which enabled his jump to the big spotlight in Rio. But Rio was an expensive mistress. Up until yesterday he'd considered taking what money he had left, packing it into a bag and running away to Europe. But that wouldn't be living. He was a man who lived to live. Otherwise, what was the point? And the only way to keep his habit going was to reach higher. All the way to Brasilia. President of Brazil. It was the kind of gamble that if it paid off would pay off in the billions. But it would take more than charisma. It would take money. Money to buy the media. Money to buy his rivals. Money to buy an army of supporters. It was this weight that prevented him from fully enjoying the thrill of the moment; and it's why, when his aide signaled that a special guest had arrived, he chose to end the speech after just one hour.

His head of security was a former Rio Police officer known as *O Touro*. The Bull. Touro was waiting at the door of the warehouse when Pesado arrived. *"Oi, Doutor,"* Hello, Doctor. He greeted Pesado using the exaggerated title of respect given to men in senior positions regardless of their education. "He's clean. No bugs. No weapons. You want me to undo the cuffs?" he asked.

Pesado considered, "Leave them on until I say so. Did he fight?"

"No. He's ready to make a deal," Touro said and led the Mayor inside.

Waiting for him was Royce Mirza. He sat on a metal folding chair facing a wall with his hands zip-tied behind his back. The warehouse had once been used to store construction supplies purchased for unfinished public works projects; supplies that were sold off to private companies. Drug vials now littered the floor and Royce was positioned so that he was looking at a wall of piss stains.

Pesado chuckled to himself. There was a reason he and Touro worked so well together.

"Enjoying the view?" Pesado asked to the back of Royce's head.

Royce recognized the voice. He'd never met the Mayor before but his videos and social media campaigns and street posters were a part of every *Cariacás'* daily life.

"I'm just trying to figure out which one is yours. I'm thinking it's that one there on the end," he said nodding toward a skinny trickle of a stain.

"Funny. Cut him loose, Touro."

Touro stepped behind Royce and used a palm sized pocket knife to slice the plastic cords. Royce took his time to roll out his wrists before standing and turning to face the mayor.

"I see you got my message, thank you for coming," said Pesado. "I'm an admirer of your work."

"I can't say the same," replied Royce. "What's this about?"

"Your friend, this Miles Ronan. I want to talk to him."

"Why don't you ask your pet, Detective Amalero? I'm told he's the one who snatched him."

"Amalero's dead. So is a diplomat friend from the U.S. Consulate. They were chopped into pieces and fed to the sharks about two kilometers out past *Ihla Grande*. Your friend escaped and is in the wind." Pesado studied Royce's reaction. The hardened cop was at a loss.

"How do you know this?"

"I received a very angry call from the man who killed them."

"Heinrik? You're in this with him? Even for you that seems low."

"I wouldn't say I was working with him. But he's offered me an opportunity. Just like I'm about to offer you."

"You want me to work for you?" Royce asked, incredulous. He then turned to Touro and gave him a long up and down look, imagining himself in his position. The former cop wore a tight polo shirt which made his biceps pop. Around his neck he had a thick gold chain which would cost Royce two years worth of salary. He was the epitome of everything that Royce hated about the Rio Police. Royce shook his head, "Yeah, I think maybe I made a mistake. I came here thinking you'd know where my friend was. But you're fishing, just like me. So, why don't you tell your monkey to give me my gun back and we can forget we ever met."

"Do you know how I've stayed in power for so long?" Pesado asked.

"By shamelessly lying to ignorant voters?"

"By eliminating threats," Pesado replied. "And there are two ways to neutralize a threat. You kill them. Or you own them."

Royce smirked and addressed Touro, "Is that right, Big Boy? He owns you? Are you his pet? Do you snuggle up to him at night when it gets cold?"

"Touro, do you have any complaints about working for me?" Pesado asked.

"Nope," Touro replied, unfazed by Royce's jabs.

"Touro, tell Captain Mirza where you and your family live."

"Barra," he replied. Referring to the strip of ocean front apartments in Barra da Tijuca.

"In a penthouse in front of the beach," Pesado added. "Captain Mirza, you made a mistake. You allowed yourself to be caught on camera committing a crime. You helped an American fugitive break into a bank's security system. The bank is pissed and my City Attorney has already filed charges against you. You're going to prison. Which means your wife and adorable little girl… Well, I don't know what will happen to them. They'll probably end up back here in *Caxias* picking trash."

Royce had faced death before. And he'd always survived. But this time was different. This time the beast had cut off his escape. He'd need to kill it from the inside.

He took a deep breath. And as he dove into its gaping jaws asked, "What do you want me to do?"

CHAPTER
SIXTY-TWO

ALBERTO SANTOS DUMONT WAS A SLIGHT, effeminate and profoundly eccentric man who lived much of his adult life in Paris. He was also a Brazilian national hero. As long as she could remember Marié had been taught that this countryman of hers was the first to build and fly an airplane. That Brazil was the birthplace of flight. It wasn't until she was in her late teens when she had traveled to the U.S. that she learned another country had made the same claim. It was the first time that she realized a narrative which she considered gospel could in fact be up for debate. It was a lesson that she was reminded of every time she landed at Rio's small domestic airport named after Alberto Santos Dumont. The airport, like the city it served, was simultaneously beautiful and nerve wracking. Its flight path weaved between the city's granite mountains and ended on a short strip of runway lined on three sides by water. The slightest of pilot error would, and occasionally did, send a plane tumbling into *Guanabara Bay*.

She'd passed the flight from Santa Catarina making edits on the interview from the night before. Her producer would be able to blur Antonio's face and alter his voice but overall the sound and lighting on the simple iPhone video worked great. Ronaldo had real talent. As the plane landed she called up Miles' email address again. All of her training told her to keep the interview to herself. Miles wasn't her partner. He was part of the story. Yet, the same people who preached these principals were also the ones who wanted her to stay in her place and report on the latest fashion trends. Miles was the one who gave her the story. He's the one who had put his trust in her. And if this story were to have a happy ending -- he needed to see this interview.

"Hey there, beautiful. Need a ride?" the man's voice whispered in her ear.

She whirled, panic flushing through her body - only to find Royce Mirza standing behind her with a sly grin. "*Filho da puta!*" she snapped. "You scared the hell out of me."

"It's good to be scared. There are monsters about," he said and then pointed to his car parked in a loading zone in front of the terminal. "I'm right here."

She looked at the VW Golf with its black tinted windows. It had a fresh scrape on the bumper left over from Miles' recent mis-adventures. Royce was already climbing into the driver's seat.

"You coming?"

"How'd you know I was going to be here?" she asked. Royce Mirza was starting to grow on her. But she still didn't trust him.

"Cop magic. C'mon, no one ever saved the world standing on the curb."

She didn't trust him, but Miles did. And she trusted Miles. "Santos Dumont," she reminded herself and opened the passenger door.

CHAPTER
SIXTY-THREE

I CAUGHT a ride back to the mainland tucked in the back of a sport fishing charter. The fishermen were sales executives from São Paulo. Drunk. Telling stories in Portuguese. After the novelty of being an American wore off I was ignored and able to doze for most of the ride. The sunset amidst the islands was a game of peek-a-boo and as we arrived at the old mining port turned tourist town of *Paraty* it was in this half shadow, half golden light that I saw Marié waiting on the pier. She looked young and fresh in white tennis shoes and a casual patterned dress that hung loose at her knees. She wasn't here to play investigative journalist. She was here for me. My heart smiled. But as I stepped onto the pier the vision dissolved... and I was alone again. It felt right. No longer was I swirling beneath the wave, unsure which way was up or down. I'd hit the hard bottom of the ocean floor. The certainty allowed me to set my feet and launch upward, the only doubt now being whether I'd surface before I ran out of air.

Paraty's waterfront dated back to the 1700's and was made up of stocky stone buildings and narrow cobblestone streets. In the dark it felt like being transported back in time; except for the steady flow of tourists in T-shirts and flip flops waddling past like fattened geese. I needed a phone. I needed a car. I needed money. The tourists offered all three. I chose my prey with care. The man was a Brit. Bald. Middle aged. Vainly fit. With a painful sunburn. His companion was a dark Brazilian girl in a short skirt and high heels who looked to be about sixteen. I followed the couple into a restaurant and made my move as he entered the restroom. An arm drag to a back take to a choke and within ten seconds he was unconscious on the floor. As I suspected his wallet was fat with cash. This type of tourist didn't pay for his pleasures with a credit card. I unlocked his phone by scanning his unconscious face and then turned off the sleep mode so the screen would stay open. I then bolted out the back of the restaurant and sprinted through the streets to the edge of the old town where I was able to grab a taxi.

The driver warned me that the ride to Rio would cost R$200. I peeled off five hundreds from the Brit's wad and the driver grinned, gave a quick touch to the rosary dangling from the mirror and pulled out before I could change my mind. The Brit's phone soon began to blow up with messages from its owner. Amongst other things, he threatened to call the police and track me down. "Good," I replied. "I can share these photos with them." I attached one of the pictures from his photo roll: a teenage girl in her underwear posing in a Copacabana hotel room. It was one of hundreds. He immediately stopped texting.

I next pulled up the internet browser and logged into my email account. There were two messages. One from my boss, Peter Wills, telling me to check in or else. The other was from Marié Alves with a subject line that read: *"Black*

Swan." There was no message in the body only a video attachment. An interview she'd made with a young Brazilian man. Unfortunately it was conducted in Portuguese. I'd need a translator. One that I could trust.

CHAPTER
SIXTY-FOUR

HE'D MET Gregor Heinrik once before. In his father Paulo Heinrik's office. The odd young man had sat in the corner staring out the window for the entire meeting. Pesado had initially thought he was retarded. But as the meeting came to a close Gregor suddenly turned to Pesado and asked, "Have you ever been to *Complexo de Bangu*?"

The question took Pesado by surprise. Bangu was Rio's notorious state prison. A black hole to hell. "*Não. Porque?*" No. Why? Pesado replied.

Gregor stared at him with a blank gaze. "We just received a letter from a client in Bangu. He ran out of money and hasn't been able to pay the cell boss. He's eaten nothing but cockroaches for the past month. It's fascinating what the human body will do to survive."

"Would you like me to call to the Warden? I can see about getting him moved to a different area," Pesado offered.

"No. He's right where he belongs," Gregor replied and turned his attention back out the office window.

It was a threat from a lawyer to a client. A warning that *they* didn't work for him -- that *he*, the client, worked for them. And today, three years later, the flat tone of Gregor's voice on the other end of the phone still gave him chills.

"Would you like to know how our client in Bangu has fared?" he asked, assuming that Pesado was still lingering over their conversation from three years ago. "It seems his deprivations have given him strength. He has risen from the mud. Killing and clawing his way back to the world of man. He is now the boss of the entire block. An accomplishment that has left him unrecognizable to his former friends and family. Most in his position would have been crushed to dust and forgotten. Or turned into a whore. Sucking and begging. It's these rare incidents that give me hope for our species. I truly believe we can be salvaged, Mayor. We only need to set aside our inhibitions and embrace our fullest potential."

"Do you have a point? Or are you just prancing around like an insane peacock?" Pesado asked. He could hear the man weighing his response. His desire for control versus his need for information.

"Do you have the gringo?" Gregor asked.

"I know where's he going."

"Where?"

"First, business. The treasure is significantly larger than your boy Mr. Barry led me to believe. I want half."

"Half... half of what?"

"Half of a billion. And just so we're not dancing around the point, that would be five hundred million. Dollars," Pesado said. He couldn't stop from smirking. He had the fucker. Heinrik was running out of time and had no choice but accept the deal. Even so, the silence on the other end of the line made his heart skip. "Did you hear me?" he asked. Patience was not one of his strengths.

"OK. Half," Gregor replied. His voice was a dull thud.

Like a right hook into a heavy bag. "Now, where is Agent Ronan going?"

"I'll tell you when he gets there," Pesado said and hung up the phone.

A jolt of adrenaline dampened his armpits. He'd just stuck his arm into the tiger cage and emerged with his fingers intact. He pocketed his phone and stepped out of the SUV. They were parked at the end of a service road near the Duque de Caxias city limits. Immediately he was hit by the smell of sulfur. The stacks of the nearby oil refinery flared against the red sunset like a factory in hell. The effect was intentional. Pesado found co-operation to be more forthcoming while posing as the devil.

His men parted as he approached revealing the reporter girl lying face down on the gravel road. Her arms were zip-tied behind her back and his newest acquisition, Royce Mirza, stood to the side scrolling through her phone.

"Did the gringo call?" Pesado asked.

"No. He won't. He's too smart for that. He'll work solo from now on. But he just opened her e-mail." Royce handed Pesado the phone. The e-mail tracker indicated that the e-mail had been received.

"So he has the video. You say he's smart. Will he connect it to the old Jew?"

"He'll figure it out," Royce assured him.

"Good. We just need to get there first." He whistled at Tuoro and waved a finger indicating that it was time to wrap up and get on the road.

"What about her?" asked Royce.

"Let me talk to her," Pesado said.

Royce grabbed Marié by the back of the collar and jerked her up to her knees. Her lip was bloody. "*Filho da puta!*" she spit at Pesado.

"Sweetheart. This attitude is not productive. Look at

Capitão Mirza. He understands. Life is a game. And in a game the importance is not in choosing to play the white pieces or the black pieces... What's important is that you choose the winning side."

"You're the loser," she scoffed.

"You and I clearly have different criteria for winning and losing," he said as he stepped back. "Mirza..."

"Yes, sir?"

"Kill her."

"Sir, it's not necessary. She gave us what we needed. She's not going to talk. I promise," Royce said.

"Don't bore me. Kill her. Or you both die."

Royce looked over at Pesado's security detail. There were five of them counting Tuoro. Each of them armed. Guns out. Aimed at Royce. This was a test.

"Please hurry. If we miss the Jew I will take it out on your family," Pesado said as he pulled out his phone, flipping on the video camera to record Mirza's final debasement.

Royce turned to Marié, "I'm sorry..."

"*Por favor...* Royce... you don't have to do this," she pleaded. Royce pulled his 9mm from the back of his pants. She went pale, in shock that this was really happening. She scrambled to her feet and ran. She immediately stumbled in the soft marsh. As she climbed back to her feet Royce fired. The first shot hit her in the back. The force spun her around. And she was hit with two more quick shots. Both square in the chest. She staggered backward -- and then crumpled to the ground.

Tuoro stepped forward shining a light. The body lay unmoving, half sunk in the tall grass and mud. "She's dead," he declared. "You want to drag her out deeper?"

"No time," Pesado said. "The dogs will take care of her."

He clicked his phone's video off and turned to Royce, "Well done, Capitão. Come. Ride with me. We can discuss terms."

"Terms for what?" Royce asked. Not budging.

"For your soul!" he laughed and headed toward his SUV, waving his phone with the video of the killing.

Royce looked out at the dark shadows of the marsh and Marié's form sinking further into the mud. He made the sign of the cross and offered a prayer. But it was an act. Prayers were pointless. What he really needed was just enough privacy to palm his phone and send Miles a message. But Tuoro's hand fell heavy on his shoulder before he could finish.

"*Capitão*," Tuoro said, "No more phones until this is done."

"Just letting my wife know I'll be late," Royce said.

"I have a man outside your apartment. We'll let her know." Tuoro stood firm with his hand out. "Pesado's orders. It goes for everyone."

"Right," Royce muttered and handed over his phone.

"Welcome to the team, Brother."

"Glad to be here, Brother," Royce said and threw an arm around Tuoro's shoulder. "Now why don't you tell me all about this apartment of yours in Barra."

Royce led him up toward the vehicles leaving behind Marié's body -- which shifted in the mud as she took the chance to gasp for air.

CHAPTER
SIXTY-FIVE

"IS THIS NECESSARY? I'm old. My circulation isn't cut out for bondage games anymore," the professor complained as I used one of his neck ties to secure him to the dining room chair.

"Do you want to tell the police that you co-operated freely? Or under duress? It's all the same to me," I offered.

"Very well. Just not so tight," he whined.

I leaned over and loosened the tie. "Better?"

"Yes. My varicose veins thank you," he joked.

His stupid grin pissed me off. Without warning I slapped him hard across the face. His chair wobbled and he fell over, smacking his head on the hard wood floor. I kneeled over him. His nose and lip trickled blood. "I need you to take this fucking seriously. A teenage girl is right now being tortured to death. All those free lunches you enjoyed with my dad? The check is due. Tell me you understand."

"I'm sorry," he whimpered. "However I can help…"

I dragged his chair up to the dining room table. "Watch this video. After you've finished, we'll go through it together and you'll translate for me." I propped his iPad on the table and pulled up my email and opened Marié's video. As the video played I moved to the balcony to peer down at the street. Professor Gabriel Martins lived in a cramped apartment on the second floor of a five story building. Directly across the street was the restaurant where Tom Jobin famously composed "Girl From Ipanema." The restaurant had renamed itself "*Garota de Ipanema*" to capitalize on its brush with history and decades later still did a steady business. It was a busy street. Even now at ten in the evening pedestrians roamed the sidewalk shouting and laughing. It was impossible to tell if I'd been tracked. The Brit's cellphone had died soon after I'd left Paraty and I tossed it out the window. I'd also had the taxi drop me at the beach two blocks away. I scolded myself. I was being paranoid. I pulled the blinds shut and returned to the table where the video had just ended.

"Oh my, this is disturbing," the professor said.

"Tell me."

The video was an interview conducted by Marié in a quaint, Bavarian styled hotel room. Someone off screen named Ronaldo was handling the camera. The young man sitting across from Maria was in his early twenties. Handsome. Dirty blonde hair. He came from money, his clothes were expensive name brands. As the video played the professor gave me a simultaneous translation:

"Marié starts by asking him about his background. He says his name is Antonio Heinrik. He's saying here that his family owns a large amount of property in Santa Catarina state. A big industrial farm. The holdings were originally purchased by his great grandfather, Gustof Heinrik who settled there after World War Two. Marié then asks him to talk about his great grandfather. He replies: he was a Nazi."

On screen I could see that Antonio was shook. This was a deep shame that he was revealing to the world. He took a moment to gather his courage.

"Marié tells him to take his time... Then he explains that his great grandfather was a German officer in WW2. That he worked in one of the concentration camps. As the war came to an end he was tasked with shutting down the camp. After they killed the remaining prisoners they raided a warehouse of stolen valuables. Gold nuggets. Diamonds. Jewelry. The life savings of these people. It was a fortune. They then hauled all of this treasure to Hamburg along the North Sea where they bribed a submarine captain to help them escape.

"Marié then asks him if they used the submarine to come to Brazil.

"Antonio says, yes.

"Marié asks, why Brazil?

"He says, according to the family stories the choice was between Argentina and Brazil but they chose Brazil because it had more Black people.

"She asks why was this important.

"For the workers. Because they could make them work and not have to pay.

"Do you mean slaves?

"Yes, they thought they could use them as slaves.

"And did they?

"Yes.

"Really? Slaves? But how?

"They built an orphanage and then went into São Paulo and Rio and other places... and collected black children off the streets and brought them back to Santa Catarina. Then as they grew up they were forced to work. They built the entire farm that way.

"My god... she says... How long did this last?

"It was over by the time I was young but it lasted a long time. I think at least into the 1980's. My dad told me that he remembered seeing black children being forced to work when he was growing up."

I paused the video to digest what I'd just heard. "Is this possible?" I asked the professor.

The professor sighed, "Sadly, it's very possible. Even now there are stories... it's not slavery like what you may picture with chains and whips... it's more like what you would call indentured servitude. Some of these remote areas still trap the workers on their farms and if they want to eat -- then they have to work. Heinrik Farms is a huge operation. I've heard of it. They may have started small but they're now a multi-national company that exports all over the world. If they built this company on the back of slave labor... it's a big story. They'd lose a lot of business. But it gets darker," he said referring to the interview. "Let's keep going?"

I pushed play on the iPad. On screen Marié handed a sheet of printed photos to Antonio.

"She's asking him if he recognizes the places in these photos."

As Antonio studied the paper the camera moved behind him to capture the images. The photos were shots of a stone farmhouse.

"He says that this is the original farmhouse which was later converted into the dormitory where the children and workers were kept. It's empty now. He says that after the workers all moved on or died out it was used for family events... which he thinks is pretty sick. He never liked to go there. Even as a kid, before he knew about the history. It still felt haunted."

On screen Marié handed him another page of photos. This one had shots of a field of tall grass. One of the shots had been zoomed in on a colorful wooden marker planted into the ground. The marker was painted in red and black swirls that resembled a surreal, melting swastika.

"She's asking if this field means anything.

"It's the field behind the old barn... it's where they buried the bodies.

"What bodies?

"The workers. When they got sick. Or died in the field. Or tried to run away. They buried them there.

"How many bodies?

"This went on for so long. So many years... probably hundreds.

"What about these markers? She's asking. They're new. They're not from the 60's or 70's.

"He doesn't know. He's never seen those before. But he hasn't been out there since he was a little kid. Like he said, the place scared him. When he was last there the field was just grass. It was always just grass. Those markers are new.

"Now she wants to talk about Gregor Heinrik."

I saw that the name put Antonio on edge. He sat up straighter. He clenched his hands.

"He's my cousin. He's older than me. I don't really know him. But..."

Antonio stopped talking and looked toward the hotel room door. He didn't want to be there. Marié set aside her comforting therapist tone and turned interrogator. Trapping him in his chair with rapid fire questions. Professor Martins did his best to keep up.

"He's a serial killer, isn't he?

"I don't know.

"But you suspect? They say he killed a classmate of his, Greta Shefer. Right?

"People say that.

"Did your family buy out Paulo's share of the farms because they were worried about Gregor?

"Yes.

"Was it a condition of the sale that they leave Santa Catarina?

"Yes.

"Are those grave markers Gregor's victims? Has he been secretly returning to bury bodies in your family's garden of shame?

"I don't know. Maybe...

Antonio looked at the photo of the field. The camera over his shoulder pushed in giving a close view of the grave markers. Dozens of them. Antonio's eyes welled up with tears. He swiped them dry and sat up straight. Taking control of his moment.

"He's sick. The whole family is sick. They're so sick that instead of standing up to him and exposing their past they're going to sell the farms before their secret comes out.

"They're selling the farms?

"It's a big secret deal. They're trying to sell it before someone - like you - finds out about their history and they lose value.

"So in order to save some money they're willing to let a serial killer go free?

"Yes.

"And who's buying the farms?

"An international company. My dad and the others, they've been meeting with this old man, an Israeli who lives in Rio. The man met their first offer, didn't even negotiate and now they're just waiting...

"Waiting for what?

"Paulo's family has a matching period -- part of the original buy out deal was they would have thirty days to match any offer to purchase the family property. But, the farms are worth so much now. The Israeli's offer is like hundreds of millions. So... there's no way he could ever find that kind of money.

"When is the matching period over?

"Thirty days after they sign the deal... which is soon. The day after tomorrow."

Marié sat back and stared into the camera for a long beat and then the video ended and the screen went black.

Professor Martins squinted at the screen, for the first time he noticed the subject line of Marié's e-mail. "What does that mean? The Black Swan?"

"It means Leticia has a chance."

PART FIVE
THE GENTLE ART

CHAPTER
SIXTY-SIX

THE TITLE WAS A MOUTHFUL, but he still liked to hear people say it: Special Agent In Charge Peter Wills. It wasn't all ego trip, although he was proud of his position and his work. Work that had started all the way back in his steel town high school where he'd gone from a failing student to the class valedictorian. He was just as proud of the work he'd put in as he rose through the ranks at the Bureau. He'd not only been a good investigator but he'd learned how to play the game. He cultivated friends. He collected favors. He made sure to never burn a bridge unless it was absolutely necessary. It was a skill that he recognized early on would separate him from his peers. While other agents, such as the one on his mind right now, put their head down and worked hard and cracked cases they were unable to see how their actions fit within a larger puzzle. Yes, he was proud of his title but he didn't need to have his ego stroked. He used it as a release valve. It forced people to slow down and take a breath before delivering their next sentence. It forced them to take him seriously.

"Special Agent In Charge Peter Wills -- it's a surprise to hear from you this late. Isn't it past your bedtime?"

"It's nine PM. I still have a half hour until lights out," he smiled. "Plenty of time to find out why you lied to me."

"You should know better than to accuse a spy of lying. Exaggerate? Mislead? Omit? Sure. But lie? Come, man. This is not how we do business," she said.

The aide from the Israeli Embassy grinned at him from across the table as she lifted the glass of wine to her nose. She was in her early thirties with green eyes and a playful but disarming intelligence. Beautiful in a middle eastern way that made it difficult to know if she were Arab or Jew. She wore a grey and black business dress with the blouse opened one button too many revealing a deep line between her cream colored breasts. Her night black hair rolled in waves past her shoulders giving her plenty of opportunities to tuck loose strands behind her ear. Female spies were always the most effective in Wills' opinion. The macho posturing of male on male interactions was gone, replaced by a distracting sexual dynamic that clouded their real motives. He knew all of this; but he still had to force himself to focus.

"You can call it by any name you like, it's still a lie. And here in my world, lying to an FBI Agent is against the law."

"Thank god I don't live in your world, Agent Wills. Don't you find it terribly dull, everyone saying exactly what they mean all the time?" she said as she finally took a drink. Lipstick lingered on the rim of the glass which, like any good spy, she wiped clean with her napkin.

"You omitted mission critical information. As a result a Deputy U.S. Consul is dead and my agent is running for his life. We need to know that we can count on your cooperation going forward."

"Or what? You'll give me a strict scolding?"

"Or we expose that you're making business deals with Nazis."

"Ahh... I believe the more accurate description would be re-acquiring lost generational assets."

"No one reads past the headline these days. As soon as I'm done here I have a call set with a friend at the Washington Post."

The clatter of the restaurant muffled her sigh as she let her façade fall away. "This is turning into how do you say, a poop show?"

"Shit show," he corrected.

"Thank you, a shit show. That does sound better. Listen, the old man is a legend; but let's be honest, Nazis hiding out in South America aren't exactly our top priority these days. Sure, it's good P.R. to catch Nazis. It gets votes. It's a deterrent of sorts. Fuck with us and we'll spend the rest of eternity not only hunting you down - but hunting your ancestors down - and then taking back all that you've ever stolen. That kind of thing. But Nazi hunters are a dying breed and strategy wise, their support is limited."

"You're telling me the old man took things into his own hands."

"I'm saying that we're not going to clean up his mess. But at the same time we're not going to blow up his operation without certain assurances."

"All right, what do you want?"

"We need to know that your boy will finish the job, no matter how dirty it gets."

"Don't worry about him. He's committed. The question is whether you're willing to let him call the shots."

"And what does that look like?"

"Agent Ronan has complete operational control from this point on."

She swirled her glass. Her thoughts were interrupted by the buzzing of Wills' phone. He held up the screen. The caller I.D. read: *Washington Post*.

"Out of time."

She reached over the table and dismissed the call for him. "What does he need?"

"A sacrifice."

CHAPTER
SIXTY-SEVEN

A PUNCH in the face can be exhilarating. I felt bad about hitting the professor but it had worked. By the time I left he was jumping to help. He gave me his car and his cell phone and promised not to call the police until the next morning. In return I left the silk tie around his wrists loose enough to escape as soon as he liked.

The drive north to the fishing village outside of *Buzios* took a little over an hour. I parked a kilometer away from Jamie Gold's house and hiked down a rocky cliff to the beach. The walk felt good. It meant forward movement. It meant I was no longer driving in circles. It meant I was coming to the end. The text from Peter Wills came through on the Professor's phone as the house came into sight.

"He's inside the house"

The message meant that Jamie Gold was home. The message also meant that Wills was able to secure Mossad's co-operation. Jamie Gold had been cut loose. I was free to move in. I crouched low in the sand a hundred yards out. It was after midnight but the lights were on and I could hear music coming from the house. As my eyes adjusted I could make out the dark shape of armed men. Two were posted on the beach side. Another two posted in front on the road. The louvered wooden blinds were shut and I couldn't see inside but it was clear that I was late to the party. Someone had taken my black swan.

I lied. My dad's disappearance wasn't a surprise. The day he left he'd come to me early in the morning. It was just before dawn and he'd slipped into our house and nudged me awake. He no longer lived with us at the time but he came and went as he pleased. I was still groggy as he led me out to his truck. Our boards and wet-suits were already loaded up and a thermos of hot cocoa was waiting for me in the console. Right next to his coffee. During the fifteen minute drive to the beach a storm had moved in and the waves, which had been glassy moments before were now full of chop. Normally he'd have insisted we paddle out on principle's sake. But this day he was content for us to open the gate of the truck bed and sit and watch the rising sun as it battled against the approaching clouds.

"Don't be taking shit from anyone," he finally said.

I remember his intensity caught me by surprise. He was a hard man, this I knew, but he rarely used swear words in front of me.

"I guess what I'm trying to tell you is that people, they're all the same. No matter where you go. No matter how big they are. Or rich. Or whatever they *say* they are. At the end of the day, we're all just bags of guts and blood. And when you get in a fight - and you will, because any life worth having doesn't come without fighting for it... Remember, that man across from you they ain't more special than you. At some point they've been scared to death. At some point they've cried like a baby. They've

bled. They've lost. And at some point they'll do it all again -
- so might as well be you that makes them do it."

Even then, I realized that this wasn't normal father son
advice. This was a man's life philosophy. The kind that
comes bubbling up before he embarks on a journey to face
the dragons at the edge of the world. Later that afternoon I
was snatched off the sidewalk by three cartel enforcers on
my way home from school. I never saw him again. So, yeah,
I lied. I knew he was going away. But at least he gave me a
gift before he left. The greatest gift a father can give to his
son. The courage to walk up and punch a mother fucker in
the face.

"They need me alive," I said to myself. "They need me
alive. They need me alive." As I walked to the house I
slowed to scoop up a smooth, oval rock from the sand. The
rock fit in my palm as I closed my fist. "They need me
alive."

"*Para aí!*" barked the man. He wore a t-shirt and jeans
with a compact holster on his waist. His gun pull was confident and precise. But he didn't speak English and I understood none of his commands. "They need me alive. They
need me alive." When I failed to stop he was forced to
holster his gun in order to free his hands - and I stepped up
and threw a right cross. The rock, heavy in my fist, gave the
punch extra weight and I felt his jaw crack beneath my
knuckles. He dropped to the sand unconscious. I whirled to
face the second guard who ran at me from ten yards away.
The sand slowed his feet just enough that I had time to
wind up and throw the rock. It hit him square in the face.
He stumbled to a knee clenching his shattered nose. I closed
the gap and finished him off with a soccer kick to the side of

the head. I then jumped to harvest both of their guns before stepping back and waiting.

The door to the house opened. Backlit by the light from the open door I could see my friend Royce Mirza standing next to another man I'd never met but recognized, Bruno Pesado. The Mayor of Rio de Janeiro.

"About time," Royce said. "Come inside. Let's talk."

"We can talk from here." I called back. "Who's your new friend?"

"Someone who wants to find a solution for everyone."

"Switzerland, huh? I find that hard to believe," I replied. "You have Jaime Gold?"

"Yeah."

"Is he still alive?"

"He's still alive. He's not happy. But he's alive."

"Does your new friend understand that Jaime Gold is the key? That nothing works if he's dead?"

"He understands"

"What about his wife?" I asked.

"She's been taken care of," he said.

"You mean you killed her?"

"What would you have done?" he asked.

"I wouldn't have killed her!" I snapped. "What about Marié? She's the one who must have told you about Gold. What did you do to her? Is she inside too?"

"She didn't make the trip," Royce replied, no longer having fun with our conversation.

"What does that mean?"

"It means, I'm really sorry."

"You fucker," I groaned. "Is she dead? Did you kill her?!"

"Come inside. My friend here is in touch with Heinrik. Let's get this over with before anyone else gets hurt."

"So this is who you are now?" I said, trying to hold back the wave of rage.

"Sometimes you just got to pull guard, my brother," he said. "Know what I mean?"

Something was wrong. Royce was too calm. Emotionless. I'd just smeared his entire moral code and this proud man had made no reaction at all. Either he'd been faking every one of our interactions since I'd met him... or... he was playing a role now. Suddenly I understood what he meant by pulling guard. And the final piece of my box fell into place.

"Have your friend make the call. I'm ready."

CHAPTER
SIXTY-EIGHT

"NO. No. No. No smashing. You are not an elephant. You are a spider. You must sting. Bring the opponent into your web," Mitsuyo told his young student. The teenage boy nodded and tucked the loose gi back into his belt as he re-set for yet another go. Carlos Gracie was skinny and pale but possessed an intensity that had taken time for Mitsuyo to appreciate. At first he'd mistaken the boy's attitude for arrogance. Mitsuyo had been traveling and living out of Japan for over a decade now; but he was still learning to read these Caucasians. This was also the first time he'd taught jiu-jitsu to a non Japanese.

He'd met the boy's father, Gastão Gracie, in *Manaus*, the capital of Amazonia, a wild frontier city filled with miners and loggers with an un-quenchable appetite for fights. Gastão made his money promoting these fights and Mitsuyo Maeda was the biggest star in the game. His exotic fighting style was a mix of ancient Japanese disciplines called *Judo* and *Jiu-Jitsu*. Everywhere he went, and he'd been all around the world: Europe, America, Cuba, South America... local champions lined up to beat this unas-suming man. But they never did. An entire fighting career had passed and he'd never been beaten. Boxers, wrestlers, catch-as-catch-can experts. They had all fallen. Now in his early 40's Maeda had finally retired and settled into the Amazon port city of *Belem*. Gastão Gracie continued to visit. This charming salesman of Scottish decent pressed him for months to take his juvenile delinquent son Carlos as a student. Gastão was desperate. His son was running wild in the streets. Without a change the boy would end up in jail, or worse.

Maeda was torn. Like all Japanese fighters he'd made a vow back in Japan to never teach his techniques to foreigners. But he owed Gastão. The man had given him his final paydays in Manaus and was an important business connection. Finally, after securing a promise from both Gracies that they would never share these sacred Japanese methods; he brought the boy into his dojo.

Now, less than a year later, Carlos was his best student. The boy routinely beat Maeda's more experienced Japanese fighters. But he relied too much on his intensity. He would fly at his opponent with no regard for his own safety and smash and smash until they gave up. Maeda realized that he'd taught the boy like a Japanese student. He'd begun with throws and take downs assuming that he'd learn the defensive fighting in time. But this had been a mistake. Now that Carlos had an artillery of offensive weapons all he could envision was the attack.

"Lay down," Maeda told him. "Like this." He demonstrated by laying down on his back with his hands defending in front of him and his knees and feet in the air. "Smash me," he ordered.

Carlos rushed in but Maeda flowed with his attack and pulled him into an arm bar.

"Again," Maeda ordered.

Carlos stormed in and again Maeda turned with the

momentum and rolled him into a triangle choke. They went on like this for over an hour. Maeda ordering Carlos to attack and then submitting the boy over and over until Carlos gave in and collapsed in exhaustion.

"What am I doing wrong?" Carlos complained.

"You do not create art with a hammer."

"I don't understand. How is fighting an art?"

"We are not fighting. A fight is chaos. You smash and smash and hope that your opponent will fall before you do. What I am teaching is to kill gently. To do this you must first paint your opponent's death; and that is art." Maeda could see that the boy was close. "Do you want to become a killer of giants?"

"Yes. More than anything," the boy replied without hesitation.

"But how? They are so big. And you are but a bug."

"I sting them...?" He was a good student and he knew the answer, but didn't yet understand the answer.

"Yes. And to do that you must lure them into this," Maeda said and held up his arms and legs. "Your web. Your guard."

A new light filled Carlos' eyes. He looked up from his teacher and out the steam streaked dojo window past the fish market and past the muddy streets and past the horse drawn carts of 1920's Amazonia - and into the future where this skinny boy with a chip on his shoulder would bring the philosophies of jiu jitsu to his countrymen; who in turn would spread them to the world.

CHAPTER
SIXTY-NINE

ONE HUNDRED YEARS later I sat cross legged on the cool, damp sand of a Brazilian beach preparing my sting. In the grey pre-dawn light I could make out the shape of Heinrik's boat sitting in the deep water off shore. Opposite, waiting on the rear porch of Jamie Gold's house, was Mayor Pesado. He sat heavy on a plastic chair and smoked from a pack of cigarettes and sipped coffee. The three of us formed a triangle. But I needed a box. I needed a fourth side. I needed Royce Mirza to be the man I believed him to be.

Movement. A black zodiac skimmed fast and low across the ocean surface. As it grew close I could see Heinrik controlling the outboard motor and Leticia sitting in the front facing forward. She was neither blindfolded or bound. When the boat ground to a stop on the sand she remained still, staring into space with dead eyes. "Almost there. Just a little longer," I said to her in my head.

"Tuoro, bring him out!" called Pesado. The details for the exchange had been been agreed upon in the night. Pesado's man with the broken jaw brought Jamie Gold out of the house. The old man's lean arms were bound behind his back and he'd been blindfolded with a rag. His face was bruised but he held his head high. Tuoro walked him across the sand until they came to a few meters from the beached zodiac where Tuoro shoved him to his knees and held an uzi machine gun at the back of his head.

"*Agora você!*" Now, you! Pesado yelled to Heinrik.

Heinrik stepped out of the zodiac. I could now see that he was wearing a bullet proof vest and had an assault rifle strapped over his shoulder. He reached back and offered his hand to help Leticia. She ignored the hand and climbed out on her own. He didn't register the insult. She meant nothing to him. "Go with him," he said and pointed toward Royce who stood opposite of me on the beach. She took in the men spread out in front of her. Strange men with guns. When she didn't move right away he grabbed her by the upper arm and shoved her toward Royce. "*Sai, cachorro!*" She stumbled and then ran. Royce was forced to run after her and sweep her up around the waist. Her escape attempt had used up all of her strength and he pushed her to the sand where she sat in a state of shock.

"Excellent," called out Pesado in a thick accent. He walked down from the porch and motioned to a plastic table set in the sand with three chairs, "Please join me, gentlemen."

Heinrik waited for me to go first. I made one last scan of the beach. Royce and Tuoro stood on opposite sides with their hostages. Waiting at the house were three more of Pesado's security detail. One of them with a bandaged nose. All of them were armed with short barrel Uzis. I tucked my two stolen pistols in the back of my pants. I then walked down to the table and took a seat. Despite the guns pointed everywhere this next part would be easy. We would all be on our best behavior until the goods where transferred.

Heinrik arrived last.

"Feels like we should start with a toast," said Pesado.

"No, thanks," I said. Stopping him from waving to his men for drinks. "Let's get this over with."

"Agent Ronan doesn't drink with strangers," Heinrik said.

"Or psychopaths," I replied.

"I prefer the term evolved," he said. "We're actually quite good company. Ask your sister."

"You may kill each other later," Pesado interrupted. "But now we have business. Agent Ronan, the password?" He pushed a notepad and a pen across the table. I gripped the pen and looked over at Royce and Leticia. I wanted just one sign that I could trust him. But he remained a statue in mirrored sunglasses. I quickly wrote out *VB6/28/91* and slid the paper to Heinrik. He had a small iPad ready. He entered the date as written. Then he stared at the screen... waiting...

"Did it work?" barked Pesado.

"It's good," Heinrik finally nodded.

"Yes," I muttered under my breath. The relief surprised me.

"Let me see. Let me see." Pesado was on the edge of his seat.

Heinrik kept a firm grip on the tablet and turned it toward Pesado.

"How much is that in dollars?" Pesado asked, squinting to understand the numbers on the screen.

Heinrik calculated in his head, "At today's rate, one billion two hundred fifty million. dollars."

Pesado gave a low whistle and clapped his hands, "*Que beleza.*"

"Since you guys have your money..." I stood to leave.

"Sit down," Pesado warned. He raised one hand in the air and snapped his fingers. Immediately the three gunmen on the porch brought their guns to the ready position. "No one leaves the table until we're *all* whole."

I raised my hands in surrender and returned to my seat. I knew he'd object. I just wanted to see what it looked like.

"Now my turn. Transfer my half," Pesado demanded. He slid a small piece of paper to Heinrik with his own bitcoin account number. Heinrik took the paper, entered in the account and made the transfer.

"It's done," he said seconds later.

Pesado check the account on his phone. Nothing. Nothing. But then a big grin filled his face. "It's been a pleasure," he said as he stood and offered his hand first to me and then Heinrik. Neither of us accepted. He shrugged. "Here is how this is going to work. We all back away and walk out of here nice and easy. Any sudden moves and my men have orders to shoot. Anybody tries to follow me - my men have orders to shoot. Understood?"

"First you tell your man to step away from my prize," said Heinrik.

"*Tuoro! Capitão! Vem comigo,*" Pesado called out.

Royce and Tuoro stepped away from their respective hostages and moved parallel to Pesado as he strode fast toward the main road and his caravan of bullet proofed SUVs. The three Uzi toting guards remained near the porch to cover his retreat.

Heinrik rushed from the table to secure Jamie Gold and I headed to Leticia who was left sitting alone in the sand. My walk turned to a jog and then a run. I collapsed on my knees in front of her.

"Leticia, do you know who I am?"

She stared at me like I was an alien.

"Do you speak English?" I asked.

"Are you real?" she asked.

"Yes. I'm real," I said. "Do you know who I am?"

"You're Miles. My brother."

"Yes. That's me." My eyes grew wet. "Can you walk? We have to get out of here. Right now," I said and reached to pull her to her feet. She flinched as I touched her but then leaned on my hands as she stood.

A bullet thudded into the sand.

"Run!" I yelled.

I pushed Leticia toward the trail where I'd arrived in the night. As she ran I pulled both guns from the back of my pants and turned to see Royce aiming his gun at us. Before I could get off a shot he fired again. It went far wide. He was buying us time. I'd guessed right. This was the man I knew.

"Go!" he yelled.

Behind him the three security guards walked down from the porch and moved toward me across the sand. I took a quick look toward the water where Heinrik had dragged Jaime Gold into the zodiac and was pushing the boat into the surf. The shooters weren't coming for him. He wasn't a threat. Me and Leticia. We needed to be silenced.

PopPopPopPop. Uzi bullets ripped into the sand at my feet. I whirled and ran. Leticia was already at the trail head and safe behind a large boulder. But I still had twenty yards to go. I wasn't going to make it. I dove to the right - twisting and coming down in a prone firing position aimed back at the gunmen. My first two shots went wide. The third one hit the shoulder of the security guard with the broken nose. He spun and fell to a knee. The other two shooters ran in opposite directions, fanning out to make me choose between targets.

Now, Royce. It's time to sting.

Royce turned away from me and fired. The shooter's skull exploded. Brain and blood splashed across the sand. The other shooter whirled in shock at Royce's betrayal; giving me time to fire off three shots. One in the leg. One in the chest. One in the stomach. He crumpled into a motionless ball. Blood forming a puddle around him.

"Behind you!" I yelled. The shooter with the broken nose rose up behind Royce. PopPopPopPop. A zipper of Uzi bullets ripped through the air. Royce dropped. I leaped to my feet and fired both pistols until they were empty and the shooter was dead several times over.

"Royce!" I ran to his side. Blood streamed down the side of his head where a bullet had grazed his temple and clipped part of his ear. But he was alive. "Royce! Wake up! C'mon!"

He groaned and pushed himself into a sitting position.

"There we go, buddy. Let's get you out of here." I pulled him up to his feet but he swooned and fell, clutching his thigh where a bullet had shattered his femur.

"You go. I'll be fine. Get the girl... Get her safe," Royce said.

"What about Pesado? He'll be back when he realizes what happened."

Royce grinned a bloody smile, "Marié will take care of Pesado."

I caught up with Leticia at the top of the trail as it emerged onto a cliff overlooking the ocean on one side and the fishing village on the other. The professor's car was parked a short walk away. She sat on the rough grass and stared out toward Heinrik's boat in the distance. The zodiac had just docked and although it was too far to make out any detail I could picture him dragging Jaime Gold onto the blood stained deck.

"He's out there?" she asked.

"Yes," I replied.

"He took that old man. Why?"

"Revenge. A long time ago that old man killed his great grandfather."

"So you traded the old man for me?"

"I guess you could say that," I replied. "It's a little more complicated. I'll tell you everything. I promise. But right now we need to go."

"Go where?" she asked.

"I…" I didn't have an answer. She had no family waiting for her. Just me. In a way she was already home.

"Could we just sit here a little?" she asked.

"Yeah. Of course," I said and sat down next to her.

"What's going to happen to him?"

"The old man?"

"No. *Him*," she said.

Heinrik's boat had turned and was heading out to the open sea.

"The old man is going to kill him," I said.

"Good," she said without hesitating.

I looked over at her. She was smiling. It was the most beautiful thing I'd ever seen.

CHAPTER
SEVENTY

HE RAN the boat at full throttle slamming through the rough chop. On the floor, the old Jew knocked his head with each thump. The old man was tough. He never cried out. Gregor found himself checking to make sure he was still alive.

The coastline had receded to a blur and it was finally safe to stop and take care of business. Jaime Gold was going to die. A slow, painful, terrifying death. It would be a new experience for Gregor. He'd never killed a man before. He'd killed Frank Ronan. And of course his own father. And the detective and David Barry. But these had been acts of war. He'd never killed a man for pleasure. He didn't think there would be the sexual arousal that came with killing women; but he wasn't sure. He was curious to find out.

He sat Gold upright and removed his blindfold. The old man blinked away the bright sun and looked at Gregor with a beatific smile.

"Stop smiling," Gregor snapped.

"But why? I'm happy."

"You're happy that you're going to die?"

"I've lived a full life."

"A failed life," Gregor pointed out.

"A failure? Oh no. God has put me right where I belong."

"God?" Gregor scoffed. "God is a fabrication of a weak mind. A way to rationalize your failures. Just one call now and the farms are mine. And that is but the beginning. My garden will soon spread throughout the world," he leaned in close to Jaime Gold, "I am the Messiah of your nightmares."

Jaime Gold laughed. He laughed and laughed. Gregor slapped him, knocking him to the floor.

"I see you God. I am ready!" Jaime yelled up into the sky and began to chant a prayer in Hebrew.

"Stop that!" Gregor yelled and kicked him in the side. Jaime took the punishment and continued to pray. Gregor strode across the deck and pulled his machete from a case built into the wall. "You'll stop that or I'll cut out your..." A light glinted off the machete blade. Gregor looked up in the sky where a faint contrail line appeared high above. A disturbing thought occurred to him. He reached down and cut free Jaime Gold's wrist ties, and there... on the inside of Gold's forearm was the raised scar of an embedded GPS tracker. All of his plans. Three generations of work and striving. All of it was about to be ruined by a piece of metal the size of a grain of rice.

"Boom," said Gold.

The missile pierced the clouds and in the amount of time it took Gregor's brain to consider that Jaime Gold had meant to be captured -- that he really was exactly where he wanted to be -- their lives were over.

CHAPTER
SEVENTY-ONE

"IT'S GOOD. Too good to rush," her Producer said looking up from the video that had just played on her tablet. "We'll run promos all day and use it for the lead on tonight's show."

"That's too late. It needs to drop right now," she said.

"Marié, it's a compliment. I'm offering you the lead on the evening news. Isn't that what you've been begging for?"

"I want to drop it on the website. Right now," she insisted. "People are counting on this. People are going to be hurt if it doesn't get out right now."

"Be serious. This is too good to bury in the morning news. That's final. Besides, it's not ready. Legal needs to sift through it, the graphics on the interview still need work. Go home. Get a shower. Breakfast. Then come back and we'll finish this thing up."

Marié glimpsed her reflection in the office window. It had been a long night. She'd been abducted from the airport. Beaten. Interrogated. Shot and left for dead in a swamp. And then forced to walk five kilometers in the dark covered in mud. But all she could think about now was

Royce Mirza. The stoic hero of her story. The look of desperation on his face when he'd picked her up at the airport had been shocking. He'd pulled the car off the side of the road and begun by showing her photos of his wife and daughter. He told her how they'd met when he was a rookie officer investigating her father's murder. How his wife's father had been the owner of a neighborhood grocery and was gunned down by a favela gang who'd been trying to collect protection money. Mirza then told her how his wife and little girl were now being threatened by another type of gang boss, Mayor Pesado. And how he had a plan to bring Pesado down. To expose his rot. To save the city. To save his family. But he needed her help. She was the key. Without her help; his family would die. Either that, or he'd have to kill Marié. But he'd already decided that he wouldn't sacrifice one innocent for another. Even if that other innocent was of his own heart. She would never forget the tears of gratitude welling up in this hard man's eyes as she pulled off her shirt and allowed him to strap the bullet proof vest over her bare torso.

All of this effort would be wasted if the story didn't come out now. Pesado had to be stopped before he could get his hands back on the levers that ran the city. Levers that turned cogs that would crush her story before it aired. Cogs that turned gears that would grind Capitão Mirza's wife and daughter into a bloody pulp and spew them across the streets as a message to anyone that dared challenge his control. All of this weighed on her story being aired *right now*. And this pretentious fuck in Italian loafers and pressed Brooks Brothers shirt and manicured fingernails was standing in the way.

"Please, Marié. You did good, girl. Hey, we'll celebrate tonight after it airs. We'll go out to eat. Just the two of us," he grinned, looking her up and down.

"I own this story," she said. "You denied my expense request for the flight to Santa Catarina. I paid for it with my own money. That means I did this on my own time."

"Now, Marié what are you…"

"I have over five hundred thousand followers on Instagram. If you don't run the story right now, as the lead on O Mundo's website; I will put it out on my own and within an hour every news agency in the country will be running with it."

"You wouldn't…"

"Watch me," she said and snatched her tablet and headed out of the office.

"*Caralho!*" Fuck! Pesado yelled. He dialed his phone again. Again the call went straight to voice mail. "Why aren't they answering?!"

Tuoro looked back from the driver's seat. "Uu ook airr ones," he said.

"What? What the hell are you saying?!"

"You… took… their… phones," he blurted, cringing in pain from his broken jaw. A purple stain had spread up the side of his face.

"*Caralho,*" Pesado muttered. "Something's wrong. Why so many gunshots? Two, three, four shots - that's all it should have took. But that sounded like a fucking war. And they should have caught up with us by now." He looked out the rear window of the SUV. The highway was almost empty.

"Wan me oo sloo owwwn?" Tuoro asked.

"What? No! Speed up. Fuck. They're not coming. Fucking Mirza. This had to be him. He fucking turned on us. I'm going to ruin that piece of shit. He's going to beg. And then I'm going to take him apart piece by piece."

He picked up his phone and called his man stationed outside of Royce's apartment building. "The wife and daughter, are they still there?!"

"Oi, Pesado." The man's voice was a whisper on the other end of the line. "They're still here, but--"

"Go get them. Both of them. Drag them out by the fucking hair. Screaming. Tie them up. Whatever it takes. Just get them and bring them out to the refinery."

"Boss, there's someone else here," he whispered.

"What? Who?"

"I think it's BOPE. There's two cars. Three guys are waiting down on the street. Two others went upstairs..."

"How did that happen? Mirza doesn't have a phone. He couldn't have called them this fast."

"Boss, didn't you see?"

"See what?"

"O Mundo. There's a report... *merde*... they saw me. I gotta go."

The line clicked dead. Dread filled Pesado's gut. He pulled up the O Mundo website on his phone. There was his photo. Top of the page. Breaking News. *"Caught On Tape Mayor Pesado Orders Reporter's Killing"* The headline was followed by a video report with Marié Alves - who, still very much alive, was standing in the dark wearing a bullet proof vest covered in mud on the road leading to the refinery. He didn't need to watch. He knew what had happened. Royce Mirza had played him. His dread turned to panic, which, to his surprise, then dissipated into relief. His career was over. There was no way he could spin this. A lifetime of work ended in a matter of seconds. But so was that starving pit of ambition that had consumed every waking moment of his life. He felt oddly free. Free to take his 600 million dollars and disappear. But before he could fully sink into the fantasy the SUV slowed down and he was jerked back to the real world.

"What is it?"

"Blitz," replied Tuoro.

They came to a stop behind a line of cars. Pesado leaned forward. Flashing police lights blocked the road ahead. "Turn around," he ordered.

"Wee oo cose," Tuoro replied.

"What are you saying?!"

"Too close! They'll see us," Tuoro grunted through closed teeth.

"That's BOPE up there. Or *Policia Federal*. And they're looking for us. So turn around and gets us the hell out of here! *Agora!*" Pesado said.

Tuoro looked from Pesado to the police blockade and back to Pesado… He'd never seen the mayor scared before. This giant was shrinking before his eyes.

"I'll pay you," Pesado pleaded. "One million."

"No."

"Two million."

"I want half."

"Are you crazy? Three million. That's dollars! Three million dollars!"

Tuoro scoffed. He'd been standing close enough to the table on the beach to hear the negotiations between Pesado and Heinrik. He didn't understand English but he did understand the word *billion*. If Pesado had taken half of a billion then Tuoro wanted half of Pesado's half. He pressed his hand on the SUV's horn.

"What the hell are you doing?!" Pesado screamed trying to slap his hand away from the horn.

"Half," insisted Tuoro.

"Ok! Ok! You can have half! Just go!"

Tuoro let go of the horn, spun the steering wheel and jammed on the gas. The SUV whipped a u-turn and they roared down the median weaving between on-coming cars, flip-flop wearing pedestrians, cyclists... a boy balancing a crate of snacks appeared out of nowhere... Tuoro yanked the wheel and they veered off the road and rolled down an incline and slammed into a cement drainage ditch.

Drip. Drip. Pesado was woken by the sound of his own blood dripping from a gash on his forehead. The SUV was tilted at an angle. In the front seat Tuoro was unconscious and pinned behind the steering wheel airbag. Pesado fought through the fog. He had to keep moving. But first he reached into the front seat and pulled Tuoro's gun. He then kicked open the door. As he climbed out his foot slipped - and he fell into the black grime of the drainage ditch. The stench was overwhelming. Vomit burst from his mouth - splashing into the stagnant water. But he had to keep moving. He stumbled and made it to the ditch's slanted wall.

"*Para la!*" Two BOPE officers appeared on the ledge.

Pesado ignored them and tried to climb - but slid down the grimy, moss covered cement and landed on his butt.

The officers thought it was hilarious. "*Oi, Gordinho.* What's wrong piggy? Don't give up! You can do it! We believe in you!"

How dare these peasants talk to him like that. Pesado gripped Tuoro's gun and stood up and fired at the officers. The recoil jerked his arm and he slipped and fell back into the muck. The officers laughed and took their time with his death. The first shot hit him in the leg. Then the arm. Then the other arm. Then as he tried to crawl away they shot him in the ass. The final shot hit him in the back and came out his chest. He flopped flat and died; his face half submerged in the piss and shit of his constituents.

CHAPTER
SEVENTY-TWO

THE DREAM HAD BEEN the same every night for a week. I was walking and walking and would look up and realize I was back in the cemetery with the white picket fence. But now the graves that had stretched to the horizon were no longer empty, they were filled with people. People I'd never met. Thousands of them. The difference between these people and those in the original graves were that these people looked innocent. They came from all walks of life: men, women, children, elderly, white, black... In the dream I was searching this field of graves for someone... but I didn't know who... and then I would remember -- I was looking for Heinrik.

And I could never find him.

"What's so funny?" I asked as I sat up on the hospital couch. The feel of cheap vinyl lingered on the side of my face.

"You were snoring," she said. "Again!"

"Impossible. I've never snored in my life."

"Marié, was he snoring?"

"Totally snoring," said Marié. She stood in the doorway. "I could hear you coming down the hall. The nurses thought it was an earthquake."

Leticia clapped her hands, delighted with the ribbing of her big brother. But she was just as excited by the shopping bags in Marié's hands. "What did you get? What did you get?"

"I wasn't exactly sure on the sizes so I got a few options. Try them on. We'll exchange what you don't like. These should keep you covered until we can go shopping together." She placed the bags of clothes on the couch where I'd been sleeping.

"I can't wait to get out of this thing," Leticia said as she hopped out of the bed. The hospital robe hung wrinkled and loose around her neck.

"I can tell when I'm no longer needed. I'll give you girls some privacy," I said. Leticia was already dumping out the bags and barely noticed as I walked to the door.

Marié touched me on the arm as I passed, "Don't go too far."

"I'll be right outside," I promised.

After the events at Jaime Gold's house I had called Special Agent Wills and he'd pulled strings with the U.S. Consulate to get Leticia a spot in Rio's best hospital. Marié had been waiting in the lobby when we arrived. After the doctors whisked Leticia away it was just the two of us again.

"Did you finally figure it out?" she asked.

"Figure what out?"

"Your black swan," she said nodding toward the doors where Leticia had disappeared.

"I did. Thank you. And congrats on your story. It looks like black swans all around."

"Thank you," she said. Then added quickly, "The story's done now. Your part at least."

"Yeah? Does that mean you and me...?"

"For an FBI agent you're not so good at reading clues," she scolded.

It was as much of an invite as I was going to get. I took her head in my hands and we kissed like that first time.

For the rest of the week she came in and out as I stayed with Leticia. The last couple days had been good but before that there were some bad days. There had been a slight opioid withdrawal over the first 48 hours and then she slept for another two days. For the past three days the doctors had been focused on pumping her full of food. And now she was begging to get out of here.

"How's she doing?"

I looked up and smiled. Royce sat on a chair across the hall from Leticia's room. His leg was in a brand new cast and a pair of crutches leaned against the wall beside him.

"She's good. How are you doing?" I asked. I hadn't seen him since I left him on the beach in a pool of his own blood.

"This thing itches like hell and every time I take a shit I have to ask my wife to pull down my pants."

"So back to normal," I said.

"Screw you."

"You're back to work already?" I said, pointing to the gold badge dangling from a chain around his neck.

"Crime never sleeps. Isn't that what you gringos say?"

"That's what my boss says. That, and get my ass back to Langley." I sat down in the chair next to him.

"Seriously, how is she?" he asked.

"Physically, she's fine. Better than you or me. The

wonders of the teenage human body. The doctors have cleared her to leave today. But psychologically... she's not as strong as she looks. It'll be a while before she can be alone. We're setting her up with Marié for now. She has an extra bedroom and her mother is dying to have a kid to spoil."

"What about you?" he asked.

"I'm working on getting her a passport. But it'll take some time. Until then I guess I'll be coming back and forth from the U.S. That part will be hard. We've gotten kind of attached to each other."

"Isn't that sweet," he teased. Then he grew serious. "I'm going to have to talk to her. Officially."

"When?" I asked.

"Now."

She didn't cry. I wasn't sure if that was a good thing or a bad thing. I'd given up trying to hold back my tears. Even Royce was struggling to stay in cop mode.

Although we already knew most of Leticia's story, hearing it from her perspective was harrowing. She explained matter of fact about the night she was taken. Then the following two weeks being held in Heinrik's steel box. She told of the mental games she used to pass the time. She showed us the scars on her fingertips. Her nails would never fully grow back. She told of drifting away to a fantasy world and how it got to a point where she resented the box being opened and being ripped away from its comfort. She told of the night when she'd stabbed me at the *sítio* and how she'd been convinced that I was trying to kill her. She told about the practice run at the bank and how she'd tried to escape and how when he caught her she'd peed all over herself. She told about how during the final few days she'd been pumped full of drugs and had thought she was already dead. She told about being tied to the surfboard but was surprised to learn that it had really happened. She thought it had been a dream. In the end it was a piece of paper that made her crack.

"I found this in Detective Amalero's office." Royce handed her an empty envelope with writing on the back. It was the note that Leticia had left in the safety deposit box. "Do you remember writing it?"

She stared at it for a long time.

"It's a map," she finally said. "I... I was trying to count the time between the turns when we drove to the bank. See... one... left... That's one minute and then a left turn. Thirty. Right. That's thirty seconds and a right turn..." she trailed off and turned to me, "I left it for you. I saw your photo. The one of you when you were a little boy with Daddy. I don't know why but I just knew you were out there looking for me. That you would find my map and come rescue me... but then you didn't come... and I was so scared..." She choked as tears streamed down her face.

"I'm sorry," I said and moved to pull her into a hug. But she pushed back.

"Why didn't you find the map?! Why didn't you come for me?!" Her face turned red with rage. She punched me over and over, "Why didn't you come for me?! Why did you leave me with him?!"

Marié rushed forward and wrapped her arms around her. "Para. Para, querida." Leticia went limp and sobbed into her shoulder. "Ta bom. Ta bom. Ta bom" Marié muttered. She then waved at me, "Go. She'll be OK. I'll call you when I get her home."

Royce and I slipped out of the hospital room and

headed down the hall and rode the elevator in silence. Each of us needing the time to rebuild our defenses. When we finally exited the hospital Royce turned to me and held up the paper with Leticia's map, "Are you coming?"

"Yes. But I'm warning you, I might burn the place to the ground."

CHAPTER
SEVENTY-THREE

IT TOOK Royce and his men a little over an hour of trial and error to track Leticia's directions from the bank to Heinrik's apartment building just ten blocks away. The building, a fifteen story modern high rise, was located in the *Lagoa* neighborhood with a stunning head on view of the Christo statue in one direction and a peek-a-boo glimpse of Ipanema beach in the other. The building's security was state of the art and black suited security guards controlled the facilities. It was the kind of place where wealthy residents whisked themselves in and out of the garage, and in and out of their apartments without ever knowing their neighbors' names.

Heinrik's penthouse was accessed by its own private elevator. The building's security boss claimed not to have a key. Royce's team didn't need their help. They simply used a blasting cap to break through the steel fire door at the top of the stairwell. And then set another blast to enter the apartment. The interior was designed to resemble a Russian nesting doll. Rooms within rooms within rooms. The madness extended to the décor with each room meticulously decorated in Germanic themes. Wagnerian steel and glass. Bavarian countryside. Medieval nobility. And of course all leading to a womb of Nazi memorabilia. Inside this sanctuary was one final room: four stark white walls no larger than a walk in closet. This is where he'd kept Leticia.

The Nazi room served as his home office. The shelves were lined with files and journals that once belonged to his great grandfather. There was also a computer set-up with multiple screens. The server and modem were still turned on, blinking and purring like a digital zombie as it spewed its dead master's sickness into the ether. Whatever Gregor had begun, it was still on-going. The thought made me dizzy, as if I was no longer standing on dry land -- but balanced on the tip of an iceberg.

"Oi Gringo! Vem ai! Rapido!"

A flurry of activity yanked me back to the real world. I ran to the rear of the apartment. The BOPE team had gathered outside a utility room. I pushed through and found Royce standing over a deep tub holding a hand over his nose.

"What is it?"

Inside the tub were bloody towels. And bloody gauze. And bloody clothes. Men's clothes that had been singed black. The fabric cut away and stiff with burnt flesh.

"It's fresh," he said. "The fucker's still alive."

Rage.

Blinding rage.

Then a cold brace of fear. He was out there, loose, hunting the people I loved. And every single person able to protect them was stuck here with me in this room.

CHAPTER
SEVENTY-FOUR

IT HURT. But he knew that the pain was the only thing that kept him going. It triggered his adrenal gland and kept him conscious. This body, that he'd groomed for so long, was now a mangled piece of meat. Barely recognizable as human. He laughed. He'd always considered himself above humanity. His survival was proof. An inferior being would have died on that boat. But those reflexes he'd trained and the muscle he'd developed, they had saved his life. His body was burned beyond recognition. But his limbs were intact. His mind was intact. Now he was truly apart. He'd become the monster. And like Grendel of lore he lurked below in the dark. Waiting. He would die soon. He knew this. His lungs rattled. Each breath tasted of charcoal. And with no skin to protect him infection had taken hold. He already shook with fever.

His great grandfather's image hovered before him. It was so nice to see him now. The great man had been his hero for as long as he could remember.

"I did it, grandfather," he said. "Your legacy is secure."

Gunther Heinrik had been a severe man. A formal man. Even now, in death, he wore his uniform. He gave his great grandson a curt nod and faded away. Gregor wanted to call out. But he stopped himself. He shook off the vision. He couldn't afford to grow careless. He reached into his pocket and pulled out the syringe. The golden liquid was a mix of cocaine and adrenaline. It would give him the strength to finish. As he had in life he would not put his fate in the hands of others.

He would avenge his own death.

"C'mon. C'mon! Answer!" I yelled into the ringing phone. But for the second time in a row the call went to Marié's voice mail. I left another message, "Marié! Call me back as soon as you get this. Something's come up. Take Leticia and go somewhere safe. Don't move until you talk to me!"

The elevator door pinged open and I exited into the building's subterranean garage. Royce had given me his car key and his 9mm. In the dim cavernous space all of the cars looked the same. I clicked the key fob. Beep-beep. There it was. Tucked into a dark corner.

The needle pierced the fresh layer of scab and entered the deep vein. As the syringe emptied the pain melted away and his entire being seemed to inflate. He could feel his heart pump energy into every cell. It rushed through his veins returning his legs and arms to steel and bringing his mind into a razor sharp focus. And as he rose from the floor he filled the backseat of the car like a wraith.

His hand gripped hold of my hair and ripped my head back against the seat. My right hand reached for the gun that I'd dropped on the passenger seat -- but he was faster. His knife sliced deep into my wrist. My arm dropped limp and a geyser of blood pumped from the severed artery. Before I could register that the blood spraying the interior of the car was coming from me he'd brought the blade up to my exposed neck. His pressure was exquisite. I was pinned against the seat and I could feel my pulse against the steel. Yet the skin was unbroken.

"Your radial artery has been cut," he rasped in my ear. "You're starting to grow cold. Soon the thirst will be overwhelming. But this discomfort will pass and within the next three minutes you'll lose consciousness. And then die. It will be just enough time for me to tell you about my garden. You thought that all I cared about was the family farm. No, my vision is so much more epic. My garden will cover the earth and it's all thanks to you. You and your father's money which is right now spreading my seed--"

My left hand, my good hand, dangled between the seat and the car door. Searching. Searching. There... I grasped the seat lever and yanked up hard while pressing back on the seat which flattened down onto Heinrik. The sudden motion created just enough space between my neck and the blade for me to hip heist, flipping onto my belly and sliding down beneath the steering wheel. He came up in a rage. And I got my first look.

He was hairless. His entire head and face and arms were covered in a red layer of bubbled scab. As he dove at me I grabbed Royce's gun from the passenger seat with my left hand and fired. Over and over. And he fell with his knife plunging down at my trapped head -- only to embed itself into the cross bar of the steering wheel.

He crumpled over the seat. Dead. One of the shots had

blown out the back of his skull. I stared at him. His repulsiveness was almost comical. How did a person come to this? Was it contagious? And what was he talking about, 'Spreading his seed?' Had he started some kind of pandemic?

The phone buzzed in my pocket and jerked me back to more important matters. I pushed the car door open and fell out onto the cement. I was so cold. I needed to stop the bleeding. I pulled off my shirt. With my teeth and my good hand I ripped off a strip of fabric and tightened a tourniquet just above the cut. Then I leaned back against the car and answered the phone.

"Hey."

"Hey back at you. What's going on?" Marié asked. "I was in the parking garage. There was no connection. Is something wrong? Are you ok?"

"I'm fine. Great, actually. I... uh just wanted to make sure you guys made it home."

"Oh my gosh. We made it but such an adventure. I got to tell you. There was a ton of traffic, so I tried a short cut but then I got lost - and I was so nervous because I wanted everything to be perfect for Leticia and I started to cry and then Leticia, believe it or not, was the calm one and figured out I was reading the map upside down. So, long story short. We made it. We're here. And I think she loves it. Leticia?!" she called into the background. "Tell your brother what you think of the place!"

"I love it!" Leticia yelled back.

"Did you hear that?" Marié asked.

"I heard it. Music to my ears."

"So... finish up what you're doing and get over here. My mom made this ridiculously huge meal. *Feijoada. Arroz. Farofa. Aipim.* We're going to need help."

"I'm on my way."

EPILOGUE

THE YOUNG MAN WAS SHY. He'd been to the store to look at her three times this month but she was so far out of his league - he hadn't even asked the clerk to take her down off the wall. But today he was ready. Today he was flush with confidence. No, the sensation was more than that. Today he'd been granted purpose.

"Sexy, ain't she?" said the Clerk.

"Yes, sir. That she is."

"Wanna hold her?"

"Yes, please. If you don't mind."

"I don't mind at all," the Clerk said already pulling the rifle from the wall. "Bushmaster AR-15 semi automatic. Couldn't ask for a better dance partner."

As the young man reached for the rifle his shirt sleeve drew back revealing a tattoo of a red and black eagle perched on a swastika. The clerk eyed the tattoo. The young man braced himself. If there was going to be a problem now was the time. But the clerk handed the rifle over without flinching.

"I personally own this very model. Perfect for home defense. Marmot shooting. And hell, just blowing shit up."

The young man tucked the rifle into his right shoulder and gripped the barrel in his left hand. He aimed it down at the floor. He took a deep breath. It felt as if his body had finally been made whole.

"A little pricey. But peace a mind ain't cheap. That one there is top of the line with a Bushnell laser scope and I'll even throw in two boxes of cartridges... let's make it $2000 even."

"Do you take Bitcoin?" the Young Man asked.

"Hell yeah. It's preferred," the Clerk replied with a yellow toothed grin.

Two hours later the young man parked in the far row of the parking lot with a clear line to the exit road. He could see the shopping mall entrance in his rear view mirror. It was early afternoon and a steady stream of shoppers came in and out. Oblivious. So fucking assuming in their safety. In the safety granted to them by what? By his restraint? They were sheep. He could almost hear the bleating. Well, today they would learn that the world had a new order to it.

"Dear Gardener, today was a great day! I got your gift! Man, it couldn't have come at a better time. I was dreaming about this AR that I saw down at the gun shop and now I can finally afford it! The extra money will go to supplies and survival gear. Like I told you my dumb ass folks kicked me out a few weeks ago. I been living in my car but now I'll be able to set up a base of operations. I'll keep you updated. The future begins now!!"

"Dear Gardener, today was a great day! I got the money!

Holy crap. You really sent it. I got to admit I didn't think you was real but fuck man, $20,000 right there in my account! I won't let you down. I'm gonna get my truck fixed and then get geared up. I'm talking tac vest and helmet and a whole crate of ammo. Then I'm gonna make you motherfuckers proud!"

"Dear Gardner, today was a great day! Your grant was received. We offer our most sincere gratitude. Our brotherhood has been ready and now we will no longer be waiting!"

"There are hundreds of these posts," explained Special Agent Linda Blaine as she scrolled down her tablet screen. "They all start the same, '*Dear Gardner, today was a great day.*' and then go on to talk about receiving money from this anonymous figure that they're calling The Gardner. The posts are coming from all over. Not just the U.S. We're talking Europe. Australia. Russia. South Africa... The most significant correlation is that ninety percent of the posters on this chat-board are categorized as neo-nazi or white supremacist leaning."

Special Agent In Charge Peter Wills looked down at his hands. The hands of a football player. Large. Knobby. Two fingers bent at an angle from breaks that were never given time to heal. They were also dark. In another era they could have been the hands of a plantation worker. "What do we have on this Gardener? Is he an individual? Or a group?" he asked.

"That's why we called you in on this, Peter." The Assistant Director spoke up from across the conference table. "We think there may be a link to your Rio affair. Agent Blaine, pull up the map."

"Yes, Sir." Agent Blaine used her tablet to call up a digital wall display. On screen was a world map with an arcing red line drawn from a rural town in Kentucky to *Rio De Janeiro, Brazil.*

"This Gardener chatter started to spike three weeks ago," continued Agent Blaine. "That's about one day after the Israeli drone strike on your target. Since then the traffic on this message board has been off the charts. Luckily we have an embed close to one of the posters. A quick look into his finances and things started to make sense. It seems that these gifts that they're talking about are money deposits coming in via Bitcoin. Now, as you know, the blockchain is anonymous. But not invisible. We were able to track the Kentucky Bitcoin deposit back to its source, in Rio... Get this, from the exact address where Agent Ronan had his final confrontation with Gregor Heinrik. From there, we were able to follow the blockchain back out to..."

Agent Blaine swiped her tablet again. The world map now had thousands of red lines. All originating from Rio De Janeiro and spreading out across the globe.

"In the five days before his death Heinrik sent out two thousand five hundred and eighteen Bitcoin payments totaling exactly $600 million in value. Most of these payments ranged from $20,000 to $100,000 - but there were larger ones. The one that's setting off the most alarms is this one here..." She swiped all but one of the lines off the map. "One million dollars to an I.P. located just outside Los Angeles."

"Long story short, Homeland wants to talk to our boy," the Assistant Director said.

"He's been a little hard to reach," Wills frowned.

"Try harder."

"Paddle! Paddle! Paddle!" I peeked over my shoulder at Leticia stroking hard. "Now dive!" I yelled and pushed the nose of my board down under the crashing lip of head high water. When I popped up on the clear backside of the wave I was alone. She hadn't made it. The wave would be sending her tumbling back to shore. Damnit. I shouldn't have pushed her. I knew that a ten minute tutorial on the sand wasn't enough. But she'd insisted on jumping right in and now I'd have to paddle back and rescue her...

"Hey, Bro! What took you so long?"

There she was. Ten meters ahead of me and already sitting on her board in the open water. Somehow she'd beaten me past the wave.

"You lied to me," I scolded as I paddled up and joined her. "You already know how to surf."

She grinned and hit a goofy victory dab. "You really thought Dad wasn't going to teach his daughter how to surf?"

"How long?"

"Forever. Since I could walk," she grinned.

I liked her. I think I've loved her since that night when she ran from me at the *sítio* but now, after spending the last two weeks with her, I realized that I liked her too. I wanted to tell her all of my plans. How the consulate was fast tracking her passport. How I'd get a bigger place so she could have her own room whenever she wanted to visit. How I was already narrowing down her college list. How I'd take her to L.A. to show her Dad's real story. But I didn't. The moment was already perfect. I leaned back on my board and let the ocean rock me in its cool embrace. If I held still I could feel the heat from the sun reflecting down off the granite guardians in the distance; as if letting me know that now I too were under their protection.

"Your girlfriend's calling," Leticia said, pointing my attention to shore.

Marié, unmistakable in her perfect bikini, stood waving at the water's edge. In her hand was a phone. I knew what that meant. The real world had finally found me.

"Race you in!" Leticia challenged. She whirled her board and with three effortless strokes paddled into a wave and disappeared down the rolling line of water.

I didn't follow. Not just yet.

MORE TO COME

THE L.A. AFFAIR

Miles Ronan's adventures continue in the THE L.A. AFFAIR! Coming Soon.

If you would like to learn more check in at: www. micahbarnett.com.

YOU CAN MAKE A DIFFERENCE!

Reviews are the most powerful tool in an independent publisher's arsenal. As much as we'd like to run big media campaigns, we just don't have the financial muscle of corporate publishers. But we do have something even more powerful... the recommendation of readers like you!

So, if you enjoyed this book we would be very grateful if you could leave a review (as short or as long as you like!) on this book's Amazon page.

Thank you very much. And until next time!